Eek! You have found me! Having done so, I hope you enjoy my little story :) Emma xx

DON'T TRY TO FIND ME

by

Emma Swift

I have a question:

Can anybody know you, I mean *really* know you, if they don't know everything about you? I am asking this because it is something I think about a lot. You see, I have a secret. A horrible, life changing secret. It's why I moved to Spain, and nobody here knows it – *nobody*. I couldn't face it if they did.

So do they really know me? Can anyone really know me, can anyone truly love me, if they do not know my secret?

Can they?

CHAPTER ONE

Why am I doing this? I ask myself, as I follow Donna out of the hotel room. *I can't believe I'm here; this is going to be everything I detest in one weekend. I must be mental.*

Donna is my best friend. This is her hen weekend. I am dressed in the hen uniform of white vest with "Hen Party – Last Chance Saloon!" written cheekily across it. The material is so thin I have to wear what I can only describe as an industrial bra, and to say it is uncomfortable doesn't do it justice. Speaking of uncomfortable, I have the highest black heels on and they are already crippling me. A black belt – sorry, skirt – finishes off my sophisticated image.

Did I say Donna is my best friend?

Now, I'm not a complete killjoy but I am easily embarrassed. If you were to rate my normal state of self-consciousness between one and ten it would be about a hundred zillion. So you will appreciate that I am feeling completely at ease and looking forward to the weekend enormously.

I'm going to have to get drunk. There's nothing else for it. My only saving grace in these situations is that after a certain amount of alcohol I become indestructible, unbelievably witty and the life and soul of the party. Often to my later regret, but tonight there's no other rational choice.

The resort we are in is dreadful. Totally un-Spanish, brash, loud and verging on the offensive. It is full of rowdy men and women dressed like – well, like me, actually. I should fit in perfectly.

I am here for Donna. I hardly ever see her now and she has held her hen weekend in Spain specially, because I live here. Not in this resort, but in a quieter spot not too far away. So I'm not complaining, and I so want to be with her and spend time with her, but I loathe this kind of thing. I mean, I'm not seventy – you would be forgiven for thinking I am – but I am shy. Donna and I are so different in so many ways, but she's a great friend and I love her. So here I am.

There are ten of us in total. I'm sharing with Donna, which is nice because I don't know any of the others. Donna knows what I'm like so will make allowances when I curl up into a cringing ball of mortification later on. I hope.

We arrive at the first bar. I'm going to get drunk but I am *not* going to drink spirits. You should see the size of the measures they pour in this place. I would be on my back in seconds. If the heels don't manage it first.

Ok, the first one is in my hand and I'm sinking it fast. Cider. Cool and refreshing. I am trying vainly to look relaxed and happy, desperate not to catch the eye of any of the gurning hulks standing around openly staring at all the girls. Not that anyone is likely to be interested in somebody who looks as hideously inhibited as me, thank God. That's one good thing.

The rest of our party seem to be having a whale of a time, beginning to mix, laughing and conspicuously enjoying themselves. Donna sidles up to me.

"You ok?" she asks.

"'Course!" I reply with a fixed grin.

She sniggers. "You need more alcohol."

She knows me so well.

"Some of the blokes aren't bad," she says. She's not looking for action - after all she's about to get married - but she knows I'm single. For some insulting reason she is never surprised about that. (Actually, if I am honest we both know why I am single. It is to do with my secret, and I am keeping all that to myself for now, if you don't mind).

I sneak a look around. She's right, although most of them are. To me, anyway. *Lighten up*, I tell myself.

It's two bars and three ciders later and I'm beginning to enjoy myself. I'm talking to this bloke who is on a birthday weekend, and Donna's right - he's not so bad, not so bad at all. In fact, we're having quite a laugh. Honestly, I can be so negative; this weekend isn't going to be so terrible. It's just a case of getting into the right frame of mind, and I'm just about there.

Then someone suggests moving on. Ok, no problem – I'm up for it. There's a bar along the road that has some kind of *Chippendale* act on. I feel my smile falter. I can already see the shrieking women and the oiled up, over-muscled performance. Not that I have ever seen the Chippendales before, you understand, but since when have I ever allowed a lack of experience to stop me from bearing judgement on this kind of thing? Since never, you can betcha. Just call me Miss Preconception.

So we all pile into the new bar. It's huge, with a big stage at the far end, and it's full of over-excited women. I go to the bar with one of the others to get as far out of the way as possible.

Ten minutes later the show starts. It's every bit as dreadful as I expected with added horror thrown in. I know lots of people love this kind of thing, and that's fine, I don't mind - each to their own. But I don't. I'm far too easily embarrassed and it makes me squirm. I just wish people would understand that and not try to make me join in as though I'm missing out on something. I mean, I don't insist they leave just because it isn't my idea of a good time. They're welcome to it.

My thoughts are interrupted as the muscly hunks (per the promotional literature) suddenly start climbing down into the audience. *Oh my God! What? Please stay away from me!* I'm already near the back and I furiously start trying to look even smaller than I am.

They are pulling women out of the crowd and carrying them onto the stage. The women are squealing and loving every minute of it. I'm in denial. I am not here. If I believe it maybe they will, too. The women on the stage are being manhandled and groped and one lucky winner has her head shoved into a male crotch. Never mind toes, my whole feet are

5

curling. If anyone tries to do that to me I don't know what I'll do, but I won't be held responsible for it, that's for sure.

Then one of the hunks heads directly towards where I'm hiding. He's *enormous*, all bulging biceps and greasy skin. I stare intently at my glass hoping he'll take the hint. Am I completely stupid? As if something that brawny could take anything as subtle as a hint.

He bends forward to pick me up, and before I can stop myself I shout, "STOP!" rather more loudly than I intend. He pauses to look at me and if I were a cruel person I'd say he's confused, but I'm not, so I won't.

"Pick someone else," I urge him. "Please."

"Why?" he asks.

"Why not?" I reply in exasperated desperation.

"I chose you," he says, as if that's his final answer, and leans forward once more.

"Wait!" I cry. "Don't! I'll be hopeless. It'll be obvious I'm hating it and that won't do you any favours." I'm almost gibbering with fear as I plead with him to see reason.

He considers this for what seems like a year while I pray to some imaginary god of furniture or something. Some of the women around me start encouraging him to pick me up. What did I say about people not trying to make me join in as if they are doing me a favour? I'm getting so agitated now I'm at risk of lashing out at someone, and I abhor violence, believe me.

"*Please* go for someone else." It's my final appeal.

Why should I?"

Aaaaargh! I've already explained, haven't I? I look up at him – my eyes aren't even on a level with his nipples. "I'll kick you in the shins," I threaten. I know how to come up with a good answer, that's for sure.

I hear male sniggering behind me. I'll deal with that later.

Finally, with a small shrug, he turns away. Thank God! I'm sagging with relief, and I never would have thought I'd willingly apply the word "sag" to my appearance in a million years.

I can still hear the muffled sniggering and it's more than I can handle. So I pull myself up tall and turn around with a haughty look and a caustic remark ready on my lips.

Oh my God! I am looking into the most stunning eyes I have ever seen in my life, and they are laughing at me. Plus he's gorgeous. The man who is laughing at me is *gorgeous*. How unfair is that? Now, please explain to me how it is that in the novels when the heroine is faced with a stunning guy her words freeze on her lips? Why couldn't that happen to me, for heaven's sake? Perhaps I was a murderer in a previous life or something. Whatever the reason, it goes without saying that my words come tumbling out of my mouth like lottery balls from a tombola. I simply can't stop them.

"What kind of saddo watches male strip shows and laughs at other people's discomfort?" I growl. Did I say caustic? Because I meant pathetic, obviously. For a moment I wonder if he's gay. I mean, he's almost beautiful, he's watching the Chip'n'Dales, and it would be just typical, wouldn't it?

His eyebrows rise a fraction and now he's laughing openly. For the second time this evening I'm goaded to hit someone - I mean something. *How the hell am I going to get through a whole weekend of this?* I wonder.

I glare at him hotly and mutter something inaudible under my breath in the hope that he might think it's something clever, before turning away. Now I realize I should have been grateful to him for one thing – while I was staring at him I couldn't see what was happening on the stage.

I hear him mimic, "I'll kick you in the shins," followed by the same sniggering, only louder this time.

I know I should ignore him, but I'm not perfect and I've had a few drinks. I turn back to glare at him haughtily again and he puts his hand over his mouth. He's quite a bit taller than me (not difficult) and I have to look up to do my glaring, which does nothing towards making it intimidating in the slightest way.

I've had enough. "That's it, I'm out of here," I mutter to myself and begin to move off.

"What did you say?" he asks, suddenly serious. He must have bionic ears.

"What's it to you?" I reply with venom.

He looks amused. "I don't think it's such a good idea for you to wander around here on your own." The way he says it makes it sound insulting, somehow. Heaven help me – what a horrible place this is. I'm perfectly safe walking around where I live.

"Is that so? How interesting." I try to make it clear I am being sarcastic, and I can feel myself climbing onto my high horse. I can't help it.

"Uh-huh. Where are you going?"

"To my hotel." Like I'm going to tell this scumbag where I'm staying.

"Seriously…" Unexpectedly his eyes do this smouldering thing which looks simply amazing. Really. I've heard of smouldering eyes before, of course I have, but I've never seen them in real life. Wow, it's quite impressive. Either that, or I'm more drunk than I thought, and come to think of it, that's a distinct possibility. "Let me walk you there," he adds.

I feel my eyebrows shoot up involuntarily in a very uncool manner. "Oh, and I'm going to be safer with you than taking my chances on my own, am I?" My sarcasm is now tangible. I gather up my reins.

"Yes, I think so," he replies levelly, and for some reason I believe him. Let's be honest, this guy has to be gay.

"Well, sorry, I'm sure," I tell him, doing my best to convey the opposite, and I urge my horse forward.

"Wait. Look, if you don't like the idea perhaps we could go somewhere else to wait for your friends. There's a bar around the corner

7

which is quieter than this," – that wouldn't be difficult – "and I really don't think you should go off on your own."

I'm staring at him stupidly now. I have no idea what to think.

"Really." He tries to push his point home.

I give up. I am not going to use the word "sag" again to describe myself. "What's the bar called?" I ask.

"Madrugada."

"First light," I muse.

Once more his eyebrows rise a fraction. "It's left out of here, round the corner and about four bars down."

You might not have guessed it, but practically every building in this part of town is a bar.

I nod. "I'll go and tell Donna."

When I come back I can't see him; he's gone. I feel a sharp pang of disappointment. Only because it means I'll have to stay here for the rest of the torture, you understand, as he's successfully put me off walking to the hotel alone. Perhaps that's all he was aiming to achieve.

Then I spot him over towards the exit talking to some other lads. He catches my eye and we head out.

I must be drunker than I thought because, apart from the fact that I am leaving the bar with a man I don't know, when the fresh air hits me (well, as fresh as it can be in the heat of a Spanish June night) I feel myself wobble for a second. Or perhaps it's the heels. *Don't worry*, I console myself, *if you know you're drunk then you're not that bad, it's when you think you are sober that you are really pissed.* I snuffle a small giggle as he waits for me to catch him up.

Madrugada is surprisingly ok. As the name suggests, it's Spanish (I'm amazed) and he's right; it's reasonably quiet. Let's face it; if I was Spanish I wouldn't fight through these drunken, sweating foreigners to come here. I'm astounded there's anyone in the place at all. We go up to the bar and I try to look sober and self-assured.

"What would you like?" he asks.

"I'll get these," I reply. I most certainly do not want to be indebted to this guy in any way at all. "After all, you rescued me from the hell hole." As I say this I notice a couple of Spanish girls eyeing him up and I'm not altogether surprised. *Don't bother*, I think ungraciously, *He's gay*.

"Why were you there if you hate it so much?"

"The others wanted to go." I look down at my vest in explanation. He nods, satisfied.

"What would you like to drink?"

"Lager, please."

I turn to the bar. "Una cerveza y un vino tinto, por favor," I ask. "Tienes Rioja? Gracias." I order red wine as they don't have cider, and Rioja to be on the safe side, as you never know what the wine will be like in these places. I shouldn't really have wine on top of what I've had already but I'm too far gone to think about anything remotely as sensible as that.

When the drinks arrive I excuse myself and make for the ladies. My bra is killing me and I want to adjust it. As I walk in I catch sight of myself in the mirror and I gasp with shock. This is so much *not* how I imagined I was looking. I stare at my awful, flimsy vest; my flushed face. My hair is a dishevelled mess despite originally being in a ponytail, and I can hardly stand up straight in these shoes. I'm devastated.

I try desperately to make some sense of my hair and splash water on my face to cool it down. I fiddle with my bra and straighten my vest. I can't bear even to think of removing my shoes to flex my feet because the relief would be so incredible that it would take a gun to my head to make me put them back on. When I walk back out to the bar I'm afraid I have far more self-awareness than before and I'm still walking like a pigeon, despite trying desperately not to.

He's sitting on a barstool. Oh, great; another opportunity to make a fool of myself. I consider staying standing but I know my feet will take me hostage if I do, so I start clumsily to climb onto the stool next to him and he stands up to help me. His lips hardly twitch at all. What a guy.

We chat for a while and despite my excruciating new appreciation of how hideous I look I start to relax. It must be the booze and I'm not complaining. Without it I would be a cringing imbecile by now. He asks how the wine is.

"Fine. Try it, if you like."

He does so. "Not bad," he agrees, and he smiles at me, for the first time without a hint of mockery. Gosh, it's dazzling, and somehow it makes him seem so much friendlier. I relax even more.

"Are you gay?" I blurt out, shocking myself again. I mean, I can't believe I just asked that. What must he think? I must be really drunk.

His eyebrows shoot up. At least I've broken his cool at last. I have to stop myself from grinning a stupid, triumphant grin.

"No," he replies, and for a moment he presses his lips together as though he's trying not to laugh. My surprise must show far too clearly. "Why do you ask?"

I've obviously had way too many to be tactful. "Derr," I say, "You were at a male strip show." At least I manage to stop myself from adding that he's rather beautiful, too.

"Ah, mmmm. The others thought it would be a good place to pick up girls." He shrugs dismissively.

"Well, I suppose it was," I point out.

"Huh?"

I wave my arm to encompass us sitting together at the bar.

"Oh. I don't think this is quite what they had in mind." He grins.

I throw him a questioning look and he shrugs again.

"It was more that they thought the girls would be - what was it? - "Fully revved, hot and horny, and up for anything"."

I feel heat rush to my cheeks. "Oh," I say ineffectually, looking down.

"Are you?" he asks.

"*Pardon?*" My eyes snap back up to his as I beckon my high horse over again.

"Gay," he explains, and he's laughing.

"Oh." *Dear God.* "No."

He nods.

"Why do you ask?"

"Derr – you were at a male strip show and clearly hating every minute of it."

Ok, so I can see his point but he's unsettled me and I'm goaded. "No," I repeat, "I am not even slightly gay. Quite the opposite." I stop abruptly.

"You were so funny," he says, saving me.

"Oh, thanks very much. My God, I don't know what I'd have done if he'd have gone ahead. I'd have died. I can't bear to think about it."

"I'd have stopped him."

I stare at him in surprise. He's tall and pretty broad, I can see that, but how on earth could he have stopped that towering hulk?

He seems to read my mind. "I would have found a way."

I'm speechless.

"Would you like anything to eat?" He changes the subject smoothly.

Suddenly I realise I'm starving. No wonder the drink is affecting me. I've had no chance to eat since lunchtime with all the rushing around and the others all ate on the plane.

"The tapas look good," he adds. He stands up. "Is there anything you don't like?"

"Seafood – well, most fish really - liver, artichoke, olives…" I tail off at the expression on his face.

"Perhaps you should choose." His eyes belie his expression and I can't make him out.

"No, you do it. Please." There's no way I'm getting off this stool for anyone, not even me. "I like tortilla, chicken – most meat actually – eggs, veg."

He does the ordering and I'm surprised to hear he does it in Spanish. When the food arrives I can hardly stop myself from falling onto it in a very unladylike manner. There's loads of fresh bread, too, which is an added bonus.

He does little more than pick and I'm ashamed to say I eat the bulk of it, but my word, I feel better for it. You have no idea. Or perhaps you do.

We've finished our drinks so we order more. *Blast, I meant to order sparkling water this time,* I think. *Oh well, what the hell. I'll just sip it; I'll be fine.*

"How long are you here for?" he asks.

"Until Monday. We arrived today."

"Me too."

"Why are you here?"

"Birthday party."

"Uh-huh, but why *here?*"

His eyes meet mine. "It's not that bad."

"You're the one who said I shouldn't walk around on my own."

"True. But most of the people here are fine."

I think back, and I know he's right. I am so used to my quiet corner of Spanish Spain that I am taken aback by this kind of thing – wall-to-wall bars and hoards of people doing everything to excess. Don't get me wrong, I like a drink (as if you couldn't tell) and I can walk to at least ten bars and restaurants from my villa, even off season, it's one of the things I like about it, but there everyone knows everyone and it's a friendly place. Even the drunks are friendly, and at times I count myself among them. And nobody's ever tempted to get horny in public, I can assure you.

We carry on chatting. As we do so I'm giving him a surreptitious looking over. He really isn't bad at all. I'm still wondering if he's gay and he was lying earlier, although I don't know why he would.

Time starts to blur. That's a lie actually; it's been blurred for a while if I'm honest.

Suddenly there's a lot of noise and a crowd of people pour in. Surprisingly they're English. Then I realise it's my party together with a number of blokes. They all look a bit astonished when they see the inside of the place, and Donna makes her way over to me.

"Are you ready to go?" I say. I can't imagine them wanting to stay in here. Looking at the way the existing customers are eyeing up the girls' attire the feeling may well be reciprocated.

"Why not have one here?" he suggests and I look at him in surprise, then I realise he's spot on. None of my lot are going to cause any trouble, they're all really nice, and I'm sure his friends will be the same. What's wrong with me? Why do I always imagine the worst in people? Actually, I could tell you why, but I'm not going to unless I have to. At least the man behind the bar is happy – he can see his takings going up exponentially. He beams a big, welcoming smile.

Donna stays and talks to us, and I can see her weighing up my new friend. When he turns to say something to one of his mates she raises her eyebrows at me approvingly. I frown. I don't want him to notice and I don't like to be seen as a foregone conclusion. Because I'm not one. You might have worked that out for yourself by now.

Unexpectedly I catch the eye of the guy I was speaking to in the bar before the Chip'n'Dale horror. I remember his name is Ray and I'm impressed with myself. He must be part of the same group. He moves over and says hello.

Mr Cool-Customer looks up. "Have you two met?" he asks over-innocently, and Ray scowls at him darkly. I smile to myself. It's always nice to be appreciated, don't you think? I chat pleasantly to Ray because he was nice to me earlier and he's clearly put out. In the end there's a few of us all talking together.

All of a sudden one of the girls exclaims, "It's nearly five!" I don't bother explaining that the Spanish are often out until much later than this, because I can begin to sound like a bit of a know-it-all, and anyway, the Spanish start much later than us, too. So it's all relative.

There's a general discussion and my party decide it's time to go. That's fine by me, although I have to admit I've had so much of a better time than I expected that it feels almost surreal. I slide gingerly down my bar stool, waiting for my feet to hit the floor. My face crumples for a second as the excruciating pain shoots through me. God only knows how I'm going to make it to the hotel, but I'll just have to. The guys are leaving too. We all head out.

I'm tottering like a baby taking her first steps and nearly crying with agony. It doesn't make me a good conversationalist and I suspect it's not a very attractive look. My new friend walks beside me in silence. Luckily our hotel isn't far away. A block or two before it is where the lads are splitting from us, and I turn to him and smile. "I've had a really good evening," I say, surprising myself, and him too, I think. He grins a reply. "So have I."

"No doubt we'll see you around over the weekend." My feet are in such agony that I can't stand hanging around any longer than necessary. The rest of my party are moving off.

"I owe you a few drinks," he points out. "I was thinking I should return the favour."

I stare at him while I weigh this up. "Ok," I reply. *Honestly, don't let your enthusiasm go to his head,* I think, but I'm simply not capable of jumping for joy. And I'm not entirely sure I'm joyful. I can't make this guy out.

"What's your mobile number?" he asks.

I look at him dumbly. Do I want to give him my number? I can't decide. But he's waiting. *Oh, for Goodness sake, don't be so pathetic,* I think to myself, and tell him the number. He rings it, although my mobile is switched off in my hotel room. "You can text me tomorrow when you are out and let me know where you are," he says, "if you like."

I nod stupidly. Technically it'll be tonight but even I'm not that pedantic - honestly. I've no idea how I'll carry my phone, but I'll find a way if I want to, I suppose.

"See you later." I know I'm being ungracious so I touch his arm tentatively. "Thanks," I add, and he can see I mean it.

He smiles. "See you."

He turns away and I wobble off to where Donna and a couple of the others are waiting for me.

Too late I realise I don't know his name. I don't suppose it matters; I'm the first one to appreciate that.

I'm nearly howling with pleasure when I take my shoes off. My feet are rubbed red raw in places and my toes feel like they have been in a vice, which I suppose they have. I crawl into bed and Donna and I talk for a while. She's telling me about what I missed with the Chip'n'Dales and I know it will give me nightmares, and we're giggling helplessly. Then she asks me about my friend and I have to admit I know little about him, not even his name. What on earth were we talking about all that time? Because I didn't tell him anything about me, I made sure of that.

Donna declares him hot, and I reply darkly that I still suspect he's gay.

"You'll have to find out tomorrow," she says with a snigger, and I sigh. I'm still not sure what I think about that. Never mind, I'm too tired now. I'll worry about it in the morning.

CHAPTER TWO

I wake far too early considering the time I went to bed. I try to persuade myself to go back to sleep because I know the hangover is going to be humongous. So I doze for a while but shortly I am firmly in the Wideawake Club and I know sleep is a distant memory.

I decide to get up and go for a swim. For some reason swimming always makes me feel better, and the hotel has a decent sized pool as well as a children's pool to keep those pesky kids at bay. Not that there should be many; it's still term time.

I creep around finding my swimming things and so on, grab some aspirin and whisper to Donna before heading out. Although by now it's almost midday by this resort's standards that's still early and it's fairly quiet. The pool is empty. Honestly, I'm constantly amazed by how few people use a pool when I'm sure they will have insisted on having one when they chose their hotel.

I dump my things on a sunbed, shower and dive in. It's the only way to do it. Although the water is in no way cold the contrast to the outside temperature is still sharp. As I swim I lazily wonder why swimming always dims my hangover, before my mind shuts down altogether. I reach that dreaded point where I feel I'm just going to have to stop and then I break through and feel like I can go on forever. I'm totally relaxed and all stress has left my body. Even wondering about whether to meet Mr Sardonic tonight is easy in this state. Not that I make a decision or anything positive like that. Don't be silly.

Eventually I know I have to climb out; I can't put off the headache any longer. I collapse on my sunbed and wait for my body to stop tingling. The aspirin must have done some good because although my headache does return it isn't too bad at all. I reckon I've got off lightly, and I start to drift into the land of nod.

All too soon a shadow looms over me and Donna gives me a nudge. One by one the rest of the girls appear, but nobody's in much mood for talking yet and I'm left in relative peace. After a while I have another swim but then four lads jump in, dive bombing and messing around, so I beat a hasty retreat. I'm feeling much better by now, anyway.

A couple of the girls decide to investigate the snack bar so they take orders and we all have something. It's a good idea. One or two start on the alcohol – I'm impressed but there's no way I'm going there yet. Things get more lively and we discuss the night before with much laughing and teasing. I know the girls better now and they're all very friendly. A couple of them met guys they like and are hoping to catch up with them tonight. That brings my thoughts back to my new friend, and I'm still stumped.

We decide we'll go out at seven, have a meal and carry on from there. No problem. At ten to I'm ready. This time I have a red vest on (same wording) and flip-flops. The vest is dark and far more substantial than the previous one so I can safely forgo the bra. Heaven. My feet are covered in sticking plaster, but they are moaning with pleasure at being in my flip-flops. In what must have been a moment of pure brilliance yesterday I packed an old money belt of mine. It's thin and unobtrusive, (and let's face it, it's not as though it's going to spoil my look), and as luck would have it my phone just fits. So I can text him. If I decide to.

General consensus goes with Italian so we find a restaurant nearby. The food's not bad, and as we eat we discuss where we are going to go later. I come in for some teasing about ducking out of the Chip'n'Dale show last night. I don't mind. I got out of there, that's all that matters to me. Jo says she saw a flyer for a live sex show tonight, and perhaps I'd prefer that. I just manage to stop myself from saying I probably would, actually, because hopefully they would stay on the stage, as it might give her the wrong idea. As I said, it's all relative, isn't it?

I can't believe there would even be a live sex show on. Yes I can - who am I kidding? I wonder if anyone actually lives in this place or if it's just a cattle market for foreign tourists. That's more than possible.

Donna asks me about you-know-who, she calls him "your mystery guy". It makes him sound quite intriguing. Perhaps he'll self-destruct in five seconds.

"Are you going to meet up with him tonight?" she asks.

"I don't know."

"You haven't got long to decide."

"I know."

"Why not?" Donna is concerned for me, she thinks I should get out more.

"I'm here to be with you, not him."

"And to have fun."

"Exactly."

"Are you telling me you didn't enjoy last night?"

"No." I can't lie.

"We are seeing plenty of each other. You can spend some time with him too," she points out reasonably.

I turn to look at her. "I'm not sure. I want to make the most of you being here. I miss you."

She looks back at me tenderly. She knows it's my fault I don't see enough of her, but of all people she understands why the best.

"But by the time he catches up with us we'll all be well away anyway, so you won't exactly be missing quality time." As always Donna cuts straight to the chase. I know she's right.

"I want you to be happy," she adds quietly.

She's such a good friend. I can't explain and she knows it. She sits back. "Anyway, it's up to you. You do what you think is best. Don't let me persuade you to do anything rash."

She means it well but somehow it sounds like a criticism to me. I'm far too sensitive. Perhaps she's right; I'm always such a pathetic

15

coward. Ok, so I have my reasons, but maybe it's time for me to try to chill a bit and go with the flow. It's easier, somehow, in this resort away from normality where I can perhaps take a chance and walk away if I want to. I sigh heavily. I'll probably go through all this self-torture and he won't turn up anyway. Or he'll turn up and be gay after all. What terrible thing do I think's going to happen, in any case? I might have a good time? Let my hair down? I'm not promiscuous, but surely I should be able to at least enjoy myself if we meet up.

Oh, God, I don't know.

But I do, really. As the meal goes on, underneath I know that after a couple more drinks I will text him and my stomach fizzes with nervous excitement. I'm a self-deluding fool sometimes, and no mistake.

We move on and try a different bar. I'm aware that if I'm going to text I should probably do it soon. Why am I so hesitant? Donna is watching me, a knowing smile on her lips. She can see my other self appearing.

I shrug my shoulders at her and pull my mobile out. Find his number and send the text. There! It's done! He probably won't turn up anyway.

Of course now I'm horribly aware that he might walk in at any moment, and I have to force myself not to glance at the bar entrance every few seconds. Honestly, I'm such an idiot. Anyway, I don't know why I get myself all worked up because he doesn't show. I'm surprised at how disappointed I am. Talk about setting yourself up for a fall.

A man starts talking to me. I'm hacked off because my mystery guy hasn't come running the minute I called – well over half an hour has gone by now - so I probably flirt more with this one than I intend. He's a big bloke called Simon. He's got a good sense of humour and we're winding each other up. He's on a stag weekend with some mates who are looking over and egging him on. I'm getting a bit drunk so I'm being incredibly witty and it makes me giggle.

The bar is very busy so he moves me over to the edge of the room to avoid being jostled. How chivalrous. I smile up at him winningly, then suddenly he leans forward.

Oh my God, he's going to kiss me!

I have no time to react before his mouth is hard on mine. Without me noticing he has moved in very close and now he's pushing me against the wall and pressing against me. Stop! Don't do this! Stop! *Stop!* I try to push him off but he's too near and I can't get enough weight behind me. *I can't even kick him in the shins*, I think stupidly. Clearly my less than ecstatic reaction doesn't go down well, because he pushes harder and moves his hand to grasp my breast roughly. Perhaps I should have worn that bra after all.

Oh God! Get off! Ouch! *Stop!* I can feel the sick fear rising. No! Oh no, not again. *Please*, not again. I can't move, but he can. His hand moves slowly, deliberately. Fear drenches me as I pray to a god I didn't think I believed in any more. Oh God, please don't hurt me. I can't shout because my mouth is silenced by his, and here by the wall my friends can't see me. I'm terrified. Nobody is going to react to a bit of hanky panky in a place like this. He pushes closer still and now I can feel his erection pressing against me. God, no!! *No!* Again I try to shove him away but he grips my breast harder and forces himself forward even further before pinching my nipple cruelly. Aargh! As the pain shoots though me the fear blocks my thoughts. My mind is churning as I try to think what I can do to stop him and I can't believe this is happening.

Suddenly he pulls away. "What the *fuck*?" he snarls.

"Fuck *you*," comes the reply, and I know that voice.

Mr Might-Not-Be-Gay-After-All punches Simon hard in the face. I stand in shock, stupefied. Then I don't know what comes over me because I move forwards; perhaps I can get a kick in, although what damage I think I'll do in my flip flops I have no idea. I should at least try to help and I'm *so* angry I can't think straight. The intensity of it is overriding my tremulous fear and I'm no longer in control. I can't begin to tell you how much I want to murder this guy, although you can probably guess. It goes against all my natural instincts but my nipple is throbbing like hell and I'm livid.

Fists are flying and I can't get near.

"Go," my guy says to me.

I hesitate.

"You're in the *way!*" He sounds furious.

I back off and watch in horror as my saviour deals with Simon with a chilling, cold efficiency. Donna finds me and puts her arm around me. She hasn't seen what's happened but she recognises my mystery guy and can appreciate my stricken expression. Everyone stands back, there's little surprise at what's happening and nobody intervenes. Gosh, I love it here.

After what seems an age Simon finally falls back against the wall and slides down it. My guy is breathing heavily as he leans over him. Simon moans, he's down but he's not out. Simon's friends now appear. Even though I'm most definitely not on his side even I think they have been conspicuous by their absence - what good mates they are. A couple of them advance aggressively, but one must have witnessed the chain of events because after checking Simon over he says, "Leave it. It was his fault."

The way the others accept this makes me think this isn't the first time and I understand their previous reticence more. Especially when put together with the sight of Mr Who-The-Hell-Are-You's effective demolition of their friend.

Simon's coming round a bit now and he looks at me blearily. "I'll get you, you bitch," he mumbles charmingly and aims a weak kick at my mystery guy. My heart warms to him no end.

Mr I'm-Running-Out-Of-Names-Now-And-I-Have-No-Idea-What-To-Think turns and moves over to me. Donna steps back but hovers anxiously.

His face is flushed and I can practically *see* his excited energy still pumping from the fight. He looks at me intently and I'm ashamed to say I'm shaking. Did I mention that I hate violence? His face softens slightly and he says, "Are you all right?" The back of his hand brushes my breast like a feather and I shiver. I find my throat is constricted and I nod.

I'm totally bewildered. Everything happened so fast and now Mr Nice-Guy has turned out to be a bit different than I thought. And although I hate violence I am very grateful; very grateful indeed.

I try to show it in my face to make up for my lack of words. His expression changes again, and then he drops his head urgently to mine. *Oh my God*, I think for the second time that night, *he's going to kiss me. I'm not sure I can cope.*

Now I can *feel* his excitement and I can taste sweat and blood. I am disgusted and aroused at the same time, and I wonder stupidly how that is even possible. I must be in shock because I don't respond at all.

He pulls away and searches my face. I'm trying desperately to show him how I feel, but it's all beyond me. Finally I find my voice. "Thank you," I say, and I can hear the intense emotion at last.

Mr Oh-My-God-In-No-Way-Is-He-Gay nods. "You don't like violence." I can't read his face at all.

I stare at him helplessly. *Does anyone?* I wonder. "That doesn't mean I can't be grateful for it," I reply. I can still see Donna hovering in my peripheral vision, and it's reassuring.

Again he nods, satisfied.

Suddenly a crowd of blokes enter and a commotion starts. I realise it's his friends and they have seen him and Simon and put two and two together. For a hideous moment it looks like it's all going to kick off again but he puts a stop to it. "Let's move on," he says, and I'm glad to see he's not so proud that he insists it's Simon who leaves. After all, he's made his point fairly convincingly.

He takes my hand and we all pile out. I've just about stopped shaking now and I'm beginning to feel a bit more in control. My swirling emotions are calming down and although I would like a quiet minute to sort myself out there's no way I'm wandering off on my own. In fact, I'm pleased to be in such a large crowd.

We find another bar and someone gets the drinks in. He brings me a brandy – no doubt he can see the state I'm in. I take a sip and feel the warmth spreading through me. I'm embarrassed now as well as everything else and wondering what on earth he's thinking. As in why I was separated from my friends and against the wall being groped by Simon, amongst other things. I cringe.

Donna is still staying close, which I am so thankful for, and when he moves away she moves in. "Are you ok?" she asks. Out of everyone she appreciates how I must be feeling. Her face is a picture of concern.

I nod. There's a lot of that going on tonight.

"What happened?"

I take a deep breath and give a brief description and she draws her breath in sharply when I mention how Simon manhandled me. Her face darkens.

"I'm so stupid," I say.

"No, you're not. Nobody would expect that. Poor you, you must have been terrified." She knows how true this is.

"God knows what *he's* thinking."

"Your mystery guy? He didn't seem too fazed. Wow, he seemed to know what he was doing."

I can't help agreeing with her and it makes me uneasy.

"Still, he's definitely not gay, you know that now." She starts to giggle. Honestly, she's awful.

Despite myself I start to snigger a bit, too. The brandy must be doing the trick. I'm beginning to feel light headed, whether as a result of relief at my rescue or the booze I can't tell. Maybe it's both.

He comes back over. "Feeling better?" he asks.

"Yes. Thank you," I reply, and he knows what I mean.

Donna turns to him. "God, it's a good job you turned up when you did."

He gives her the strangest look. "Yes," he says.

I cringe again. I wonder at my immense propensity for making a fool of myself. I've probably spoiled everything. *Not that there was anything to spoil*, I remind myself harshly. *It's not as though you were gagging to meet up with him, and I dare say he could tell.* Hence his speedy response to my text, no doubt. Even so, Donna's right, it *is* a good job he finally turned up. I look up at him gratefully.

Unexpectedly he smiles, and once again it's so warm and friendly I'm taken aback, albeit in a good way. I reach up tentatively and touch his face just above his eyebrow where he has a cut and some bruising is starting to show. Despite being petrified by the fighting I'm very impressed at his defence of me. God, it's confusing. I look away.

He takes my hand and pulls gently. Still I can't look at him, goodness knows why, it should be the least I can do. He moves around until he's in my line of vision, and his face is tender. My stomach turns over. I see Donna slide away unobtrusively and I curse her silently.

"I'm sorry," he says unexpectedly.

I stare at him. "What for?" I ask.

"The fight. I can see it has upset you."

No! I don't want him to think that. "Christ," I splutter, swearing in my agitation, "I think you'll find I was already upset. I'm so grateful I can't put it into words. Please don't imagine I mind. Bloody hell!" I'm furious at myself for letting my feelings show. In fact I didn't think I had. Not those ones, anyway. Who is this guy, Derren Brown?

I'm thoroughly unsettled and pissed off with myself. I'm horribly embarrassed that he had to rescue me from my unladylike situation, and feeling a sickening mixture of shame and excitement. Mixed emotions just isn't in it.

There's a still moment while we stare at each other, and then he drops his head again and this time it's different. I want it. I want it desperately. Despite my horror of the fight I am obviously worked up and totally blown over by his sticking his neck out for my sake. Not that I'm sure he stuck his neck out that far. The controlled way in which he dealt with Simon, taking him out quickly but not causing too much damage, was alarming. I push the thought out of my mind. It doesn't prevent me from being aroused by all the excitement and adrenalin that was pumping around. I can feel it in him, too.

I slide my hands up around his neck and kiss him enthusiastically. He gives a little grunt, and is either not inclined or too clever to enclose me in his arms. God, he feels good. It's been far too long.

All too soon he pulls back and it's as if my favourite childhood toy is being wrenched away from me. I'm breathing heavily and incredibly surprised at myself. Once more I look away. I'm feeling sick again but for a different reason. I don't know what to do. Why am I always so useless?

I don't want any more brandy. The bit I've had has been great but any more and in the morning my head will feel like there's a huge cushion squashed inside my skull trying to burst its way out, and I don't want that.

"Cider?" he asks. He's exceptionally astute.

I nod and off he goes. Donna returns instantly and gives me a knowing look.

"Well, then," she says. I've never really understood what that means. I return her look blankly.

"What do you think now?" she expands.

"I've no idea." This is the truth. I am so utterly bewildered with everything.

She nods. "Take it as it comes," she says. I've no idea what that means either. She sees my expression. "Do you like him?" she asks.

I look at her helplessly. I'm not sure "like" is the word. I'm unsettled, uneasy, excited and apparently ridiculously turned on by him. Or by what he's done. Is that the same as like? I have no bloody idea. I shrug.

"Oh, very helpful," she says sarcastically.

"I'm confused," I say, and for a hideous moment I think I'm going to burst into tears.

"Chin up." She looks at me intently. This has a strong meaning for us and I gulp, pulling myself together just in time.

"Thanks." I take my cider from him and have a large swig. The cold helps to clear my head. Donna and my mystery guy strike up an innocuous conversation that almost makes me laugh. Ray also comes over with a few of the others and I'm allowed to stand quietly as the conversation flows around me. I steal a secret look at Mr. Surprising and wonder what the hell will happen next. I run my mind over the events of the evening in the hope I can sort myself out, but it does the opposite. I am astounded that I even thought about trying to join in against Simon, it goes completely against everything I believe in, never mind the fact that these days violence or aggression leave me a dithering wreck. For heaven's sake, I can't even watch Tom and Jerry without getting upset.

I can't make *him* out at all. Last night he was all mocking composure and seemed quite cultured, if you know what I mean, looking after me and suggesting the Spanish bar. I even thought he was gay, for heaven's sake. That seems incredible now. Tonight - well, he's still composed, that's for sure. And, I suppose, he's still looking after me, too. But I never would have expected the outright aggression, however justified. Or that it would be so controlled and furious. I shiver.

He's watching me. "Perhaps you should go back to your hotel," he suggests. He thinks shock is setting in.

Oh boy, he's a bit late. Shock set in the minute Simon pushed me against the wall, it's high-tailing it out of the resort now. Really, it is. I can feel it. Once again I feel a rush of light-headedness coming over me, if that's possible, and I giggle stupidly.

Donna is looking concerned again so I smile easily and shrug. "I'm fine," I say, as reassuringly as possible. Looking at their faces I've been about as reassuring as an open flame in a petrol station. Never mind. It's not their problem.

The girls want to move on. There's a bar further up the road with a dance floor and DJ. Fine by me, I like dancing once I've had enough booze to dim my self-consciousness and it might release some of my stress.

I dance for ages. Perhaps it's the combination of giddiness from my escape and alcohol, but I let my hair down and I know I'm the best dancer in the world, ever. I feel light, rhythmic and fantastic. There's always a few of the girls up with me and at times some of the blokes join us. Mystery guy doesn't; I guess chilling violence and sinuous dance moves don't mix well in the same evening. Who knows?

Anyway, it has the added bonus of stopping me from drinking so fast, because I can feel I'm already well on the way.

Eventually I fall off the dance floor and rejoin the others. My mystery guy is still here with his friends, and I'm inordinately pleased. I still don't really think I've shown my appreciation as much as I should have, but I'm not sure how to do it. Buy a rose from the tacky bloke who comes around selling them? Send him on a day at the spa? Remove my clothing sensuously and treat him to a private pole dance? I mean, what *is* the etiquette when someone has taken out a man who was molesting you? I simply can't believe I forgot to bring my copy of Debrett's with me.

He moves over to me.

"Dance?" he murmurs, and I realise the music has slowed right down. Now usually I can't stand it when a man eyes you up all night but doesn't bother to dance with you until he knows he'll have the opportunity for a good grope. But then usually said man hasn't possibly just saved me from a fate worse than death. So I nod. And smile a secret smile of anticipation.

When we get on the dance floor he stands very close but again doesn't put his arms around me. Somehow it makes it more intense, not less, and I'm not sure what to do. If I touch him will he be disappointed? Because I'm gagging to, I can tell you. It appears this time it's me who's up for a good feel.

He's watching me as all this is rushing through my head like the 5.45 from Paddington. I can see a smile playing about his lips. I want to touch them. Oh, hell, I'm so out of practice with this sort of thing. I'm so *pathetic*. I wish I had the confidence to just do what I want to do without worrying about what other people think. Particularly what he thinks. I'm still wondering what he made of finding me and Simon clutched against the wall. I only hope –

My thoughts scatter as he puts me out of my misery. *He's kissing me again. He's kissing me here on the dance floor. Don't let him stop.* My hands are twitching as I have to forcibly keep them from exploring under his t-shirt. What's got into me? I still don't know if that will be welcome. *What kind of complete idiot am I? What must he be thinking of me? Can Donna see me? Stop it! Stop worrying about what other people think, for God's sake! Just stop it!*

Now I'm kissing him back and moving forward like the terrible hussy he probably already thinks I am. Maybe he's only doing this because he's seen that I must be an easy target. Suddenly it's all clear. *I don't care.* I don't care what he thinks. I don't care what *anyone* thinks. I just know that I am going to thank him in the best way possible and I can't wait. Whatever the consequences; I have no doubts. None at all. God, I nearly take his hand and drag him off there and then. What *has* got into me? I haven't slept with anyone for three years; I haven't let anyone *near* me.

Scrap that – I didn't say that. It isn't something you need to know.

I'm almost panting with excitement, and he seems to feel the change. Dear me, it's so palpable to me I imagine even the barman can feel it. He steps back and looks into my eyes. "Let's get out of here," he says, and I know it's a corny line but I can only nod urgently and want to gallop straight out of the bar.

He stops me. "You'd better tell Donna."

He's right. At least one of us is thinking straight. I look around for her and of course she's staring right at me. I meet her eyes and she nods. She looks rather surprised but she's not stupid. Or blind.

We head out. "Where shall we go?" I say idiotically, "I'm sharing with Donna." I giggle nervously. I have made the assumption that we are going for more than just a drink and I wonder if I'm jumping the gun. Oh, God, what will he think? *For heaven's sake, stop worrying about what everyone is thinking, you imbecile.*

"I'm sharing with Rob," he tells me, so he has worked out where my mind has gone. Not that I made it difficult.

"Do you think Donna and Rob will mind sharing?" I say, and start to titter like a mental case. I'm losing my mind.

"We'll get a room."

Oh my God, we're going to get a room. I've heard of this kind of thing. My stomach churns uncomfortably with scared anticipation. I feel sick again. *What am I doing?*

The first hotel is full and I stand next to him feeling like such a slut. I mean, it's obvious what's going on here, isn't it? I know I am looking defiant to hide my cringing shame. For Goodness sake, they must see this all the time; they're not going to care, are they? Why am I bothered?

The same happens at the next hotel and now I'm beginning to waver. It's making me feel so awful; so cheap. *One more*, I think. *One more*.

He knows how I'm feeling, I can tell. He takes my hand and kisses me. It's what I need. At the third hotel I stand away from him, I'm too horribly embarrassed to go through it again. And this hotel has a room. Thank God. *Oh, shit.* I'm *so* scared. He doesn't know. He doesn't know anything about me. I have no idea what's going to happen; of how I am going to react. I have never been so frightened in all my life.

No, that's not true either. Another thing you don't need to know about right now.

CHAPTER THREE

We stand against opposite sides of the lift, staring at each other. My breaths are coming short and fast. I daren't go near him.

We find the room and he opens the door. I walk in first, and I'm surprised. It's really big and airy with two armchairs and a massive telly and so on. The open curtains reveal a huge balcony. "Gosh, this is really nice," I say, gazing around, and I'm instantly thinking, *What are you saying? You are about to have sex with a stranger and you're admiring the room, you stupid cow.*

The bed is huge. I stare at it for a brief second, transfixed, before turning to him.

He's leaning against the closed door and his eyes are hot. I feel my body start to throb. What's happening to me? For the umpteenth time that night I don't know what to do. I mean, I know what I want to happen, but I've no idea how to go about it.

He looks like a leopard waiting to pounce. It's apt, because I feel exactly like the gazelle caught in his eyes. He advances slowly. This is not what I expected. He puts his hands on my waist and I see surprise flicker across his face as he encounters my money belt. The catch is like a Chinese puzzle – the idea being that it will be difficult for a thief to whip it off me – and if he tries to remove it we'll be here all night. I give a ridiculous giggle as I picture us having steamy sex with me still wearing it. I'm going to pieces.

"I'll do it," I say, and of course I'm so on edge that I fumble clumsily and it seems to take forever. Perhaps it would have been better to leave it to him, after all. He waits amazingly calmly until finally it's off.

Then his hands start to move. At last I feel him touch my skin. They are under my vest and slowly heading north, feeling their way and taking my vest with them. I'm almost beside myself and I'm bursting to rip his clothes off, but he's looking into my eyes and it's unnerving. I try to, but I can't break the connection, it's like he's using superglue. Then he reaches my breasts. Now he looks down. *That's not fair*, I think absurdly, *how come he can look away so easily when I can't?*

He slides his hands up and automatically I raise my arms so he can remove my vest. I see his face darken for a second and I look down. Angry bruising is starting to show. As he did in the bar, he brushes my breast softly with the back of his hand. I catch my breath and he meets my eyes again.

Then all hell breaks loose. I can't wait. I can't wait any longer. He is scrabbling at the back of my skirt trying to undo it. My hands are under his t-shirt and it's every bit as good as I imagined. Then his t-shirt's off and I'm grappling with his shorts. My skirt is round my ankles and I nearly fall over as I try to kick it away. I'm panting and flushed; I've never in my life wanted someone like this. His hands reach for my knickers and I'm almost sobbing with desire. Then suddenly we're both naked and he pulls me

24

onto the bed. Bloody hell, he's fit. His body is hard and exciting. *Oh my God, oh my God.* I'm ashamed to say I'm gagging for it, encouraging him shamelessly.

In seconds his face is above mine. He moves urgently and I'm wide-eyed, sick with anticipation. Then suddenly he stops. *Fucketty fuck! Why? Why is he stopping?* I can't stand it. *What have I done?*

"Are you sure?" he says.

Bloody hell! If I hadn't been that question would do it, and no mistake. I nod urgently. "Which part of my body language did you find ambiguous?" I ask.

He grins.

"Slowly," I say, suddenly shy.

I have to stifle a giggle. He looks like I've just asked him to pull out one of his own teeth.

"It doesn't matter," I add quickly, "if you don't want to, or can't. Sorry."

But he can. Ooooh, oh my God, he can. *Oooooh.* I think I've died and gone to heaven.

I have no idea how much later it is. I'm lying on my side. He's in front of me, facing the other way. The sex has been extensive and fantastic and I'm sated and deliriously happy. I look at his silhouette; I can hardly make it out in the dark of the room. As I look I wonder what he thinks. I can't help it – I'm always worried about what people think. I hope to goodness he doesn't just get up and walk out in the morning. I've heard of that kind of thing and it sounds hideous. I mean, I don't mind him going - he has to, doesn't he? - as long as he's nice about it.

To be honest, whatever he does he can't take this night away from me. It's been brilliant, *he's* been brilliant, and I'm so grateful. And I didn't fuck up; thank God I didn't fuck up.

Very slowly, very gently, I ease myself over to lie on my other side. I still must disturb him because he stirs, and then turns over too, curving his body around mine. It's dark so I know he won't see. He kisses my head, and it's so the right thing to do. Now I know he won't just get up and go tomorrow as if I'm worthless.

He puts his arm across my waist and his hand drops against my stomach. It flutters in response and I feel his fingers start to move, and I'm quivering with eager anticipation. And I thought the night couldn't get any better. How wrong can you be?

It's morning. I'm lying on my back and it's quite light because, although at some point last night we pulled the curtains, in our haste we didn't make a very good job of it. He is on his side, turned towards me, his arm curled around my waist. I have the biggest grin in the world plastered across my face. I can't seem to help it.

Unexpectedly I wonder what he looks like, lying next to me. I mean, I've only ever seen him after a few drinks, maybe I've been wearing beer goggles the whole time. I have to suppress a nervous giggle at the thought. He might be really ugly.

I have to look now. Carefully I turn my head. I let out my breath slowly. If anything, he looks better than I remember. Perhaps it's the after-sex glow. I'm glowing so much I feel like the *Ready Brek* kid off the adverts. I move my head back so I am facing the ceiling again, my eyes closed, the grin still refusing to budge.

Presently I feel him start to wake. His breathing changes and his hand twitches. I lie still, giving him time to come round undisturbed. After a few minutes he lifts his head and I open my eyes.

He's looking at me, and he smiles. "What's so funny?" he asks. He can't be that thick, can he? I start to blush and his smile widens – now he's got it. "Ah," he says. "Mmmm," I reply.

He lowers his head and kisses me. I *knew* he wouldn't just go off without so much as a goodbye. I'm a better judge of character than that.

He tightens his arm around me and pulls me slightly towards him. I find my hand is running up his arm, along his shoulder, down his chest, and onwards. He makes a deep sound and pulls me on top of him. This man is insatiable. God, how fantastic is that?

Later he gets up for a shower. I lie bashfully under the sheet and watch him as he moves around. He's magnificent, and I shiver with pleasure. As I hear the water run he puts his head around the door. "Join me?" he asks.

Oh no! Did I mention that I'm a bit self-conscious? For a moment the mockery of the night I met him emerges. "Don't tell me you're embarrassed," he says, "It's a bit late for that."

He's right, of course, and I have to climb out of bed. This is no time for shrinking violets, and I've come this far. *I hope he doesn't notice,* I think in panic, *please, please don't let him see.*

He's already under the water. That's good. I step in and he takes my face in his hands, kissing me. He picks up the soap and takes his time. If I wasn't so profoundly anxious I'd be enjoying it immensely. As it is, I can't help enjoying it quite a lot. To me this is the best bit. I've never been keen on sex in the shower; I spend the whole time worrying that I might slip and fall over. He turns me round, and I'm sure he hesitates, just for a split second, and I shrink inside. *Oh, God, he's noticed; he's seen the scars. Now he'll know there's something wrong with me. It's not fair! It's not fair.* For a moment I want to dash out and run away, but I can't.

To my amazement he simply carries on. He doesn't trace the lines with his fingers, nor does he ask about them. I'm curled up with misery, waiting for him to react, but he doesn't. Maybe I imagined the hesitancy, I was dreading it so much. Perhaps he can't see because of the running water; I know they've faded a lot now. His arms slip around me and he pulls me against him. I turn round and now it's my turn. He has a fabulous body and this is a pleasure. Now I can relax and enjoy every inch of him, except that of course I've gone back to wondering if he'll want sex in here, and if so, if I'll fall over. God, I'm so pathetic. I hate myself sometimes.

I wonder if he can read minds. He turns the shower off and picks up a towel. I do the same and we face each other, starting to dry each other off. We don't even make it to the bed. I've had more sex in these hours than I would ever have had in a week - even a good week. I don't want it to end. It's like I'm in a dream and I don't want to wake up.

But I have to. I'm aware that time is running on and I want to see Donna, too. We dress and sit on the balcony for a while and I text her. The girls are around the pool and not going anywhere until seven again. She tells me not to hurry back, but it's not that easy. I want to see her as well and I'm torn. Also, it's not only about me; perhaps he's ready to go, too.

I glance over and he's watching me with the strangest expression on his face. He's very good at unnerving me at times.

"You want to go," he says.

This unnerves me even more. I want to explain, so he can understand the conflict, but I've never been any good at it and I don't want to give too much away. I can't tell him why I hardly ever see Donna, so he can't appreciate the way I feel. He stands up. "Text me tonight?" he asks, and I nod. "Do you think you can manage not to get yourself into any trouble this time?" he adds sardonically.

I cringe, and he laughs. To my relief he appears to be unfazed. I look up at him and by his expression I think my face must say all the things I've been unable to put into words. I reach up and once more tenderly trace the cut above his eyebrow. He drops his head for one last kiss.

I go to my hotel room and change into my swimming things. It's funny, but I'm no longer so bothered about strangers seeing me, I suppose because what they think doesn't matter. It's a bit like going topless – easier to do in front of strangers than someone you know. I've always thought that was odd. Anyway, the only thing this lot are going to wonder about is why I am wearing such a high backed costume when I am quite clearly sunbathing.

Of course, as soon as I'm back I'm wishing I'd stayed with him longer. I do that all the time. Someone once told me that whatever time I left I would always worry that it was too soon. I think they might have been right. Is everyone so messed up or is it just me?

Donna's pleased to see me and bursting to hear all the gory details. You will have guessed by now that I'm not good at that either and I have to disappoint her, but I know she gets the drift and she's pleased for me. She tells me about the rest of her evening, and it sounds as though everyone had a good time. Jo and Trish want to go to a bar at the far end of the resort tonight to meet the guys they like. I don't think it will be a problem, the resort is fairly compact.

At seven we head out. Blue vests this time, substantial and dark enough for me to go bra-less again, which is a relief because I am sore.

We eat and head off to the chosen bar. I send my text, and start to glow again as the warm anticipation starts to grow. My stomach is fizzing as I imagine how the evening will go.

But he doesn't arrive. I know he might be a while, because he was last night, and we are probably further away than we were then, too. But as time goes on I realise he isn't coming at all. *Why? What have I done?* Did he see the scars after all? My stomach twists with misery and my whole body seems to shrink into itself; I feel utterly wretched. I try very hard to hide it because it's our last night and I don't want to spoil it. Donna is watching me closely and it takes all my energy to put on a brave face while I curl up with despair inside. It's not so much that he doesn't come, although that's bad enough; it's that he doesn't even bother to text me, to tell me he's changed his mind, or broken his leg, or whatever other excuse he might choose to give to get out of seeing me. At least then I'd feel he cared enough not to leave me uncertain, rather than have me standing here knowing he's so unconcerned that even a text is too much trouble. I feel hideous, thrown away like a dirty, used nappy.

I keep getting very angry, too. That *bastard*. Who the *hell* does he think he is? I'm furious, wretched, vitriolic and meltingly disappointed.

I get through the evening somehow. Alcohol is a great healer and I become indestructible after a while, conspicuously enjoying myself and letting my hair down. In fact I'm trying desperately to drive the desolation out of my head, and it works, to an extent.

I'm so utterly glad when the evening's over. Watching Jo and Trish with their men, arranging to get together when they are back in England, doesn't help. Not that I was expecting more than a weekend with my guy – no way would it have extended beyond this resort – but I didn't expect it to end like this and be left feeling like, well, like shit, actually.

The next morning I feel better, mentally at least. I have a horrendous hangover, that's to be expected, but I am more resigned to what's happened. It's not the first time I've been let down by a man, and after a night's sleep the memory of our night together is emerging, and nobody can take that away from me. The fact that he seemed genuinely to like me spoils the balance, somehow, but then again, I wouldn't have enjoyed it so much if he hadn't. Let's face it; I wouldn't have even been there. *And maybe he did like me, at the time*, I think. It's easier to believe that. At least I've done it. I thought I'd never be able to go there again, and he's given me that.

Donna and I have a good chat while we pack up our things. She is sorry about what happened, but I shrug. "I had a good time," I say.

She's relieved I've taken it so well and I ask her about her coming wedding to distract her. She still has a lot to do and she's very excited. I haven't met Mike, her fiancé, because she met him after I moved to Spain, but he sounds lovely and I'm happy for her. We hug and there's almost tears, probably because we are both a bit weary after the rigours of the weekend.

I wait with the girls for their minibus, and then they're climbing on board and waving frantically as they disappear out of sight. I'm holding myself together as I find my car but by the time I'm climbing in my vision's blurred. Finally alone, in the security of my little metal box, I fall to pieces.

I make it home in the end and it's a comfort to enter the familiar rooms and leave my experience behind me. I'll go out tonight to the local bar, and maybe Paulo and some of the others will be there. That'll cheer me up and it will be better than staying in and moping.

I've known Paulo for a couple of years and I think he has a bit of a soft spot for me. He's always attentive when I see him, and I know if he's out I will be looked after. When we first met I was hopelessly useless at socialising, plus my Spanish wasn't so good, and it was some time before I cottoned on to how he felt. He has never once made advances to me, and that makes me wonder if I'm wrong, although I don't think I am. It may be because I was so excruciatingly inhibited when we first met that he is waiting for me to show I am ready. He's that kind of guy. In addition he has never seen me with anyone else, so there's no threat in that way and nothing to make him feel he has to push things. Or perhaps he thinks I'm gay and just likes my company. Who am I kidding – I don't have a clue what's going on in his head, do I?

My local, Paco's, is unusual in that it is frequented by a mix of Spanish and British. That's one of the reasons I like it, and why I was pleased it would be my local when I was house hunting. Although my Spanish is good now, it's nice to have some British people to talk to, because whatever anyone tells you, our cultures are quite different. Even if just at the level of discussing British TV or football, it's not until you move abroad that you realise how much you have in common with your fellow countrymen. Or perhaps a better way of putting it is how little common ground you have with the locals - the easy conversation which you need when you first move somewhere and perhaps you're shy or your language skills aren't so great. Or both.

Most of the Brits here are retirees, and that drew me to the place, too. You don't get many retirees kicking off and fighting. The Spanish are not aggressive generally, even when drinking, so I am comfortable in Paco's, and indeed in this place where I live. I have made a lot of friends amongst the Spanish and British here, and they are all pleasant people. The culture difference matters less now I can speak the language more and am part of the life here.

There's a good mix in the bar tonight and it's not too busy. Paulo is there and he's pleased to see me, asking me about my weekend. Perhaps I'm reacting to what happened, because for a moment I am almost tearful at his clear affection for me, and I'm probably warmer to him than usual. I expect this to please him but a couple of times I see him eyeing me anxiously, and I wonder if he senses anything.

The evening passes quickly and memories of my weekend are driven out for a while. I'm grateful, and I surprise myself by having a good time.

Donna rings me the next day to see how I am. In fact she rings me a few times over the next week or so and I know she's worried about me. She has no need to be. I'm back in my secure little world. Ok, so I am still absolutely furious with my mystery guy, and perhaps disappointed, too, but I'm getting over it and the feeling of degrading worthlessness is fading. In any case, I could never have had a relationship with this guy. I can't have a relationship with any guy. The whole weekend is beginning to feel like a dream, although I am trying to hold on to the memory of the sex. I grow hot every time I think about it.

It was so fantastic to see Donna and I'm gutted that I won't see her again for ages. She must be thinking the same thing because she says, "I wish you could come to the wedding."

She's so kind. She uses the word "could" not "would", even though technically I can go. I'm silent.

"Sorry," she says.

"It's ok. I do, too." I can't begin to put it into words and she knows that.

She changes the subject.

But somehow she's planted something in my head. It's not as though I haven't wished I could go before, but hearing her say it like that has made it seem more real. An annoying part of me wonders if I should be grateful to my mystery guy (or *Scumbag* as I prefer to call him now) because having successfully overcome one hurdle perhaps I feel I could face another.

Whatever the reason, the idea keeps niggling at me. Underneath I know I can go to her wedding, it's just that I swore I would never set foot in the UK again. At the time I was so traumatised that the thought of being there scared me to death. I knew I wouldn't be able to cope. They say time is a great healer, and perhaps they are right. Three years have gone by since it happened, well over two since I moved to Spain, and the picture of Donna's delighted face if I turn up and surprise her almost manages to overrule the fear. I can't stop imagining her and how much it would mean to her.

Oh, bollocks. I know now that I will regret not going more than I will regret going. I can arrive the day before, attend the service, see Donna, meet Mike and be on a flight back by the evening. Nothing can happen in such a short time, and it will be worth it. After that, if I find it's as bad as I'm dreading, I need never, ever go again. Perhaps I should try going anyway – at least once. And if so, what better time to choose?

I feel sick as I book the flights. Luckily I can do exactly as I hoped. I book a hotel near the airport and a car, too. I'm scared stiff but proud of myself. I'm so looking forward to seeing Donna's face when I turn up. I can't wait. And I could wait forever. It's confusing.

A week to go.

The flight is ok. I buy a load of sandwiches at the airport, pick up my car and drive carefully to my hotel. It's a long time since I've driven on the left and it takes all my concentration.

Once there I lock myself in securely. I'm not leaving again until I have to.

The next day is bright and sunny. I'm pleased for Donna's sake and also because I have brought a summery dress hoping it would be warm and now I can wear it. I have a jacket and matching shoes, and a big hat. This is very important. I don't want to be recognised if any of my old friends are there. That would be too awful.

I know I look different now. The bump in my nose (which I hated anyway) was thoughtfully not put back, I'm tanned and slim and my hair is longer and bleached by the sun. I have used a *champagne* rinse for the past week, too, just to be on the safe side.

I'm almost trembling with trepidation as I leave the hotel. I've given myself plenty of time to find the place, although I want to sneak in as late as I can and hide at the back. I park up and sit in the car waiting, winding myself up nicely.

Eventually I have to get out and I arrive at the church just as the stragglers are entering. Perfect. I slide into a pew at the back with my hat pulled well down. I won't let Donna see me until afterwards in case she faints with shock or something. My stomach is tingling excitedly at the thought of her pleasure, and despite everything I feel an anticipatory smile spread across my face.

After five minutes or so the organ starts and Donna walks in on the arm of her father. I feel a horrendous pang, and for an awful second I think I'm going to keel over. This is something I hadn't thought about. But Donna looks beautiful, and I am so proud and happy for her that it overrides my shock and I watch surreptitiously as she passes and walks up the aisle.

The service is lovely, only slightly marred by my worrying about exactly when I should reveal myself to her. I wouldn't be happy if I didn't have something to worry about. Anyway, not on her way out, that's for sure. Don't want her bursting into tears the minute she's married, that wouldn't look good. I'll wait until they are outside, do it then.

The service finishes and she and Mike lead the way out. It's the first time I've seen him and I'm impressed. I am one of the last to leave and I search for my friend - it's more difficult because I'm not tall.

Then I see her. The happy couple are standing together talking to someone, and thank goodness it's no-one I know. I move towards them and raise my face so it is no longer shadowed by my hat.

For a hideous moment I actually believe Donna is going to have a heart attack. She stares at me with her mouth open and her eyes popping out of her head. Mike sees and looks over. I walk quickly towards her and she whispers, "Em," then puts her hand over her mouth. There are tears in her eyes. I'm *so* pleased I came.

We hug, as well as you can hug someone in a huge white dress, and she whispers in my ear, "Oh my God, I can't believe it. You came! You came to my wedding. It's the best present ever. Thank you so much."

"I wanted to," I reply, and move back.

Mike is watching us with open curiosity. Donna turns to him. "This is Sam," she says.

His eyes widen and I know Donna has told him. Ok; that's fine. So she should, under the circumstances - I mean, they're husband and wife, aren't they? Family. "Sam," he says, holding out his hand, "I'm really pleased you made it." He looks at Donna with such a tender expression that I draw in my breath. *I want that*, I think. He knows how much this means to her. I can see I'm going to like him.

"Can you come to the reception?" Donna asks eagerly, "Only it wouldn't be any trouble because Don's ill and he and Maria had to cry off."

"No," I say, "I'm flying out tonight."

Her face falls and I feel really mean. But even though up to now it hasn't been so bad I don't think I could face that. The knowledge of my impending escape is definitely making all this easier.

"Did you bring your guy with you?" she asks unexpectedly.

"My guy?" I repeat blankly.

"I thought I saw him – the one from my hen weekend."

I stare at her, and she can see from my aghast expression that I most definitely did not bring Scumbag with me.

"Oh," she says quickly, "it must have been someone who looks like him. I wasn't sure."

"You *know* how that ended," I mutter darkly as Mike is listens in with interest.

"Of course, sorry. I don't know what I was thinking."

"We could fit you in, I'm sure, if you could stay." This is Mike, wanting Donna to be happy.

I gaze at Donna. She knows, and I simply can't speak in front of him, so what do I do? My mind churns. Mike takes the hint and moves away slightly. He really does seem very nice.

"Someone might recognise me," I tell her.

"But you look different now. Nobody will be expecting you to be here, and you look so different."

I knew turning up like this was a bad idea.

Donna takes in my expression and adds quickly, "Sorry, I know. It's just so wonderful to have you here and I want it all." She takes my hand and squeezes it, making me gulp. "I'm so glad you came," she whispers.

Oh, God, I feel really mean. I want to stay for her, of course I do, but if anyone sees me I'll die. I can't face the possibility. She can see my dilemma and knows she's being unfair.

"Whatever else, you came," she says. "It means so much to me. Thank you." Her eyes are shining into mine, and then their focus shifts and she's looking past my head. For the second time in ten minutes her mouth drops open. I glance behind me to see what she's seen.

Oh my God! It's him! It's Scumbag! *Scumbag* is standing there; standing there, staring.

CHAPTER FOUR

Oh my God, oh my God, what am I supposed to do? I feel sick anger welling inside me and he's using superglue again because I can't look away. I'm like a rabbit trapped in the headlights. My feet are nailed to the ground and my stomach is trying to escape.

Donna moves and stands partly in front of me, staring back at him defensively. Mike sees her, and moves forward automatically to back up his new wife. I'm frozen like an utter half-wit, staring stupidly. Donna moves again, turning her back on Scumbag and moving between us so I can no longer see him. She's looking at me, Mike's looking at her, I'm having palpitations and Christ knows what Scumbag's doing.

"What's he doing here?" Donna asks and I look at her like she's mental. *How the bloody hell do I know?* I think. *It's your wedding.*

"Did you invite him?"

I know it's a ridiculous question but I can't think straight. She gives me a wounded look and says, "No, of course I didn't, but anyone can come to the ceremony, can't they, churches are public places."

It dawns on us both at the same time. Oh fucketty fuck, I can't believe this is happening. *What am I going to do?*

"Perhaps you should see what he wants," she suggests.

"Why the hell should I?" I retort angrily. How dare he put me in this position at my best friend's wedding? How *dare* he?

Donna shrugs. She turns back to him and now I can see him again. He holds his hands out placatingly. "I only want to speak to you," he says, "Please."

I don't know what the bloody hell to do. The last thing I want to do is speak to him, and yet I don't want to refuse and cause a scene or anything on Donna's big day. If she thinks I should speak to him then maybe I should – the bride is supposed to get everything she wants today, right? Oh, *shit.*

"Please," he repeats, "I'd like to explain."

Donna turns to me. Perhaps the romance of getting married is getting to her, because she isn't telling him to piss off like I would expect her to. She gives me a pointed look. "We are going to have to go and do the photos," she says quietly. "It'll take about a quarter of an hour and then I'd like you to come and have yours taken, too. Is that ok? Do you have time?"

I nod submissively. I'm going to have to speak to him, I can see that. The photographer is calling Donna and Mike and they move off. I stand and stare at Scumbag. I don't want to go anywhere near him. I'm furious, all the hurt and degradation is being dug up again, and the sight of him is making me feel sick. I'm also very confused. My brain is shouting out, rebelling against my forced proximity to him, but my body is saying something completely different. It remembers our night together and it knows exactly what it wants.

"There are some benches around the side of the church," he tells me, "We can talk there."

"I only have a few minutes," I say, wanting to keep it short.

"She said fifteen," he corrects me, nodding after Donna.

Bloody hell, he *does* have bionic ears.

I follow him to a quiet bench and he sits at one end. I go to nearly the far end. Only nearly because despite myself I know that going to the very end would be rude. Dear lord, if I don't stop worrying about what other people think I'm going to do myself a mischief. I should be *wanting* to offend this guy, and I'm worrying about bench etiquette.

He gives me a searching look for a moment and then turns to stare out over the gardens. "That night," he begins, "I know I must have upset you. I'm sorry."

I draw in a sharp breath. Upset isn't really in it. I have so many brilliant, caustic, vitriolic things to say in reply to this that I'm dumbstruck. I stare at his averted face, struggling to keep calm.

"I didn't mean to," he continues.

Still I say nothing. He's getting no help from me. And anyway, suddenly I can't think of anything to say.

"I was by the pool. A few of us were heading out earlier than the others to eat. The rest had been out for lunch and must have drunk quite a bit. They were going to follow us on. We were arranging where to meet when we noticed Shane. He must have dived into the pool, but into the shallow end by mistake. He wasn't moving and there was blood."

Scumbag (and I'm just beginning to have the tiny thought that this name might be a tad unfair) narrows his eyes for a second before carrying on. "I was nearest so I dived in. John followed and we pulled Shane out but he was unconscious and bleeding. We didn't know how long he'd been in there before anyone noticed. Ray has done first aid so he worked on Shane while we waited for the ambulance. Christ, it was awful." He pauses and rubs his nose as he remembers.

Oh, God, the cold realisation is creeping through me, followed by hot little sparks of excitement. I can't help it.

"I went in the ambulance because I speak the best Spanish. The others followed. It was touch and go for a while. In the end we stayed all night and into the next day until we knew he was ok. I couldn't contact you because my phone was in my pocket when I dived in. It was ruined, so I'd lost your number. As soon as I could leave for an hour or so I caught a taxi to the airport but I knew I'd missed you by then."

He'd have missed me whatever time it was, given that I wasn't flying anywhere, but he wasn't to know that. I'm staring at him dumbly, wondering what to think.

"I'm sorry," he says again.

"Don't be," I reply, "It wasn't your fault."

He must be telling the truth. Nobody would make something like that up, would they? Anyway, I can check it when I get back, there should

35

be something in one of the papers. Not that that helps me now, of course. But still.

"How is he? Shane? Is he ok?"

"Yes, he's fine. Stupid bastard."

For a moment I can see how angry he is, then he sighs. "I wanted you to know."

He sits up straighter and turns to me and I don't know what to do. For heaven's sake, I never bloody well know what to do. I just look at him, and God knows what my face is saying.

He moves to stand up, and I'm thinking, *Don't go*. What's wrong with me? I rack my brains for something to say, to make him stay a bit longer.

"Thank you for telling me." It's weak, but it'll do.

"I didn't want you to think I'd deliberately stood you up."

I look down. I remember the hurt and shame and I can't keep up. I don't know why I'm drawing this out because I can't be with him, I know I can't.

"I did think that." I hear my voice catch. *I'm giving myself away,* I think, *Stupid cow*. "So I'm glad I know now," I finish with more composure.

He nods. He has the strangest expression on his face. "Can I make it up to you?" he asks, and looks surprised. What on earth does that mean?

I suck in a breath. If it means what I think it might then it's kind of what I want, but I'm stumped. I'm flying to Spain in a few hours. And anyway it's no good. I'm silent.

He looks puzzled. "After the reception?" he suggests.

God, he's a bit forward, I think, and almost giggle.

"I'm not going to the reception," I tell him.

He's shocked, I can see. "But I thought Donna was your best friend. Why wouldn't you go to the reception?"

"I wasn't even coming to the wedding." I stop abruptly. I'm saying way too much.

"Why?"

"I'm flying to Spain tonight."

"Again?" I can tell he's confused.

I look down. "It's a long story."

"I have time."

"Well, I don't." I'm crying inside, trying to think of a way out of this horrible mess I've got myself in to. I'm not going to say I don't know what to do, because that would be pathetic.

"Weren't you invited?" He's incredulous.

"Yes."

"Then can't you change your flight?"

Oh, *Christ*, this is so unfair. "You don't understand," I say.

"No, I don't." I don't like the look he gives me. I'm floundering and panicking. A little part of my brain is wondering if, were I to miss my flight, he would come to the reception with me.

"When are you back?" he asks, and he's got me. I'm well and truly stuck.

I gulp. Tears are welling up and I push them back. He's watching me and I can't read his expression.

He turns away. "It's ok, I can take a hint. I don't suppose I blame you."

"It's not that." My voice is a whisper but old bionic ears hears me anyway and turns back. I'm going to have to be honest. "I live in Spain," I tell him, "I'm going home."

He isn't expecting that. He raises his eyebrows and thinks. "Surely you don't have to go back today? Don't you want to stay until tomorrow? To be at the reception?"

"Yes," I reply, because suddenly I do. Suddenly I want to very much. Nobody will recognise me, I'm being paranoid, and it'll be worth it. I'll have the double whammy of making Donna happy and spending more time with him. It's win-win. I can face the reception if he will be with me.

"Well then," he says, and I understand it no more because it's him saying it rather than Donna. "Go and see Donna and tell her you're staying, I'm sure she'll be pleased."

"Will you stay? If I miss my flight and go to the reception will you come with me?" I'm holding my breath.

"I thought you'd never ask."

I glance at my watch. "Oh shit! I'm supposed to be having my photo taken."

I stand up in a rush and bump into him in my haste to go. I freeze – and I don't mean cold, no way José, I mean like a statue. My brain is saying *hurry up, hurry up, hurry up*, but my body refuses to budge an inch. It thinks it's finally getting what it wants.

"I know," he murmurs, and then he takes my hand and we half jog around the church to find the others.

Donna's eyes nearly fall out of her head when she sees us together and I can tell she's pleased. I feel a moment's doubt. *What am I doing? This can't go any further. What am I doing?* But I don't care - despite knowing that, I want this evening, this night, if I can have it, and worry about the rest later. He knows I live in Spain, so he can't be expecting any more, can he? Of course not. He only came to explain, for God's sake.

The photos seem to take forever and Donna makes sure she has a few of just me and her, which is nice. Some of the girls from the hen party are there and it's good to see them. We catch up while the photographer gives directions and takes the photos. My guy waits patiently while all this is happening, and our eyes keep meeting. Finally I'm done and Donna tells me how to get to the reception. "What's his name?" she asks, "In case I have to introduce you?"

Oh! I realize I still don't know. I'll almost be sorry to find out, there's something mysterious and exciting about not knowing his name. "I'll ask him," I say, wondering if I really will. What am I thinking? I'll have to, now.

I start to walk over and the girls are with me. Jo sees him and stops dead. "What the hell's *he* doing here?" she snarls. "He stood you up. He stood you up and he didn't even *text*."

"It wasn't his fault," I tell her. I'm hoping he can't hear us, but he has bionic ears, hasn't he?

We carry on walking. "How difficult is it to send a text?" She's spitting venom, and I'm ashamed to admit that a little bit of me is pleased because it's on my behalf.

"Not so easy when your phone's at the bottom of a swimming pool," he replies calmly, and she stares at him as though he's something she's stepped in.

"Really," I add, "there was an accident and he had to go to the hospital."

"And you believe him?"

"Yes."

Not only do I believe him, but I realise now that I wouldn't care if he was lying. It's not as though I'm going to marry him, for God's sake.

We travel in our separate cars and park up at the big hotel where the reception is being held. Once we are inside and each holding a glass of champagne I say to him shyly, "I don't know your name."

His eyes glint into mine. "I know," he replies.

"What if people ask? I can hardly say I just picked you up in the street and we haven't got round to names yet."

"Why not? It's true, isn't it? Or would you rather say we're more into rampant sex than conversations?"

I blush furiously, and my stomach jumps at the word "sex". I can feel a smile starting.

"You can call me Tom."

"Is that your real name?"

"No."

"Oh." I giggle. "Then you can call me Sam." I have to say this, because that's how Donna and her family now know me.

"Is that your real name?"

"No."

"I see."

I sincerely hope he doesn't. We have another glass and I'm glad because I need the Dutch courage. I keep expecting someone to look at me and exclaim with surprise, trying to hide their shock and embarrassment. I've never understood why what happened to me should embarrass other people, but for some reason it does. It's one of the reasons I had to get away.

After a while we are called to our tables and I'm relieved to find I'm on a table of complete strangers. I don't know whether it's something Donna has managed to achieve or happy chance, but I'm grateful. I spotted a girl I used to know earlier on, but so far no one has looked at me twice so it appears I might be safe.

Surprisingly I have a good time. There's no doubt that having him here with me helps enormously. I find I don't really want to think of him as "Tom" if it isn't actually his name, so I try not to. Scumbag hardly seems fair now, though, does it? A couple of times he rubs my leg under the table. I do it back to him once and he leans over and whispers, "I'm not sure I'll make it to the evening at this rate." I flush dramatically, sure everyone will notice, but if they do they're far too polite to let it show. Thank heaven.

Then the speeches start. This is something else I hadn't anticipated, goodness knows why. When Donna's father stands up it's like someone has punched me in the stomach. My Dad will never get to do this, my Mum will never buy the hat. I can feel myself going to pieces. How I wish they were here. How I miss them. How many times in the past three years have I wished that those evil bastards who broke in had finished me off after they were done with me, like they did the rest of my family? I was sure they were going to. I was *hoping* for it. For a moment I'm back there and I can feel the incredible pain as the knife cuts into my back. God only knows why they did that after everything else. The main scar is shaped a bit like a wonky "S"; maybe they wanted to leave a message. The police think perhaps they were disturbed, and that's why they stopped and Mark and I survived, although we were left for dead, I know that. It certainly killed our relationship; Mark never got over having to watch. Poor Mark. I feel a fresh stab of pain at the thought.

This is no good. I try to rearrange my stricken face and glance up to see if anyone has noticed. My guy is looking at me with that strange expression which I can't make out. Oh God. My focus changes and I see Donna. She mouths, "Chin up," and I nearly burst into tears. But, thank goodness, it's what I need, and somehow I manage not to.

Finally it's over. I've been furiously picturing how this evening will go, as that seems to be the most effective way of driving out my other thoughts, and I've recovered my equilibrium. I know that later on, when I am with him, I'll be glad to be alive.

Donna and Mike are doing the traditional thing and heading off on honeymoon tonight. She doesn't know where they are going, it's so romantic and I'm delighted for her. She's really excited and very happy. I want to stay until they leave, around nine o'clock, she tells me. My guy raises his eyebrows at me and his meaning is clear - he's not sure he can wait until then. I'm in full agreement, but he'll have to. We both will. I'm amazed and a little disturbed by how quickly my feelings can change from utter despair to lust and excited anticipation, but I'm not going to let that bother me now. I've got enough on my plate without that.

"Oh, shit!" I suddenly exclaim.

"What?"

"I don't have anywhere to stay tonight."

This is really not like me, but so much has happened, and with all the worrying and fear I just clean forgot. I must be going mad. I giggle nervously and wonder where he lives. Is he planning on going home tonight? Somehow I think not.

He smiles. "I sorted out a room earlier," he says. "It seemed the best thing to do and I thought I'd spare you the experience. I can still remember your revulsion at having to go through it in Spain."

He's perfect. I nearly suggest taking our things up now but I stop myself in time. We'll never make it back down if we do.

Oh, God, there's the hire car too. Luckily I have the phone number in my mobile and I leave the reception room and find a quiet spot to ring them. He follows me and waits while I sort it out, then suddenly he leans forward.

Oh my God, he's going to kiss me. I've been waiting for this. I'd almost forgotten how good he tastes. I can feel the rush of desire but of course I spoil it for myself because I start to worry that he's actually going to want to have sex with me here in this corridor and someone might walk round the corner. I'm such a dickhead. I mean, he's clearly very turned on but he's not stupid.

A bit of heavy breathing later we return to the reception room. I can feel I'm flushed and hope it's not too noticeable. My body has woken up and is pounding nicely, or at least it would be nice if I wasn't in a room full of people.

Someone wanders over. It's one of the girls I used to know before it happened. *Oh God! No! Please, no.*

She peers at me. "Excuse me," she says, "but I'm sure I know you."

I smile at her as blandly as I can while it feels like my heart is about to leap out of my chest and run away.

"No, I don't think so." Even to me my voice sounds a bit weird and Tom or whatever his name is shoots me a look.

"Really, you do look familiar. How do you know Donna?"

I'm starting to curl up into a ball inside. I should have anticipated this and had my answers ready, but then I hadn't expected to be staying, had I?

"We have mutual friends," I explain, and it's uninformative enough to be true without actually saying that we went to school together and giving everything away.

"Perhaps I know some of them," she hints.

"I doubt it," I say abruptly, and I know I'm being rude but I'm in such a panic I can hardly breathe. If she recognises me I'll die. I can already picture the expression of horror and pity on her face and I can't bear it.

She gives me a searching look. "I know who you remind me of," she says slowly.

Shut up! Please stop. I'm trying desperately to keep my expression blank so I don't give myself away, but I'm not sure I'm managing it.

Then her look turns to confusion. "No, you look different, and anyway, she disappeared. God, it was awful, what happened."

I'm speechless. I mean, half the time I don't know what to say and the rest I'm incapable of saying anything anyway. Feeble isn't in it. *Please*, I entreat, *please don't say anything else; please*. I have no idea if I'm still managing to look normal when he steps in. "Sam," he says, and perhaps I imagine the deliberate way in which he says my name, "I think we should have a word with Donna while she's free."

"Yes," I reply quickly, "You're right. Excuse me."

He takes my hand and leads me away to where Donna is standing. My heart is thumping horribly and my mind is in a whirl; once more I'm wondering if he's Derren Brown, or have I been that obvious? *Please, God, no.* I push the thought away for now. Perhaps he really did just think we should catch Donna while we can, and he's right, because once the evening party starts properly we won't get a chance.

While we are talking to Donna and Mike her parents see me. "Sam!" they call, and rush over. Scumbag (I know I really must stop calling him that, but it's habit. I mean what if I cry it out during sex or something? I suppose I could pretend it's an ex, but come to think of it that could be worse) shoots me a look at the name "Sam" and I think maybe I should have used the word "original" rather than "real". Christ, I can't get myself in any more of a mess, can I? He must be wondering what on earth's going on.

Donna's parents are really nice to me. Of course they know what happened to me and they are two of the few people who know I changed my name and moved to Spain. Most people just think I vanished off the face of the earth. They are extremely caring and I'm wondering more than ever what Scumb – I mean Tom or whatever his bloody name is – must be thinking. He probably has me down as some kind of deranged loony and is regretting ever agreeing to stay for the reception, and I can't say I blame him.

Time is running on. The evening party starts at seven to give Donna and Mike time to see people before they head off. Donna's parents wander off with Mike. Donna wants a quiet word with me, I can tell. My guy goes to the bar (he's really quite astute at times) and Donna draws me to a secluded corner nearby.

"Thank you so much for staying for the reception," she says, "I know you've missed your flight."

"That's ok, I wanted to, really, I just wasn't sure if I'd be able to."

She nods. She understands. She glances over to the bar where he's getting the drinks in. "What about him?" she asks.

"What about him?" I reply, because I have no idea.

"Do you like him?"

"Like" still isn't the right word. I want him, of that I'm positive, but like? God, I hardly even know him, I realise.

Donna's waiting for my response. "I don't know," I say. It might sound hopeless but it's the truth.

"You asked him to stay with you," she points out.

She's right. But I'm not sure that I asked him for the right reasons, if you see what I mean.

"So what are you going to do?"

"What do you mean?" Perhaps the unexpected occurrences of the day are getting to me, because I can't think quickly enough.

"Are you going to see him again?"

"How can I?"

"These days flying to Spain isn't such a big deal."

"I can't." I know I sound feeble, but I can't help it. It's difficult to put into words that I can't face him disrupting what I have, now that I've finally managed to create a life away from the horror of what happened.

"You could tell him," she suggests quietly.

"No!" I stare at her, I can't believe she would even say that. *Nobody* knows, *nobody*.

"Do you want to be alone for the rest of your life?"

I know the romance of her day must be getting to her for her to say this, but it's below the belt and I'm almost angry.

"No," I say again, in answer to her previous question, and there's no doubt in my voice. God, even if I wanted to tell him I wouldn't be able to.

"I'll tell him, if you like."

I stare at her again. "You'd do that for me?"

"I'd do anything for you, Em, I want you to be happy."

"Don't call me that, please."

"Sorry."

"I can't. I can't do it."

"I can."

I can't believe she has offered to do this, it really is above and beyond the call of duty and it takes all my anger away. But it's too much for me. I shake my head. Tears are starting to form in my eyes.

Then Donna does the strangest thing. She takes hold of my face, leans forward and kisses me gently on the lips.

You have to understand she's never done anything like this before, and neither of us is even slightly gay, at least to my knowledge (she got married today, for heaven's sake) and anyway, the kiss isn't sexual, even though it's loving.

I hear a noise beside me and he's here with the drinks.

Oh, wonderful; this is just splendid. What the bloody hell must he be thinking of me now? *Thank you, God, thank you so very much. This just can't get any better, can it?*

CHAPTER FIVE

"Just think about it," Donna says, totally unfazed. I'm wondering if I even know her. "I'm not back for two weeks anyway."

"I love you," I say, moved beyond sense, but at least I have the wit to whisper it so very quietly that even bionic ears won't hear. *Surely.*

She nods. "Thank you so much for coming. You've made my day."

"Me too. Have a great time on honeymoon. I like Mike, he's lovely. Be happy."

She looks up as Mike calls her, and we hug a very big hug. She takes her drink; "Thanks," and turns back to me. "I'll call you when I get back. Think about it."

And off she goes.

My mystery guy is giving me such a funny look that I almost giggle out loud. I have to say I don't blame him. If I'd seen me from the outside today I'd think I was completely deranged. I wonder if he's having second thoughts. Oh God, I hope not. I didn't put myself up for all this not to get my reward at the end. This time I do giggle out loud and I wonder if he'll call an ambulance to take me away.

But he doesn't. He kisses me, and I can tell he's aroused, and that shuts me up because I'm not sure why.

Soon after this people start arriving for the evening. Speaking to Donna on her own becomes impossible, but it doesn't matter. We've said all we wanted to say and the main thing is I'm here. I will wait for her to go and then be glad to disappear again.

We hang around the bar, more biding our time than anything. Don't get me wrong, we're chatting and everything, and I think we're both enjoying ourselves, but neither of us is giving much away and the conversation's generic. Then some of the people from our table at the reception join us and we're having a pleasant time. Nobody else claims to know me, even though I know they are there, and with each hour (and drink) I'm relaxing more. Apart from beginning to worry about how I am going to escape tomorrow, of course. There's always something I can worry about. But I try to put it from my mind and not be so hopeless. I'll think of something. Meanwhile the excitement's building, and I can sense it in him, too. I'm tingling inside and can hardly keep still.

Finally nine o'clock arrives. Donna and Mike appear and she's wearing a beautiful powder blue going away outfit. She looks stunning and Mike looks very handsome. You can see how in love they are. There's much cheering and confetti-throwing and she makes sure I get a final hug before they climb into the car and disappear out of my life for the next however long. I'm grinning happily for them and slightly tearful, and I'm ashamed to say this might be as much for my sake as theirs, shallow pig that I am.

Anyway, I don't have long to think about this because he's already taken my hand and is leading me away. I want a final word with Donna's parents before I go and he tries nobly to be patient although I can feel his agitation growing. Donna's parents and I exchange a few meaningful sentences and looks and then it's big hugs again. Goodness knows what he's thinking, and I know I shouldn't worry about it but I do. I'm beginning to think that my mind isn't the thing he's most interested in, anyway. What's taken me so long to cotton onto that? You must think I'm really thick.

Once we're clear of the party I half expect him to throw me over his shoulder and scamper to our room, but he shows great restraint in hardly bundling me into the lift at all. Let's face it, it's not as though I'm in disagreement. Once more we face each other as we ascend and then he follows me into the room. I'm starting to worry again. *What if it isn't the same? What if I disappoint him? Oh God, will I be all right this time? What should I do now?* I really am a half-wit.

He's close behind me and he slides his arms around my waist, kissing the nape of my neck. "Fuck me," he breathes, and it rather jars with the romance of the day. I can't tell if it's an expression of relief that we're finally alone or a request. I'm hoping it's both.

I throw my jacket and hat onto a chair and he begins to slide the strap of my dress off my shoulder. I'm quivering with anticipation as his mouth follows the strap's progress and I'm almost beside myself. I've always thought that's a strange expression – I mean, how on earth can you possibly be beside yourself? Unless you're Mystic Meg or someone, of course. I can't believe I'm thinking this as he's undressing me. I must be finally going bonkers.

Now he's at the other side and I know that if he doesn't undo the zip my dress isn't going anywhere no matter how many straps he removes. Part of me wants to turn around and start on him, and part is taking too much pleasure from what's already happening. I'm not going to say I'm wondering what to do. He decides for me, and it's just as well. I feel the zip go and then he slides his hands inside my dress. God, I can hardly cope. His mouth is still on my shoulder and I'm starting to worry about him seeing my back, but there's no way I'm budging for a moment or two. Oh, no.

I turn round before he can move. I'm itching to get my hands on him and suddenly it's like before. Our eyes meet and it's pandemonium. Of course I have far more to go at than him – buttons, ties, belts, socks – he only has my knickers and a dress and that's already half off. He takes pity on me (or perhaps he can't wait either) and fumbles at his belt while I make a complete mess of his buttons. Then my hands are on his chest, his trousers are off, my dress falls to the floor. Finally he's naked and he rips my knickers off (I've always wanted to say that).

In a nice touch he picks me up and carries me to the bed. He pushes me back onto it and advances, once more reminding me of a leopard (and I don't mean he's spotty), as I watch him, mesmerised like the gazelle. Then all of a sudden his face is above mine and I wonder if he'll remember.

Ooooh. Oh God. Mmmmm. Oh yes. He remembers all right.

Fuck me.

I've no idea what time it is. I'm lying on my back with that silly grin on my face again. I'm spent and happy and my legs feel like they've been taken off and put back on again but not quite in the right way. I'll be walking funny for days but I don't mind, it's worth it. He's been, in the main, gentle and considerate, with gratifying moments of urgency thrown in. Not once has he been remotely rough or forceful, and it's just as well. I wonder if he's exceptionally good at reading me (perhaps he's Derren Brown's brother) or it's simply happy chance that everything he does is right.

As he sleeps next to me I start to wonder what the bloody hell I think I'm doing, and find I don't care. For once in my life I actually don't care. Whatever happens next, however I am going to get out of seeing him again (and I'm assuming he'll want to see me, that's the kind of vain cow I seem to be just at this moment), it doesn't matter. I realise now that if Donna was to ask me, yet again, if I like him, the answer is becoming dangerously close to "yes". And I can't risk that. I simply can't.

But I can still enjoy tonight, and boy, that's exactly what I'm doing.

I turn my head slowly to look at him. It's dark but not pitch, and I can see his outline and the shadows of his face. I feel a rush of gratitude for this pleasure he has given me, not to mention the confidence, not only from being able to be with him without running screaming into the distance, but also from him actually coming back for more, and it almost overwhelms me.

I move my face to his and kiss him. He stirs, and I feel him smile. He reaches out for me and pulls me nearer. He's stroking my back gently and I'm getting so turned on. I can hardly believe I can really be wanting him again so soon, but I am. It appears the feeling's mutual. I don't know what this man has done to me but I like it. I like it very much. I like what he's about to do to me even more.

It's morning. I'm stretched out across his chest, face down. Goodness knows why, and I'm instantly aware that he might see my back. I wonder if it really matters. Normally if someone sees the scars I blame them on a car crash. Now that there's only a few really noticeable, and I make sure most of those are mainly hidden by my underwear or swimwear or whatever, I don't get asked so often. The worst one is the "S" shaped one; it was the deepest and starts too high to be hidden by my underwear. Perhaps I should just let him see them and get it over with. Now that he's come back for more I feel more confident about it. But no. For some reason I don't think I'll be able to lie to him like I usually can. Why would that be? Anyway, I don't want to wake him so I lie still and wait.

Perhaps I should get a tattoo. I've never been keen on them but they are very fashionable and I could hide the scars that way. Perhaps I could have a heart with "Sam" and "Scumbag" on each side. One of those would do the "S" nicely. Without warning I snigger loudly and I know I've woken him. He shoots me a look and I'm not surprised. It must be a bit disquieting to be woken by a girl lying across you and sniggering at nothing.

"What's so funny?" he asks, and I try to convey that it's pleasure at the sex like last time, but I can see he's not buying it. He gives me a dark look that only makes me worse. It's not being able to tell him that makes it so funny, you know? And I definitely can't tell him.

He sighs and starts stroking my back again. It's soothing and I start to calm down. At least while my body is across his he can hardly lean up and look at it, can he? I can move when I need to. But, of course, other things take precedence and in the end he's not interested in my back at all. I should have known - honestly I can be dense, sometimes.

It's still fairly early, which is nice. Let's face it, it's not as though we came to bed late, and despite all our activities I reckon we've both had plenty of sleep, on and off. I lie there, completely at peace.

Presently he gets up for his shower. Once more I watch him as he goes to the bathroom and starts the water, and this time I join him without him having to ask. He picks up the soap, and doesn't turn me around but reaches both arms around me to do my back. This means I'm pressed up against him and it makes me giggle, and I'm very aware of his response. I'm not going to say I'm starting to worry that he'll want sex in here because that would be so feeble, and anyway loads of people must have sex in the shower, it's very popular, and hardly anyone ever falls over. As far as I know. So I try to ignore myself because he didn't want it last time, did he, so why spoil things?

Now it's my turn and I take great pleasure in the excuse to explore him. Did I mention that he has a fantastic body? He's already geared up, if you'll pardon the expression, and it's not long before, thankfully, he's turning off the shower and heading for the towels. We don't do much drying off though, I can tell you.

Afterwards he asks if I want breakfast. I'm surprised at how hungry I am, but then again, I suppose I've had quite a bit of exercise, in a way. He orders it from room service, which is a nice idea. While we are waiting he asks me, "What are you going to do today?"

It's a strange question. I mean, I'm flying back to Spain, aren't I? I'm puzzled, but in case all the sex has addled his brain (I know it's done something to mine) I reply, "The flight's not 'til six but I can always go to the airport early. I guess I'll have to anyway to book a seat. I don't know what time you have to check out of here."

"Twelve," he tells me. Good, that gives us plenty of time "I could come with you to the airport, see you off."

"No," I say, a trifle too quickly. I'm not having him see which airport I'm flying to. "There's no need," I add, more kindly.

"Or you could stay until tomorrow."

I stare at him. This is something I hadn't considered and I don't know what to say.

"You could come to my place," he offers.

Oh, God. If I don't want him in my life I certainly can't intrude into his, so what can I say? Thoughts are dashing around my head and I can't catch hold of any of them to enable me to turn one into words. I continue to stare deeply like some kind of bovine philosopher. God only knows what this guy sees in me.

"No," I repeat. All that thinking and this is the best I can come up with? Why don't I try letting him down gently?

But now small threads of silver excitement are joining the thoughts in my head. The prospect of another night with him is making my body tingle.

"You have work on Monday?" he asks.

I haven't - there's nothing like having your whole family murdered to leave you in a position of financial stability - but it would be a good excuse, wouldn't it? I shake my head. For some reason, as I suspected, I cannot lie to this man.

"Don't you?" I say hopefully.

"I work for myself."

That's a surprise. I wonder what he does, but I don't ask. I don't want to be nosey or to start a session of twenty questions.

The excitement is beginning to overcome the reticence. I knew it would. That's why I was excited in the first place. If you ever manage to work that one out please let me know.

"We could stay here," I suggest. "It's reasonably handy for the airport." Too late, I realise I don't know where he lives. If he has a flat above the control tower how on earth am I going to get out of going there now?

He gives me that strange look of his. I don't like that look, it makes me nervous. I shuffle a bit while he ponders.

A knock on the door makes us both jump and I leap up to put on one of the fluffy robes provided in the fear that room service will have a key and just walk in. He gets up with more decorum and grins a superior grin as he puts the other robe on and opens the door. Gosh, it smells good and in no time I'm tucking in enthusiastically.

"All right," he says, and I wonder what the heck he's talking about.

"Huh?" Still, at least I know how to coin a penetrating question to find out.

"Let's stay here."

Oh. My body does that tingling thing again, and then I have a thought. "You have no spare clothes," I say. In fact, he doesn't have anything with him at all – why would he when he only turned up to explain?

"I don't suppose I'll need any," he replies coolly, and I nearly fall into my bacon and eggs in shameful glee. The tingling has turned into pounding lust. How on earth does he do that? Does it really matter?

Now I'm starting to worry that tomorrow he'll suggest staying another day, and another one, and so on and so forth. Because if this guy works for himself he can give himself any number of days off, can't he? And while the thought of staying in this room with him for the rest of my life is sorely tempting, I know I have to go. I know I can't get too attached. I wonder how I can find out what his plans are.

"I have a meeting tomorrow afternoon so I'll have to leave for that," he says, and now I'm really convinced he's Derren Brown's brother. I try not to show my relief, and somehow looking disappointed is possible, because in a way I am. It's a good job I'm used to being confused or I'd be really mixed up by now.

We finish our breakfast and he puts the telly on. It's Sunday morning so I expect the choice to be rubbish, but of course the hotel has satellite and amazingly we find a film that looks promising. I'm almost feeling normal, lying on the bed with this man in our matching robes and watching a Sunday film. It's unnerving. Heaven help me that I might ever actually enjoy something without finding it unsettling. I'm beginning to think spoiling my own good time is my one greatest talent.

That said, I could lie here all day, I really could. Which is just as well, isn't it, because I probably will. I shiver at the thought.

I won't bore you with all the details of the day. Suffice to say we have sex more times than I can tell you, we order more food to be brought up to the room, we watch more telly and chat, and I worry about him seeing my back and how I will get away tomorrow without making any promises I can't keep.

I have the best time ever.

In the evening we decide to eat in the restaurant and actually get dressed. I've forgotten how good he looks with his suit on. I'll enjoy removing it later, too. We drink plenty of wine and that helps things along as we talk about nothing personal. I'm beginning to wonder if he has more to hide than I do, or if he's merely reacting to my lack of forthcomingness (is that actually a word?) Anyway, you know what I mean.

As we eat I take sneaky glances at him and try to work him out. This man manages to be both cool and funny, and I'm impressed at his apparent ability to respect my boundaries without me even having to point them out. I'm becoming uncomfortably aware that I am beginning to like him, at least as much as you can like someone about whom you know practically nothing. *Not even his real name*, I think with a gleeful frisson, and I know it's a good job I'm leaving tomorrow and that I'll have to make sure he can never find me again.

Christ, I think, *sometimes life is so fucking unfair*.

When we return to our room it's different. Not the room - that's the same as we left it - but us. Our urgency has gone and we undress each other with slow delight (or at least I do). When we have sex he's almost tender and I can hardly stand it. But, oh God, it's so good. I can't begin to tell you how good it is.

Later on I'm lying close to him in the dark and I'm not sure if he's asleep. His arms are around me and it feels wonderful, and I know I'm getting myself into a complete mess. Our physical intimacy is incredible and I'm tormented by the fact that I'm going to have to walk away tomorrow and I'll never be with him again. On top of that I'm panic stricken about how I'm going to achieve it without either of us getting upset. (By either of us I mean me, mainly, to be honest.) But I'll have to. I nestle a bit closer into his chest and he grunts and his arms tighten around me just a little, and I know that if I leave it any longer I'll be too late. And I simply cannot set myself up for anything like that ever again.

I loved Mark. I loved Mark with all my heart. We'd been together for over three years and he was everything to me. After it happened, and I was lying in that hospital bed, the only thing that made me fight, the only person I had left to hold onto, was him. When I learned that he was in a bed in the same hospital all I could think of was to get myself better - to a state where I could go and see him. He had been through it all with me, and we would be able to gain strength from each other and help each other to come out on the other side. Our love would see us through.

The first day I was allowed in the wheelchair I begged to be taken to see him. I was shocked when I realised he was in a wheelchair too, and could have come to see me earlier. I'll never forget the look on his face when I was pushed in. I can't possibly describe it to you; I don't have the words. Suffice to say he turned me away. He could hardly bring himself to look at me. He blamed himself, and the sight of me made him feel so guilty he simply couldn't bear it. I tried to tell him that it wasn't his fault – it was their fault, for God's sake – how the fuck could he help me with two broken legs and knives at both our throats? But he wouldn't listen. He couldn't even look at me without seeing what they had done to me and knowing that he hadn't stopped it. I never saw him again.

I'd lost everything; *everything*. The one person I had left, who I thought loved me most in all the world, let me down. I know he didn't mean to, that he couldn't help it, but it didn't change the fact that he did. I wished I'd died along with my family that night, and I'll never forget the emotional pain, in some ways even worse than the physical torture I had already suffered.

I will never, ever, *ever*, set myself up for anything like that *ever* again.

By now tears are brimming over my eyelids and I'm cursing myself for remembering and digging it all up again. What am I hoping to achieve? I'm hoping to hell he's asleep and doesn't know I'm crying. What on earth will he think? He wakes up to me sniggering and goes to sleep to me crying. He'll think I'm some kind of mental case. Perhaps I am. Anyway, he's very, very still, so he must be asleep. Thank God. I lie there and try to forget, and in the end I relax, and I sleep too.

At some time in the night I wake. I'm lying next to him now and it's a good job because I've been dreaming some horrible dreams involving hospitals, knives and me trying desperately to leave him as he follows me ceaselessly. God knows how much twitching and jerking I've been doing. I move away from him slightly and carry on worrying about how I will get away in the morning.

I consider getting up now and sneaking out. He seems to be pretty deeply asleep. But I can't do it to him. I can imagine how I would feel if it were reversed, and it's just too mean and cowardly, especially after him bothering to come and find me to explain about standing me up. Anyway, what if he were to wake up half way through? I shudder at the thought. It seems, whatever I said, I'm cowardly enough to let that possibility put me off.

I know it's going to be difficult to lie to this guy so I decide the best thing to do is try not to promise anything and make sure I don't give him any telephone numbers or anything. If the worst comes to the worst I'll have to make a "mistake" with one of the digits. I really don't want to upset him, though. Although I don't know if I will, as he might be quite content with just our weekend together, mightn't he? I wonder if I should leave him a note just in case, but I don't know what I would say. "Sorry I refused to see you again but I'm starting to like you and that's no good" simply doesn't back anything up, does it?

Oh God. Why am I so hopeless? What if I really do upset him? Perhaps a note *is* a good idea, at least it shouldn't do any harm. I know there's some hotel stationery on the side so I sneak out of bed and into the bathroom. I close the door and put the little light on over the mirror in the hope that it won't disturb him. If I hear anything I can pretend I'm vomiting, and if that doesn't put him off coming in nothing will.

I rack my brains for what to say. Best to keep it simple and quick, especially as I'm panicking in case he wakes. I can't think clearly. In the end I write:

"Tom" (Sadly I think putting "Tom" in speech marks is pretty sardonic and clever.)

Thank you for the perfect nights and incredible pleasure you have given me. I can't see you again, I'm sorry. I hope you'll believe me when I say that this is not because of anything you have done.

There is a part of you that will always be inside me, and know that I will think of you often, and that when I do I will always be smiling.

Please don't try to find me.

Have a great life,

Sam

x x

I'll forgive you for feeling sorry for me that after all my deliberations this is the best I can come up with.

Too late I realise the second paragraph could be construed as to be a bit rude, and I get myself into a right tizz wondering if I can fit "my head" in where I've put "me". But it doesn't look like I can without the whole thing looking crappy and infantile and I'm not doing it again because I've stupidly only brought one piece of paper in and I'm scared he'll wake up before I can put it in his suit. At least I don't have to worry about that, there's nowhere else to put it. Except, of course, that when I do get to his suit I can't decide which pocket to put it in. If I put it in his inside jacket pocket he might not find it for ages, but if I put it in his outside pocket he might find it before we leave and I'll die. I consider his trouser pocket but there's no benefit there. Then I wonder if I should write another quick note to put in his outside pocket, telling him there's a note in his inside pocket and he mustn't read it until he's alone. Then I realise what an utterly stupid berk I'm being and wonder if I really should be committed. *Then* I hear him move and I shove it into his inside pocket (not finding it for a million years is less of a crisis than him reading it in front of me) and quickly scurry away and creep back into bed. My heart is pounding and I'm cursing myself for being such a useless imbecile.

Christ, I feel weird, because I really don't want to go but I can't wait to get out of here. How bizarre is that?

CHAPTER SIX

It's morning. When I wake he's there before me. He's lying on his back and seems uncommunicative. By uncommunicative I mean not welcoming communication rather than simply not wanting to communicate, if you get my drift. Although how you can seem like that lying on your back doing nothing I have no idea.

I'm already feeling wretched and he's not helping. Unless I'm imagining it as a result of my feeling of wretchedness, which is distinctly possible.

What with my wretchedness and his uncommunicativeness (do I win an award for a word like that?) we're heading for a dandy morning. Perhaps I should just get up and run screaming from the room after all.

I move my arm slightly and he turns to me and his eyes are guarded, and for a horrible moment I wonder if he senses something. After all, he's Derren Brown's brother, isn't he? Derren Brown's brother with bionic ears. Perhaps he can hear my thoughts. That would be awful. I almost snigger at this but I reckon waking up to me sniggering at nothing once is enough. Christ, I hope to God he didn't sneak up in the night and read my note. I go cold at the thought.

I must be looking apprehensive because suddenly he smiles and all my worries high tail it out of the building. I love the way he has that effect on me. I reach up and touch his face where he was cut in Spain, although there's nothing there now, and he just knows. He kisses my palm and suddenly everything is all right and everything is wrong and I don't know what to do. That makes a change, I hear you say.

This time it's me who pulls him to me and I'm touching him and stroking him and I want him desperately. I don't want it to be my last time and I almost hope that the fire alarm will go off so I won't have to experience that *last time* feeling. Although it's early yet, and knowing him it isn't the last time anyway. I wonder when he has to leave, he wasn't specific yesterday. I know we have to check out by twelve, though, so that gives me one possible deadline. While I'm thinking all these stupid thoughts I'm trying hard not to let my feelings show; after all, he doesn't have to know it's the last time (or next to last time, or whatever), does he?

We have our shower with the same result as before and it's all feeling beautifully, horribly familiar. Afterwards he tells me he doesn't have to leave until twelve, and I'm pleased. I tell myself that's because I wouldn't want to stay here in this room on my own, and that I'm going to have long enough to wait at the airport as it is. Assuming I can get a flight. And I'm positively not going to start worrying about that. Not yet, anyway.

We order breakfast and he finally asks me what my plans are, and I'm pretty sure he doesn't mean for the next few minutes. I've had all night to think of what to say and I'm still stuck. I stare at him silently like some kind of abandoned ventriloquist's dummy.

"I mean, do you tend to come to England much?" He tries to help me out as I've obviously lost the ability to respond to such a vague question as his previous one.

"No," I reply vacantly, and I'm trying not to sound too negative (for heaven's sake, how much more negative than "no" can you get?) without lying.

"Don't you ever visit your family?" he asks.

"No," I repeat.

"Never *ever?*" He looks astonished.

"I don't have any family," I say, and although I try not to, the way I say it stops him in his tracks, I can tell.

He looks at me thoughtfully and I look away. For a moment I think he's going to say something but he changes his mind. I have no chance of saying anything, I've been completely struck dumb, this time physically as well as mentally. My stomach is contracting into a tiny, sickening ball.

I try to pull myself together. I mean, I may as well write, "I never want to see you ever again in my whole life!" in big letters across my forehead. I'm better than this and I want to leave on a good note, even if I'm not showing it very well. I've come through worse situations than this one and the least I can do is make sure this guy leaves feeling good about himself. He might not realise it but he's given me so much.

I smile at him. "It's difficult," I say, and for sure I'm not lying there. "I'm not sure how I'm fixed yet, so I'll have to let you know."

He nods, and I don't know if he knows I'm fobbing him off or not. I hope I'm a better actor than I always thought I was. I've had more practice now.

"Ok. Just let me know when you do. Or I can always come to Spain, or somewhere."

I'm moved by his offer, and the possible shrewdness of "or somewhere". Perhaps he thinks I'm married or something. Maybe it would be easier to encourage that thought. But surely somebody married wouldn't have been so obviously sex starved as me, would they? Perhaps they would.

For a mad moment I consider arranging to meet him "somewhere", anywhere, where it wouldn't impact on my life and I could still see him and enjoy the sex every now and again. I'm utterly shocked at myself, and I suddenly realise it isn't only about the sex. If I carry on meeting him I can't help feeling that I'm going to like him more, and that's a no-no.

Breakfast arrives and it's like a Godsend. We are distracted from the conversation (and I use that word in its loosest possible terms) as we start to eat. It's very good and I can't help wondering how many pounds I must have put on this weekend. Then I think perhaps I've lost weight because of all the sex and I look at him with far too much fondness, and he sees it and smiles. In a way I'm glad because he looks happier now and it was the right thing to do. Then I wonder if I'm torturing myself for no reason and imagining his reactions because of what I know I'm about to do, and that maybe he wants to end it now too and we're both in the same situation and putting a face on. Then I tell myself to stop thinking and to stop worrying what he's thinking and to enjoy our last hour or two together.

Perhaps he's thinking that too. Christ, it's exhausting.

We finish breakfast and he puts the telly on and we lie on the bed in our robes like yesterday morning, like a normal couple. I can't stop myself from snuggling up to him a bit and he kisses me, and suddenly it's urgent again and, oh boy, it's such a sweet pleasure.

I'm not going to go into the next hour or so. We have fantastic sex (no surprises there), shower again and all too soon we're having to dress and get ready to leave. I have a mini heart attack when I think he's going to put his hand in his inside jacket pocket and find my note, but he doesn't and I manage to carry on without keeling over. I tell him I'll get in touch when I know I have a weekend free and he gives me his number without a murmur. Perversely I'm disappointed that he doesn't ask me for mine to be on the safe side, but clearly he trusts me. I guess that as he made the effort to come and find me to explain why he stood me up he expects the same from me. I feel like an awful, wicked cow because I am going to run out on him and he doesn't suspect it. Stupid, blind fool that he is.

We're out by our cars now and it's goodbye. I feel tearful but I have to hide it or he might guess. He drops his head for one last kiss and I try to savour it so I can remember the taste of him for as long as possible. Then he says, "Call me," and we climb into our cars and he drives away without a backward glance.

I sit in my car for some time. I'm exhausted with everything and wondering if I've done the right thing, although I can't see what else I could have done under the circumstances. It goes without saying that I'm also wondering what he's thinking. I consider throwing his telephone number away to remove all possible temptation, but I'm weak and I can't do it. Not yet. I only hope to God he doesn't find my note before the flight and race back to the airport to see me. Always assuming he would be bothered anyway. I consider waiting somewhere else until nearer the time but I've already gone back to worrying about whether I'll even be able to get a flight and I know I'll have to go and see, and that once there I won't come away again. Maybe I'll be able to check in early and go through passport control to get out of the way.

In the end I get a flight with no trouble. Nobody turns up at the airport to stop me and my flight is fine, arriving early in fact. I'm walking into my house by midnight Spanish time and although here in summer there will still be bars open and children running around I am too tired even to consider going out. I am sad and happy in turns as I go over my time in England, and on balance I reckon I've been extremely lucky to meet someone who has made me feel so good.

I never would have dreamed that going to Donna's wedding would have turned out like this and I go to bed remembering the best bits, and believe me, that's not so bad at all.

The next evening I go to Paco's and it's busy now because it's mid July and the holidaymakers are arriving in force. Paulo is there and he asks me about my weekend. I don't know whether he notices the glow that is still left over or whether he simply puts it down to how pleased I was to be able to surprise Donna and how happy she was to see me. He doesn't ask why I wasn't going to the wedding in the first place; one of the things I like about him is his distinct lack of nosiness.

I think I'm still on a bit of a high and I have a great time, and for the first time this year when I get home I go for a night time swim. The sea is warm now and I enjoy swimming in the inky black water, watching the moon and the few lights reflecting off the surface and lying on my back looking at the stars. For me this is one of the real pleasures of summer and I feel a little pang of gratitude for my father who worked so hard to build up a business, which then meant that I was able to afford this sea front villa for my new life abroad.

As I lie there I wonder if my guy has found my note yet, and I hope he does so before too long, because although it doesn't explain it does at least apologise, and I can't bear to think of him waiting for my call in the weeks to come and not knowing. If he's bothered at all, that is, and although it's pointless I can't help hoping he is.

The days go by. The resort is heaving with people now; the population here goes up from about two thousand people in winter to more than fifty thousand in summer. I know that's hard to comprehend, but it's true. Every single apartment and villa is occupied, and it's ninety five percent Spanish. Bars and shops open for these months which you wouldn't know existed otherwise, and now instead of ten bars and restaurants I can walk to over fifty from my villa. It's hardly worth moving the car because it takes forever through the congested streets and when you arrive you can't park. Even shopping takes ages because of the queues. I love it. I love the buzz, and the fact that the squares are still busy even at three o'clock in the morning, and I even love the fact that most nights I can't sleep because of people partying on the beach outside. And most of all, I love the fact that on the thirty first of August they will all disappear in one long traffic jam until next July, leaving only a few stragglers behind. And we'll all return to normal.

Donna rings me when she gets back from her honeymoon. She's had a fantastic time and she's so happy, and I'm happy for her. They went to the Maldives and spent lazy days on the beach and snorkelling and so on, and no doubt there was tons of sex and emotional intimacy and she's madly in love and I'm delighted. I tell her I am back into my routine, helping out the Brits where I can (because I speak Spanish) and working now and again now that everywhere is so busy, going to Paco's and other bars because there are so many to go at, and picking up on my regular Tuesdays out with my friends Lydia and Ali. We under sixty's have to stick together, you know.

Then Donna asks me what happened in England after she left. I tell her about my stolen two days and I can tell she's pleased for me. She can hear what a good time I had in my voice. I tell her that it's funny, I expected to feel really down after leaving him, but perhaps because I am here and it is a different world I just feel very happy for the experience and I can think of it without sadness, in fact, quite the opposite. Donna likes this and I can tell she feels a bit smug because it all stemmed from her wedding. And, in fact, from her hen night, too.

Then I tell her that I am never going to see him again.

"Never?" she asks.

"No. I can't. I was starting to like him."

"Is that a bad thing? Surely that means you *should* see him again?"

"No. I really can't."

She's quiet as she digests this, and I tell her about my note. Well, not about the wording and how I worried about changing it and which pocket to put it in, but the fact that I left it for him so he would know.

"Sam, I know I will never fully understand how you must feel, but surely if you like Tom you could give it a go? He seemed to be really into you."

"No. I can't do it. I can't rely on someone like that again."

"So you are never going to allow yourself to be close to someone again, *ever?*"

"I don't know. I can't say how I will feel in ten years, can I? But as I feel now – no. Oh, and his name isn't Tom."

This distracts her. "What is it, then?"

"I don't know. He didn't tell me. So perhaps he wanted to be able to disappear, too."

She's quiet. I can tell she's not happy, but also that she wants what's best for me and she isn't sure what that is.

"Do you think he will have found your note?"

"I don't know. I hope so. That's why I wrote it."

"Well, I'm sure he won't mind if you decide to ring him anyway. See how you feel in a week or two."

God, she doesn't give up, and she's right, she will never fully understand.

We change the subject and after another ten minutes or so she rings off. She has successfully managed to make me feel sad about leaving him for the first time since I got back to Spain. Stupid cow. I can be an ungrateful bitch sometimes.

Over the next week or so Donna rings me a few times. I can tell she's anxious for me and although she says nothing definite I can sense that she is not sure I'm doing the right thing. But it isn't up to her, is it?

Then she rings me and it's different. Her voice is strange. "What is it?" I ask, immediately concerned.

"Your guy," she says, and my stomach turns over. I have terrible thoughts that he might have been in a car crash or something like that. I mean, why would I think such a thing? Why not that he might have won the lottery or married the Queen? God, I frustrate myself sometimes.

"He came to see me," she says.

I'm gobsmacked. I can't begin to tell you - really, truly and totally gobsmacked. "How did he find you?" I ask.

"God, we didn't make it difficult. I mean, the order of service for the wedding had our full names and everything, it wouldn't take Einstein."

She's right. "Bloody hell," I say, "What did he want?"

"You. He wanted to know where you are and how to contact you."

"Hadn't he found my note?"

"Yes."

For a moment I'm livid, because I expressly asked him not to try to find me, and I thought he respected my boundaries. *How dare he?* I think, *how dare he go against what I have asked and bother my friend into the bargain?*

"What did you say?" For a horrible moment I wonder if she will have spilled the beans because she thinks I should see him again, but I push the thought out of my mind. I can trust Donna better than that.

"I refused to tell him anything. He got really angry for a while, although he didn't threaten me or shout or anything, I could just tell. Then he said even if he could have an email address, something he couldn't trace back to you, because he has things he wants to say, he would be happy with that.

"In the end I had to promise to speak to you and tell you he wants to contact you. It was the only thing that would make him go."

Oh, Lord. I don't know what on earth to do or say. Poor Donna, put in this position because of me. "I'm sorry," I say.

"It's ok. He's coming back next week."

"You could always get Mike to throw him out."

"Do you even *remember* the way he dealt with Simon? I don't think so. Anyway, I think it's only fair to see him this time. So he knows."

"God, Donna, it's very good of you. I'm sorry."

"So you won't let him contact you? Not even an anonymous email address?"

"I can't. What's the point of that anyway? If I'm never going to see him again there's no point starting a chat line, is there?" Honestly, Donna can be dense sometimes.

"I wondered if you might have changed your mind."

"Well, I haven't. And I'm not going to. You can tell him that, and that I'm sorry."

"He wanted to know why, too." Donna says this very quietly.

Oh, fucketty fuck. "It's none of his business why."

"It is, in a way."

"No it isn't!" I'm getting cross now because I feel I'm being backed into a corner, and Donna should be supporting my decision, not trying to undermine it.

"I'd tell him, if you wanted me to."

Perhaps she thinks that is what this is about, the fact that I can't speak about what happened. I know underneath my anger that she's trying to help and she wants what's best for me, or at least what she thinks is best for me. "No," I tell her.

She's quiet so against my better judgement I try to explain. I think I've mentioned before that this isn't one of my strong points, plus I only want to tell her part of the reason, but something I think she will understand. "As things are we had a fantastic time. He remembers me as I was that weekend. If you tell him what happened he will picture it, he won't be able to help it. And then when he thinks of me all he will think of is that, and when I think of him I will see him picturing it, instead of how he was when I was with him. I don't want that."

Still she's quiet and I can tell she's mulling this over. "Ok, so can I tell him anything?"

"You can tell him that you have spoken to me. You can tell him I had a fantastic time with him and it's nothing to do with him. You can tell him thank you and I'm sorry. And you can ask him to leave me alone."

"Ok."

"When's he coming?"

"Next week some time. I told him I didn't know how long it would take me to contact you. It makes you sound more difficult to reach. I didn't know if you would want to think it over."

"Oh, Donna. I don't want to think it over. I'm sorry to put you in this situation, but if you'll see him next week then that should be it. Thank you."

"That's ok. I want you to be happy."

"I am happy, honestly."

"That's not what I mean."

"It's the best I'm ever going to get."

She knows she isn't going to get any further so she changes the subject.

All the following week I keep thinking of him. I'm glad he's found my note, I'm angry with him for bothering Donna, and a perverse part of me is pleased, too. And, despite my mixed feelings, I do quite a bit of smiling.

I'm on tenterhooks as time goes by, waiting for Donna to ring me and tell me what happened.

"Your guy came last night."

"Oh." My stomach lands on my feet with a thud. For a split second I see him in my mind's eye as clearly as if he's standing in front of me.

"I told him what you said."

"What did he do?"

"Nothing. He heard me out and said nothing. I couldn't tell what he was thinking at all. He gave me his contact details in case you ever change your mind. I have his mobile number, his email address, even where he lives. He said if ever you want to you can get in touch by whichever means you feel comfortable with. Shall I email them to you?"

"No! Throw them away."

"But – "

"I don't want them." God, I still have his mobile number and that's bad enough. Perhaps now I can get rid of it if Donna has it, and then any moment of weakness I may have will be futile. Because I've had a couple of those already.

"Ok," she says, and I just know she isn't going to throw them away. "He asked why again."

Oh, God.

"I didn't tell him anything, only that it was something you couldn't help and that you were sorry."

"Thanks, Donna."

"It's ok. He said he'd like to stay in touch every now and again so I gave him my number."

"You gave him your number?"

"It's better than him turning up at the house. All that pent up energy. It makes me nervous sometimes."

I know what she means.

"I owe you one," I say.

"That's all right." She sounds sad and I feel wretched and I change the subject. She's coming out to visit me for a weekend at the end of October and although it's still a while away yet we are both excited and it cheers us up thinking about it.

Life goes on. September arrives and most of the Spanish holidaymakers disappear, replaced by a small number of Brits, Germans, Dutch and others who find July and August too busy and hot. It's nice to catch up with people who we count as friends because we see them regularly on and off.

My guy rings Donna every now and again, just to check in, but she doesn't say much about him. He's starting to fade into the past for me and I'm sad about that, but I still remember our times with a smile and I try to hold on to the memory of the sex, if nothing else. I'd forgotten how much I enjoy sex, to be honest, and I wonder occasionally if I will ever find anyone else I could have uncomplicated sex with. No one here, that's for sure. Everyone knows everyone else here and uncomplicated just wouldn't be in it. That's one of the problems with Paulo.

October's here and Donna and I are excited about the prospect of seeing each other. She's coming on her own, although of course I told her Mike's welcome, but this is much better and I like him for being so understanding. Actually it's more likely that the thought of being with us two going on and on together repulses him, and he's glad to get out of it.

The week before she rings me.

"Your guy rang last night," she says.

This jolts me. She hasn't mentioned him for a while and I'd been wondering if he had stopped contacting her.

"Oh?" I say warily, wondering why she's mentioning it now.

"He said that he can take a hint, and the next time he calls is going to be the last."

Even though I hadn't really known if he was still ringing her this jolts me even more. I don't know what to think. For a moment, unexpectedly, I feel really sad. I can't explain it.

"What do you want me to do?" she asks.

"What do you mean? Nothing."

"Don't you think you should tell him why? He always asks. It might give him closure."

Dear God, I hate that expression. Why can't he just forget about it and leave me alone? Do we all have to analyse everything these days? Shit. I'm getting angry and I know it's because a tiny bit of me wonders if she's right.

"We can talk about it when I'm there," she says.

Oh joy. Now he's managed to take the edge off me seeing Donna. *Thank you, Scumbag, thank you so very much.*

"He doesn't know you're coming, does he?" I blurt out in horror.

"Of course not!" Donna sounds really affronted and I don't blame her. What was I thinking to ask such a thing?

"Sorry!" I can't think straight. I don't want him to stop ringing her. How utterly selfish can you get? I try to pull myself together. "I didn't even know he was still ringing."

"Mmmm. Every now and again. I've got used to it now."

God, what a weird situation this is. How I wish my life was different. I have a horrible feeling I'm going to have to go out and get drunk tonight, and believe me, I'm already looking forward to it.

CHAPTER SEVEN

I do, and it's a great release. Nobody minds people getting drunk in Paco's and we all do it now and again. Plus when there are British holidaymakers around they are usually going for it; I mean, they're on holiday, aren't they? The drink in this part of Spain is so much cheaper than in the UK, and the measures are huge. I think I mentioned before that I won't drink the spirits here. If I had even one I would be on my back, and I'm not exaggerating. How some people manage to drink here without killing themselves I will never know.

I notice Paolo eyeing me a couple of times. Whilst I have been known to get drunk before, and I'm sure you're not surprised to hear that, it's usually on one of those occasions where there is a planned party, or even better, when there just happens to be the right mix. You know, one of those unexpected times when the people and the atmosphere and the whole evening just gel, and a spontaneous celebration occurs. Of course, then it isn't just me getting drunk, and I think that's what's bothering him tonight. He can see that I'm doing it on my own, and I think he suspects that it's deliberate.

He walks me home. This is not unusual. I don't mind walking on my own - as I said this is a very safe resort (that's one of the reasons why I picked it) and I never feel threatened. But more often than not somebody is walking my way, and more often than before it's Paolo. And to be fair, he does live about five minutes away from me and my place is barely a detour. He never comes in – well, he's never invited – but it isn't like that anyway. I mean, Sergio, or John, or Lydia, or anyone might be walking my way and it doesn't mean I have to entertain them. That's how it is here; everyone looks after everyone because most of us (Brits, anyway) don't have any family here. We are all one big family to each other.

I say goodnight to him outside my gate as usual, and he looks at me strangely for some reason, and I am aware that, perhaps because I'm drunk, he watches until I'm inside before he walks off.

Of course the next day I have a terrible hangover and I make myself go swimming even though the sea is starting to get cold now. I stay in for about an hour and when I come out I'm freezing but I feel much better. I'll never understand how that works. I spend the day lazing about, thinking about Scumbag and looking forward to Donna's arrival. Despite everything I'm excited and I know we'll have a fantastic time together.

Friday arrives and I pick her up at the airport. We are so pleased to see each other and chatter excitedly as I drive back home. We are going to go out for a meal tonight so that we can catch up, and then hit the bars tomorrow. We have a lovely evening and Donna tells me how much she loves being married and how happy she is with Mike, and I'm really pleased. I tell her what I've been doing and there's no mention of my guy at all. I think we're both avoiding the subject for now. We go back to the villa and sit outside drinking wine and getting drunk and we just have the best time.

The next day is a late start. I swim again but Donna isn't very keen and she sits in the sun and watches. We have a lazy lunch with a bottle of cava, and only then does she mention him. Very tentatively she asks if I've thought any more about it.

What can I say? I don't want him to know what happened, but a bit of me thinks that's selfish. Or is it kinder not to tell him? I can't make up my mind. I repeat to Donna about not wanting him to have to imagine me in the horror, and she kind of gets it. She's not stupid. I say that I think it's better to remember what a good time we had and leave it at that.

Then Donna says that perhaps, for once, she knows better than I do. I'm a bit taken aback, to be honest, and I'm not proud of this. I'm so used to it all being about me, I suppose. She says that as she is not me, perhaps she can see his point of view better than I can - looking in from the outside, as it were. She has a point, doesn't she? I feel a bit ashamed.

She adds that she is the one who has spoken to him, and although he hasn't gone on about it and only speaks for a few minutes each time, she thinks she has come to understand a little. She says it's easy for me to dismiss it (well, that isn't true at all, but I know what she means) and he only wants to understand, and is that so awful? And of course it isn't, not when you put it like that.

Bloody hell. I don't know what to do. I find it hard to tell her that I don't want him to know because then he will be put off me for good, and I will lose even the small comfort that someone out there wants me, even if only for sex. It sounds so selfish, and underneath I know that's because it is, and I know that by the end of the weekend I will agree that she should tell him and when she does I will lose him, even if it's only the memory of him, because I can't hold on to the memory once I know he doesn't want me any more. I'm in a god-awful hole and I can't dig myself out. Also I like him, and if what Donna says is true I can't let her not tell him if that's what he wants.

Fucketty fuck, I *hate* this.

Donna lets the subject drop. She knows she's winning, and did I mention that she's not stupid? I love her for being such a good friend, for caring for me so much, but also for sticking up for what she believes is right and putting me straight because I can't see what she can. I'm grateful to her. We all need to be told sometimes, don't we?

That evening we go to Paco's. Paulo is there because he knows we will be coming in. Donna has met Paulo a few times and they get on well; they are pleased to see each other. As luck would have it it's one of those evenings which just gels, and everyone ends up drinking and dancing and laughing together. Everyone dances with everyone in Paco's, because everyone knows everyone and there are no undercurrents or ulterior motives. Donna and I really let our hair down and have a great time, and I'm very pleased because I know she loves this kind of thing and

I want her to enjoy herself. The time flies and in no time it's four in the morning and we are a bit pissed to be honest but very happy. We walk home arm in arm with Paulo and a few of his mates and it's one of those times when I love living in Spain with all the wonderful friends I have made. I love everyone.

The next day is an even later start than the one before. Of course, last night we promised to go back to Paco's today because it seemed like such a good idea at the time. For now we are not so sure. We lounge about chatting, and I'm so pleased that Donna is here because she's my best friend, the only person I could bear to keep in touch with from before, who never looked at me with pity or embarrassment, and we go back such a long way. I can even talk with Donna about my family and the times before it happened because I am utterly, utterly comfortable with her and she's understanding enough not to try to understand, if that makes sense. I want to make the most of it, so in the end we do go back to Paco's but not until later on, and there are more than a few weary people there and we all laugh about the previous night's antics. Paulo turns up and he and Donna chat together for a while. It's all very pleasant, and in the end we spend most of the evening there again, although it's much quieter than the previous night. Back at the villa we drink some more wine on the patio and, perhaps because I am a little bit drunk and mellow I agree that Donna should tell Scumbag what happened. I trust her judgement and I reckon that on this one she's closer to it than I am.

We discuss what she should say. Only the bare minimum – what happened but no details. He must promise not to look at any newspaper archives or anything because they were too sensationalised and awful I couldn't bear it if he did. Really it shouldn't take long to give him the basic facts, and then he won't want to know any more and he won't want to know me and it will all be over. And it's probably for the best, I know that really, but I can't believe I am sitting here discussing it calmly and I must be more drunk than I thought.

The next day Donna's leaving and the weekend seems to have gone so fast. It has been so good to see her and we've both had a brilliant time. We promise to do it again soon, but neither of us suggest I go to England. No prizes for guessing why. I see her off with tears in my eyes, and I know she's the same, and when I return to my villa it feels empty and quiet and I'm ashamed to say I feel very sad and full of self pity and I find myself crying for half the evening. It must be the after affects of all the drinking.

In fact I don't feel like going out at all for the next few days. I mean, I don't usually go out every night, even if I make it sound like I do, but it really isn't like me not to want to go out at all, not these days. I know that I'm dreading Donna ringing me to tell me that my guy has been to see her, and I keep imagining that he is there as I am thinking it, and picturing his face. I know how to torture myself when I want to. For heaven's sake – what am I losing? I wasn't going to see him again anyway. Stupid cow.

She rings on Thursday. He had called around the previous evening and I don't know why she didn't tell me straight away but perhaps I can guess. I feel my insides tighten as I ask her how it went.

"I told him you're not going to contact him, but you've agreed that I should tell him why you won't see him. I explained that you didn't want to, but that you agreed because it was what he wanted, and you hoped it wouldn't spoil things for him. Then I told him what happened, as we said. No details, just the bare facts."

"What did he say?" I can hardly get the words out.

"Nothing. He sat through it with no reaction at all. I couldn't read his expression or anything. It was almost spooky. I told him that you asked that he doesn't go and look it up in any archives or Google or whatever, and why, and he promised he wouldn't."

I am silent. I don't know what I expected but somehow it wasn't this.

"I told him you're very sorry. I explained that you hadn't wanted to tell him because you didn't want him to picture you like that. I hope that's all right, but I felt he should understand your reluctance, I don't know why, it just seemed the right thing to do. Then I told him that you know he won't want to see you again, and that it's all right, that's why you disappeared in the first place. I said that you want him to know again what a fantastic time you had with him, and that perhaps now he can appreciate what he gave you because it was something you had thought you would never be able to do again. I told him you will always remember him with a smile on your face."

We are both crying now, we are such sentimental fools.

"I made a list," Donna says awkwardly, and my heart goes out to her because she was so concerned that she told him everything I wanted and she has put herself through this hell for me.

"His face never flickered. I'm not kidding, it was eerie."

I'm glad, because I would rather picture him with a deadpan expression than with the look of pity I had dreaded.

"I told him you will never contact him and that now at least he can understand that it's for the best. He didn't like that at all."

Oh, God. Poor Donna. I'm silent, I don't have the words.

"He asked if they caught the men who did it. Then he asked what their punishment was. I told him that two of them got life, but the other two, the younger ones, were deemed to have been led on, and that they got six and seven years respectively."

Tears are streaming down my face now as all the horror, shame and disillusionment flow through me again.

"Chris, Sam, I thought he was going to explode. He was *furious,* and it was such a cold, controlled fury, I was scared, although it wasn't aimed at me. I was glad Mike was in the house, I can tell you."

"God, Donna, I'm sorry to have put you through it. You're such a good friend."

"It's ok. I wanted to, in a way. He asked if he could come back if he had any more questions, given that you didn't want him to go looking anything up. I agreed, because I didn't see how I couldn't, really. He wants to know their names, and I couldn't remember them all, I'm sorry. Also I didn't know if you'd want him to know."

I know she means she's sorry because she feels bad that she can't remember their names when they will be branded on the inside of my head forever, and therefore I must think she doesn't care enough. But why should she remember their names? It didn't happen to her. I can't see any harm in him knowing, especially if it will stop him trying to find out from elsewhere, so I tell her all four, and I'm crying, and she can tell.

"So he's definitely going to come back for those, then?" I blub.

"I guess so, and anything else he thinks of."

"No gory details though," I say.

"Of course not. I couldn't, anyway."

We change the subject and discuss what a great time we had when she was here, and that cheers us both up a bit before we ring off.

The next night is Friday, and thank God it's always a good night at Paco's because I've gone from not wanting a night out to needing one desperately. Paulo isn't there and I'm very surprised, it's unusual to say the least, and I wonder if he has a woman. It would be just typical, wouldn't it? Excellent timing. Ok, so I'm being selfish again because I don't think I could ever be with him, but I could do with his unquestioning affection tonight, I really could, and I suspect that the main reason I came out was to see him. Sometimes life's a real bitch, and no mistake.

Anyway, there's plenty of other people there and in fact I have a good time and quite possibly I mix more because of Paulo's absence so perhaps there's a silver lining of a sorts. I have plenty to drink and almost convince myself that I'm glad now that the whole episode with Scumbag is nearly over and I can move forward free of his influence. I don't get home until after three and collapse on the bed and I'm out for the count.

The next day I wonder if Paulo is going to be in Paco's that night. I don't know whether to go down or not. I don't normally spend both weekend nights there, but I missed him and it makes the prospect more tempting. God, I'm mixed up. I realise that he has become a constant in my life and that gradually I have come to depend on his friendship more and more, but that also I don't know if I could ever give him what he wants, so that's not fair. Assuming I'm right about what he wants, and that's one of the problems. I mean, he's never ever made a pass at me or anything remotely like that in all the time I've known him (although for the first year I was so emotionally inhibited only a blind idiot would have been so stupid as to try), and I only think he fancies me because he's always so nice to me and makes an effort when I'm around. But I can't be sure. I'm going to look like a complete moron if I get drunk one night and tell him he's wasting his time because I could never be with him in that way, only to find he had no intention of anything of the sort. I can just see his incredulous, mocking face as he tells me he's not interested and looks at me as though I'm some kind of mental, vain cow.

And that's another problem with Paulo. He's so much a part of my social life now that if we tried and it all went wrong the disruption would be devastating for me. So many of my friends stem from Paco's and to spoil things there would be a disaster. And now he might have another woman and I might be too late anyway. Dear me, what a mess. Confused isn't in it.

So, of course, I do go to Paco's and I'm relieved to see Paulo's there and he's no different and neither of us mentions his absence the night before. It's not as though I have any right over him, for God's sake. In fact, there have been a couple of occasions in the past year or so when I have been asked out by someone who has interested me but as soon as they have tried to get close physically I have been unable to stand it. That's one of the reasons I'm so grateful to my guy for being able to break that barrier (and, boy, did he break it); whether because it was the right time; because of what he did, defending me in a position of a similar type to the horror albeit much, much less extreme; or because of something in him; I don't know. And to go back to my original point, I've made sure I've kept anything like that away from Paolo, too.

The next week I'm waiting for Donna to ring again and I really am beginning to think that being free of my guy will be a good thing. He seems to be constantly on my mind at present. She calls on Thursday again, and it appears that Wednesday is his regular slot. She tells me that she gave him their names.

"Did he want anything else?" I ask.

"He wanted to know your real name."

"Sam. Sam is my real name now." God almighty, I hope she didn't tell him.

"I know. That's more or less what I told him, and I refused to give him your surname either."

I breathe a sigh of relief; I knew she wouldn't let me down. "Was there anything else?"

She hesitates, and I know it's going to be bad.

"He wanted to know if they..." Her voice tails off.

I start to cry huge, racking sobs; I can't help it. I hang up the phone. I know Donna will understand, in the beginning it happened quite a lot. She knows to leave me to it and I'll ring back when I have control of myself. She doesn't want to sit there and listen to my anguish any more than I want her to hear it, does she?

Finally I call her and she answers in seconds. She's obviously been hovering by the phone in distress. God, she's such a good friend.

"That's none of his business," I manage to say, as if there's been no pause at all.

"I know. I think he knew too, really. I think he was just trying to understand fully how you must feel."

I don't know what to make of that. Oh, Christ, I'll be glad when this is all over, truly I will. I know I had a fantastic time with him and everything, but I'm hoping now that he will go away and let me enjoy my memories of him without torturing me any more. Not to speak of poor Donna and how difficult this must have been for her.

"Then he said to tell you goodbye. He said thank you for telling him, and he knows it must have been a difficult decision, and he's so very sorry, and yes, he always remembers with a smile on his face, too."

That nearly finishes me off. I gulp hard, and once more Donna understands and stays quiet.

There's not much to say after that. We're both exhausted and know it's better to finish quickly and speak another time when we're feeling better.

I'm ashamed to say that when I put the phone down I burst into tears again. I am so *horribly* upset and angry and hurt and disappointed, and I know this is the last time we will ever speak of him, and that he will never want to see me again, and that despite everything, and I may have mentioned this before, just having that stupid, vague possibility that someone out there wants me had helped me more than you can ever imagine. I know I've done the right thing, and it was only fair to him, but I'm just so pissed off that I've had to and about how fucking unfair life is.

Fuck, fuck, fuck.

It's not a good evening for me.

Thank God the next one's Friday. Friday drinking sessions are becoming a bit of a habit for me at the moment, and I dare you to challenge me about whether that's a good thing.

So now the only thing left to look forward to is Christmas, and even that's not straightforward for me. I can't help thinking about my guy now and then, and wondering what he's thinking. I hope I've done the right thing, and for once I think I have.

It's cold now. The houses here aren't built for the colder weather with their tiled floors and concrete walls, but I'm not complaining. The Brits gear up for Christmas much earlier than the locals and Paco is always persuaded to put up his decorations earlier than normal. Everywhere is becoming festive and it's cheering.

My first Christmas here was the first one after it happened. If I'd still been in England I would probably have gone to Donna's parent's house and that would have been ok. As it was, I couldn't face being anywhere. I'd never had a Christmas without my family in my life. I received loads of invites (which was very generous because at the time nobody knew me very well and I wasn't letting anyone anywhere near me, either) but I turned them all down. I'm afraid I stayed at home and wallowed in self-pity, and perhaps at the time it was the best thing, to be honest.

The following year I received loads of invites again and this time I accepted because I had come to realise that a lot of people are alone here, so I wasn't going to be sitting on the edge of someone else's family as I had dreaded, but rather that as friends we would form our own family. What I mean is, some Brits go back to the UK for Christmas, some have family here to stay, and the rest of us get together and have our own celebration. This Christmas I have even received a couple of invites from the Spanish (Paulo being one) but I have politely refused, because in that situation I will be on the edge, watching another family and feeling wretched. But, of course, they don't know that and they are being very kind in thinking of me.

Boxing day is always good fun as everyone takes food to Paco's (there's always lots of turkey sandwiches, turkey curry, turkey pie…) and we have a great old day playing cricket, or football, or boules, or whatever else on the beach, and some mad fools always go for a swim, and believe me, the water is freezing. The alcohol flows and everyone laughs about their Christmas days and lets their hair down. Anyone who fell out over Christmas, and there's always one or two, makes up, and hopefully if they don't overdo the alcohol they are not arguing again by the evening.

Paco always says he might as well not open the day after Boxing Day because we're all too hungover and tired to go out. However, I have it on good authority that someone or other always manages; his customers are made of sterner stuff than that.

So Christmas passes and it's quiet afterwards. I go out with the girls but there's not a lot happening because everyone is focusing on New Year. Last year someone had a party on New Year's Eve but this year we all decided that it wasn't fair on Paco. This is because he opens practically every day, summer and winter, and we're all grateful for that, and it isn't a very good way of showing it to take most of his customers away for what is potentially the best night of the year.

I still manage to enjoy New Year's Eve. I don't find it as traumatic as Christmas because once I was old enough I didn't usually spend it with my family, always having a party to go to.

This year I'm determined for it to be a proper step forward. I am going to completely forget my guy (I still can't help wondering if he still thinks of me, and if so if he has a smile on his face) although I am allowed to remember the sex, and I am going to look forward instead of always tending to look back, or at the very least get myself into the present. These are my intended resolutions:

1. Look forward not back.
2. Have a purpose.
3. Stop thinking about Scumbag.
4. Stop worrying about everything and especially about what everyone else thinks.
5. Make a decision about Paulo (I'm not sure about this one).

6. Be more positive (by this I suppose I mean stop wondering what I should do, and in effect therefore stop worrying about what everyone else thinks).

Oh, God.

And so New Year's Eve arrives.

I head down to Paco's at about nine because I know it's going to be a late night (or early morning depending upon how you prefer to look at it). I know Paulo is going to be there, which is good, because there have been a couple more absences which I've tried not to worry about (and next year I am definitely not going to worry about). When I arrive the party's in full swing and the place is packed, with people also spilling out onto the patio despite the cold weather.

I fight my way to the bar and I know nearly everyone in there and it's great fun. The girls are there as well and we quickly down a couple of drinks and loosen up ready for the dancing and fooling about which is sure to come.

Twelve o'clock arrives, and Paco puts the radio on for the countdown. Everyone is smiling and happy and expectant and I'm standing by the bar with the girls on one side and Paulo and his mates on the other. There's loads of other people around and it's extremely cosy.

Then the clock strikes twelve and suddenly Paulo's there, right in front of me. He says "Feliz Año Nuevo," and then he drops his head to mine.

CHAPTER EIGHT

Oh my God, I think, *he's going to kiss me.*

I don't know why I think this in particular, because everyone kisses everyone on New Year's Eve, don't they? It's normal. But it's something about the way he moves in, very determined and full of intent, and for a moment I panic and then his mouth is on mine.

Blimey, I think, *he's jumping the gun, and I'm not supposed to have to decide about this until at least tomorrow.*

Then my thought is wiped from my head, because as I suspected he's kissing me, I mean, really kissing me, properly, and I don't know what to do. (Don't go there, please.)

His arms creep around me while I flounder and worry, and because I'm so hopeless and unsure I kiss him back a little bit, and it's not unpleasant. Then I think, *what the hell am I doing?* and I start to wonder if anyone is watching. So I try very gently to extricate myself and immediately he drops his arms. Before I can think or do anything someone else grabs me and someone grabs him and we are separated for ages as everyone wishes everyone else, "Happy New Year!" or "Feliz Año Nuevo!" depending on their persuasion.

My mind is whirling and I'm anxious about finding myself back with him now because I don't know what he expects or how I should behave. But we are both sidetracked for ages (and I might just talk to everyone else slightly more than I would normally) and by the time we find ourselves near to each other again I, for one, have had a couple more drinks and have more or less forgotten about it (or at least that's what I tell myself). Nobody says anything to me, and believe me, in a small place like this if anyone is seen even shaking hands with someone too fondly it's noted, and I'm relieved.

Then the dancing begins and everybody's up for it. Paco plays a mixture of Spanish and English music to try to please everyone, and at one point Paulo pulls me up for this Spanish dance (which he has done before, to be fair) and there's lots of twirling and spinning and I find his hand on my waist perhaps slightly more than usual. Then the music changes and I dance with John, then Lydia, then Pepe, then Mick, then practically anyone else who wants to dance, and it's great fun and I'm on fire.

I also dance with Paolo a few more times, and that's nice too, because I don't want things to become awkward; no way.

He doesn't try to kiss me again, and I'm grateful for that, but I'm starting to worry about walking home in case it's just me and him and what might he expect then? Oh, Lord.

In the end the party doesn't finish until after five, we're all exhausted and boozed up and happy and relaxed, or in my case at least three out of the four, and I needn't have worried because in the end about five of us are all walking the same way and I'm safe. Lydia is with us and only when we have dropped back a touch does she whisper to me, "What's with Paolo, then?"

"Shhhh," I say, in what I'm sure is probably a stage whisper, and giggle because I'm drunk. "He kissed me. Paulo kissed me." I cringe later when I remember this because I wouldn't be surprised if not only Paulo but the whole of the resort heard me, and I'm only glad I was too confused to give Lydia my opinion of his kiss as well. Dear me, can you imagine how awful *that* would have been?

So New Year's Day arrives and we all crawl down to Paco's yet again to deal with our hangovers because it's a pact and anyone who doesn't make it is a pathetic wimp. Paulo comes in after me and gives no outward indication of what happened, so maybe it's in my imagination that I think something infinitesimal has changed. I can't put my finger on it, but he seems just a tiny bit different. Or perhaps it's me reacting to what happened. I don't know, because let's face it, I never do. Perhaps to him it was just a New Year kiss, albeit an enthusiastic (and perhaps merely drunken) one, and I'm making a meal out of nothing. Except that I don't think I am. But I'm not sure.

Over the next few days and weeks the feeling doesn't change. I can't describe it exactly, the word proprietorial is *way* too strong, but I wonder if, for the first time, he has some belief that I will be his. And I really don't know what I think about that. I mean, I know I had him on my resolutions list, but I wasn't expecting to have to deal with it so early on. Let's be honest, does anyone ever actually expect to have to deal with their list at all? I thought it was just a way of filling the time between Christmas and New Year.

This is borne out by the fact that I definitely don't know what to do. I wonder if I should encourage him, because I know I'll never find anyone kinder or more gentle, or more concerned and considerate. Paulo makes me feel safe and secure, and that's what I need, isn't it? To be sure, it was only one kiss and I could be blowing everything out of proportion, but now I am more convinced than ever that he has feelings for me - anyone who will wait for over two years must be besotted or mental - and I know I am very, very fond of him, and perhaps in time that will grow into something more. Some people say the kind of love that grows in that way is the best love of all, don't they? Not that I ever worry about what anyone else thinks.

Oh God.

A little, tiny part of me, deep down where I won't acknowledge it, wonders if, had I not met my guy, I would go for Paulo now. But as you know I'm not allowed to think of *him* this year, either.

Now we are in the quietest time here in our resort. Only the minimum of bars and restaurants are open, the roads are quiet and the shops are more or less empty. I have my nights out with the girls, and I go to Paco's at least once a week, usually at the weekend, and occasionally somewhere else for a change. I'm still not sure what to make of Paulo, but he hasn't tried to kiss me again or do anything remotely romantic in any way, so I have relaxed and wonder if it has all been in my imagination.

My guy is fading into yesterday, and although I do think about him now and again I'm remembering the good times we had with a smile, and that's allowed. Only very occasionally do I wonder what he's doing or if he has a girlfriend, and that's the kind of thinking I meant in my New Year's resolution that is definitely *not* allowed, because that's the kind of thinking that can make me sad and that's why it was on my list in the first place. Then one day when I am thinking the thoughts of him that are not allowed I get angry with myself (because it's a kind of self flagellation) and I fetch his number, which I had hidden where I couldn't find it in a shoe right at the back of my wardrobe, and in a moment of strong resolution I throw it away. Because Donna has it anyway, doesn't she?

St. Valentine's night is coming. I *hate* St. Valentine's night, I always have. Even when I was with Mark we would prefer to stay in rather than suffer the appalling special evenings the restaurants in the UK always seemed determined to put on. Mark always managed to do something clever and romantic, but I don't want to think about Mark because that will make it even worse. Luckily the Spanish aren't really into St. Valentine's night so I know Paco's should be safe and certainly better than staying in and torturing myself with old times.

So I go down at about eight and there's a few Brits in, and a few Spanish, and to my surprise Paulo is there, too, with a couple of his mates. That's a bonus. Lydia also arrives, probably for the same reason as me, and we are having a good time and I'm glad I came out.

We come in for a bit of teasing from the Brits because we're not out on romantic dates and I reply perhaps a little more sharply than I should that just because they are over sixty doesn't mean they shouldn't make an effort any more. That shuts them up. Then I feel bad because I didn't mean it to sound like that and I get myself in a right mess digging deeper and deeper and they're laughing at me, but in a nice way. Then they ask me why I don't have a young man to take me out tonight and I give them a look that would stop a clock. I'm wondering why they're not asking Lydia the same thing and starting to take it personally and I'm aware that the rest of the bar is listening (especially Paulo) and I'm getting embarrassed and more upset than I will admit. I'm convinced that everyone is looking at me and feeling sorry for me and wondering what's wrong with me. Lydia goes a bit earlier than me because she has an early start in the morning (or more likely she is making a run for it before they start on her) and in the end I walk home with Paulo and I'm relieved to get out of there.

He's quiet as we walk and I'm wondering what he's thinking and what he thought of the things that were said in the bar, and if he now thinks there must be something wrong with me, too. So when we reach my gate and I turn to him to say goodnight I'm keen to get into the house and be alone.

But he's giving me such a strange look that I pause because I don't know what it means. Before I can react he leans down and I'm thinking, *Oh my God, he's going to kiss me* again, and coming on top of the evening and all the comments I really and truly don't know what to do, and I think for once perhaps you can't blame me.

For a second he's hesitant, and I think he's trying to gauge my reaction because he's that kind of guy, but I'm so messed up that I can't think quickly enough to give him any meaningful feedback so he must decide to carry on. Suddenly his mouth is opening mine and his arms are around me and he's pulling me in to him. I can sense his increasing desire and for a short while I respond. Although I won't admit it I do feel lonely sometimes, and perversely although human contact can be the thing that terrifies me, I also miss it. I like and trust this man and so I welcome his touch and his mouth and the fact that he wants me.

Then something snaps. I don't know why – perhaps he does something that my subconscious mind picks up on and reminds me of the horror - I don't know. Poor Paulo. All of a sudden I can't handle it. I panic and I'm almost hysterical, scrabbling to get away from him and making the most ridiculous noises. Lord knows what he's thinking, he must have me down as some kind of contrary retard.

Of course he lets go of me immediately and I back right off. I can't look at him because I'm mortified by my behaviour and although my head is telling my body to calm down it won't listen at all. It's shaking and still making stupid noises and I almost sink to the floor. God, I always thought that was some kind of overdramatic thing they do in books and films, I would never have believed your legs could actually disobey your brain to the extent that they would let you down so much. Luckily I do manage to give mine a stern telling off just in time and it also serves to pull me together just a fraction as I try to calm myself and stop acting like such a complete and utter half-wit. I don't know why I have reacted like this, it's taken me by surprise as much as him (well, perhaps not quite as much, to be fair, and at least I don't have the added feeling that I must be so repulsive that with one kiss the girl is running screaming out of sight) and I still don't know what to do. I am so utterly hopeless. For the most hideous moment I think of Scumbag, and this is so unfair on Paulo that I almost gasp. How come I could do it with him but not with Paulo, who I know so well and trust completely? Maybe that's it; I can do the sex but not the relationship - the emotional intimacy. Maybe I'm too frightened of messing up my hard earned life here. Maybe I'm not ready. Maybe he just pressed the wrong button. Maybe I'll never be able to do this – the sex and the emotional intimacy with one man. I nearly burst into tears at this thought (that would just about push poor Paulo over the edge, wouldn't it?) and it's a good job I'm used to being confused because out of long practice I manage not to.

Of course I'm also wondering what the hell Paulo must be thinking and when I finally look up to meet his eyes I'm glad to say he's giving nothing away because I don't think I could handle much. My mind has gone blank; it's as if having struggled so hard to make my body behave it's exhausted now and has ceased to care. I tell it harshly that's not fair and to get a grip, because I know I have to say or do something, because I was the one who suddenly behaved as though Paulo was public enemy number one and it's the least I can do.

But he comes to my rescue, this kind and good man who I really don't deserve. He moves closer and for a horrible moment I think he's going to try to kiss me again, which just goes to show how befuddled I am because Paulo just wouldn't *do* that, and he takes my hand in his. He stands there patiently, and the touch of his hand is soothing, and gradually I calm down and God only knows what he's thinking. I expect the minute he knows I'm all right he will turn and run as far away as he possibly can and never come back. And I won't blame him one little bit.

But he doesn't. He waits, and when finally I say, "I'm ok now," he gives me a look of such tenderness that I nearly swoon. For a stupid, stupid moment I nearly ask him in, because I'm clearly totally deranged and I want to be able to give him what I think he wants, and heaven knows what would have happened if I had.

Paulo says nothing. He doesn't ask questions, he doesn't judge me, and I'm so grateful I can't put it into words. He leans forward again and gives me the standard two kisses, one on each cheek, that the Spanish do (I mean, have you ever seen a Spaniard say goodbye to a party of people – it takes about half an hour), drops my hand, says "Buenas noches, cariña," and walks away. I can't tell if it's good night or goodbye, but it's nothing new for me to be wondering what the hell's going on.

I watch him go, collapse into the villa, and I'm ashamed to admit I burst into tears. I have a horrible feeling Paulo is going to give up on me very soon, and I couldn't possibly object.

So time goes on. Paulo and I slip back into our old relationship. He seems to have taken a step back (there's a surprise, I hear you say) and I see no resentment or complaint in him. Half of me is now convinced that he loves me and is waiting, and half of me thinks he has me down as a lunatic and is more than happy to go back to being friends. In a way I'm happy not to have to worry about my guy or Paulo and I'm more settled than I was, except sometimes when I am less so. I know that sounds mental, but I'm happy in my own way, with no outside pressure on me, but occasionally I wish my life wasn't like this and I could have a man and enjoy him.

Not that life and happiness are all about men, you understand, it's just that when you feel you are incapable of it, it's sod's law that at times it's going to piss you off.

Then one day I wake up and the air is warm. Winter has left us and everything seems brighter, somehow. Easter is in April this year. Easter's a big deal in Spain and we get quite a few holidaymakers, both

Spanish and northern European. We get used to people walking into Paco's who perhaps we haven't seen for six months but who have apartments here and will come over regularly now for a while, and it's good to catch up. As I said before, they always liven the place up because they are on holiday and up for a good time.

Donna and I speak regularly and I know she worries about me. As promised, my guy never contacts her again, and I don't ask if she has kept his details because I don't know which answer would upset me more. She is blissfully happy and I am delighted for her, and I know she wants the same for me. I try to explain that I am happy, in my own way, but I know she isn't satisfied and she'll never understand that this is the best I can hope for, and under the circumstances it isn't so bad. She is planning to come and visit again before the summer and this cheers me up. She just has to sort the time off with work and make sure it fits in with Mike's schedule, and that's how it should be. We plan on June some time because the weather is good then but it isn't too busy, or maybe early July at a push. She suggests we could do the same weekend as her hen party as a sort of annual thing, and I'm not sure what I think about that. Then I think it's a good idea, because now she has reminded me (thanks very much, by the way) I'd rather spend it with her and be distracted.

It makes me wonder for the first time in ages if he has someone now and if he will think of me on that weekend and how brilliant it would be if we could meet up annually and have fantastic sex and I know I'm losing my mind.

Paulo has never said anything about what happened that night, and we are still friends, and I still wonder what he thinks. Some weekend nights he doesn't come into Paco's and I wonder if he has a woman, and a part of me hopes he has, because clearly if he was to wait for me he might be drawing his pension before he sees any action, and that would hardly be fair. But he is still a close friend, second only to Donna, who makes an effort when I'm there and looks after me, and who I look forward to seeing and I'm always pleased when I spot his face at the bar.

May arrives and now the weather is really hotting up. It's great to be wearing flip flops and t-shirts again, and the sea is warm enough for swimming and the place will gradually get busier with Brits and other northern Europeans before July arrives and it's chaos with an extra forty five thousand or so Spanish arriving.

It's a late May Monday evening and I'm standing at the bar. I ended up here by accident, Monday not being a day I normally go out on, but I went swimming and for a walk earlier and bumped into someone and one thing led to another and here I am.

I know I look a bit of a sight because my hair is salt water messy and I'm still wearing my costume, albeit with a long Indian type dress over which is quite nice in a casual kind of way. For some reason they only have foot showers on this part of the beach and so my skin has a bloom of salt on it where I haven't licked it off. (Yuck, I hear you say, but I like it for some reason, so there.) It goes without saying that I haven't any make up on. Still, one of the nice things about this place in summer is that you can turn up looking like you've been dragged through a hedge backwards and nobody bats an eyelid.

Paulo is here. Lydia's going out with one of his mates now, and I wonder what he thinks about that sometimes, and if it reflects on me. I know I can be too sensitive, but I am sensitive where Paulo's concerned. There are a number of Brits in, too, and it's surprisingly lively for a Monday. A shadow looms in the entrance and we all look up to see who it is. And my heart stops.

Because it's him. It's Scumbag. Scumbag is standing there staring straight at me.

CHAPTER NINE

Oh my God, oh my God, oh my GOD! What the bloody fuck is Scumbag doing here?

I can't believe my eyes. I nearly drop my glass. I'm not kidding. That's another thing I thought only happened on the telly – I'm learning a bit about over dramatics these days. I swear I feel it start to slip and thank goodness my brain seems to be able to do some things without direct orders from me because it kicks in and tells my fingers to grip harder. Luckily my glass is one of those half pint ones with a bulge near the top and that saves me. Because how embarrassing would that have been? Don't even go there.

But I digress.

His eyes grip mine for a long moment and I can't read his face at all. Then he looks away, turns round and walks out.

And I just watch him. I'm so *utterly* useless. I'm rooted to the spot and I stand there like an idiot, like a rabbit caught in the headlights, or the gazelle within the leopard's grasp, or whatever creature I think I might be now (actually I think dolt headed sheep would be more appropriate), and I simply watch him leave. Because he knows now, and he can't want me, can he? But still my head is shouting, *Stop him! Stop him!* and gawping at myself in incredulity, but my legs won't budge an inch. I watch in horrified disbelief, but he doesn't go. I nearly faint with relief as I see him walk to one of the front tables and sit down with his back to the bar, looking out to sea. Paco goes to take his order.

My heart restarts and is making up for lost time. I stare blindly at my drink. My ears are throbbing and I'm sure everyone must have seen my reaction and will be watching me with fascination and wondering what on earth is going on. I'm wondering that myself, actually. I simply can't believe he has turned up like this, and I'm appalled that I must look like a scarecrow with straggly sea hair and salty, sandy skin and no makeup. Then I'm appalled that I'm actually thinking about this in the middle of such a crisis. I didn't think I was so vain. Then I remember how I looked the night he met me and I realise it's nothing new to him, and *then* I suddenly realise that I didn't see a flicker of pity on his face at all and I can't work that one out. I try to compose my own face and finally I look up.

God, I'm *such* a half-wit. I should have checked where I was looking first, because I stare straight into Paulo's eyes, and they're not happy eyes, not happy eyes at all, I can tell you. I suppose I shouldn't be surprised, but I am, and I don't know what to do. Life has been ticking along fairly pleasantly recently and I think I've gained a bit of a false sense of security, believing I've been in a certain amount of control; but now I see it was all a lie, because Scumbag is here, Paulo is worrying me and without a second's pause I immediately don't know what to do. Oh, and I'm worrying about what everyone is thinking, too. Where are my New Year's resolutions now, I hear you ask?

I try to give Paulo an unconcerned grin, but by the look on his face my application to RADA won't be successful. My heart is pounding, I know I look flustered and I daren't look outside. I daren't, and yet I have to, and when I do I see him put his arm out to the chair next to him and pull it back ever so slightly. I know it's an invitation, and I'm well and truly stumped.

I'm not going to say I don't know what to do again, but I really don't. I can't face going through it all again. I *can't*. My thoughts are careering wildly through my head and I can't control them. I don't know what I'll say to him. I don't even know why he's here. He might have come to find me or it could just be chance. Perhaps he has a girlfriend now, I mean, I don't know, do I? Bloody hell, he might have had one before, for all I know. That thought makes me go cold. He might not even want to speak to me, although that movement makes me think he does. But what can I say to him? He knows now, and it's different. Will he still want sex? – no, he won't, not now. Not now he knows what they did to me. What's Paulo thinking? What does he expect from me? All this is galloping through my head so quickly I can't keep up, and the tiny, shiny sparks of excitement are there too. I can feel them although I'm trying desperately not to admit it. I feel sick.

But I can't go out there, I simply can't. My brain is screaming against what's happening and the stress it's being put under. My body has no such problems. It wants to go out there, it wants to be close to him and feel his touch, and that's not helping one little bit, I can tell you.

So I stand and watch and dither. I stare at my drink a bit more as if it's suddenly going to turn into a genie and help me with a wish or two. For heaven's sake, even if it did I wouldn't know what to ask for, I'm so absolutely hopeless. In despair I look up again, and I haven't learned any lessons because it's straight into Paulo's eyes once more, as if they're some kind of magnet and I'm too stupid and weak to stop myself and spare him from witnessing my emotions. Dear God, this can't actually get any worse. I wonder if I'll see anger, pain, anxiety, or even simply curiosity, but all I see is concern; concern for me. He's watching this ridiculous soap opera and feeling concern for me. He is either the most kind, compassionate man I have ever met in my life or a complete and utter imbecile.

"You know this man?" he asks, and now I think imbecile must be the right answer because I would hardly react like this to a complete stranger, would I? Doh! I immediately feel shocked at my callousness, which I can only put down to the disorientation of the day. Paulo has asked it in Spanish, no doubt because he expects my guy, like most of the English, to have no grasp of the language, and straight away I start to worry, because not only does he speak Spanish he has bionic ears, too, remember? So he might hear us. So I turn my back on Scumbag (I know, I know, I really must stop calling him this, but it's difficult with Tom not being his real name and everything, and anyway I can't think straight) and I don't know why because all I do is nod anyway. I think perhaps I've lost my voice.

"From when?" Paulo asks, and for an unkind minute I think, *what's it to you?* Because I've never enquired into his past, not once, it's none of my business. But under the circumstances I suppose it's a fair question, even though Paulo has shown no interest in me for months now, and so I manage to say, "From England," and hope that he will take this as meaning from before I ever came to Spain rather than from Donna's wedding last summer.

Oh no! Then I have a *horrible* thought: I hope to hell he doesn't ask me how well I know him. I mean, I could say, "I know him more intimately than you could ever imagine," or I could say, "I've only met him twice," and I realise with shame that both answers would be true. I nearly giggle out loud at this, I'm so overwrought. Oh, God.

I turn away and watch as my guy finishes his drink and I wonder if he'll leave. The sick feeling twists in my stomach as I can't decide what I will do if he gets up to go. I wonder what he's thinking, and I'm panicking so much and trying not to let it show. Paulo has turned away now, and I'm not surprised. God only knows what he's making of all this.

Paco goes out and he must order another drink, because when Paco returns he places a beer in front of him and another drink in front of the empty chair beside him. And I know it's a cider. And I know it's for me.

Oh fucketty fuck, what do I do now?

Without stopping to ask for permission my legs save me by making a unilateral decision (can two legs be unilateral, do you think?) and propel me outside. I'm too confused and exhausted to respond anyway, and a bit grateful that at least somebody (or something) thinks they know what to do.

I sit down on the chair next to him and I panic hysterically to myself. I can hear my heart banging like a hammer inside my chest and wonder if he can, too. If so, he gives no sign of it. In fact, he does nothing. He says nothing. He continues staring out to sea in silence. Gradually I calm down. The sea is quiet and it's soothing. It appears nothing is expected of me for the moment. My breathing slows and my heartbeat becomes more regular. I won't go so far as to say I start to relax, but it's a big improvement on ten minutes ago, believe me.

I pick up my drink to take a sip. It's a normal, familiar movement and I feel better still.

When he finally speaks I nearly knock my glass over with fright.

"Nice place," he says.

I don't know if he means Spain, the resort or the bar, so I start to worry about how to respond. For God's sake, Scumbag's just appeared out of nowhere, Paulo's in the bar no doubt watching every move we make, I can feel curious eyes burning holes into the back of my head and I'm worrying about whether he's talking about the bar or the resort. I must need my head examining.

I've forgotten that he's Derren Brown's brother. "Very peaceful," he says, and I know now that he means the resort. "I can see why you like it," he adds.

I'm not even sure this requires an answer, and I think it's just as well because my throat is constricted. At the sound of his voice my body nearly went into spasms, whether of shock or lust I'm not sure, and I've more things on my plate for the moment than I can handle. It goes without saying that I don't know what to say.

It appears it doesn't matter. We continue to sit in silence, and he's right, it is peaceful, or as peaceful as anything can be when it feels like you have a herd of elephants charging through your head trampling on every coherent thought you have and trumpeting so loudly you feel like you'll never be able to form a complete sentence again. I'm very glad to find he isn't expecting much from me, because apparently that's exactly what he's getting.

For heaven's sake, as we sit there we don't even look at each other. We stare out to sea in silence like a pair of statues, but somehow it isn't awkward, it's right. And his lack of attention on me is definitely helping me to relax.

"Nice bar, too," he says, "Friendly." I'm not sure how he works this one out because I'm sure any looks he's getting from Paulo won't be terribly warm and the rest of the clientele probably have their eyes out on stalks and their mouths hanging open. They've never seen me actually know anyone except Donna before in all the time I've been here.

Anyway, did I say I had more things on my plate than I can handle, because I omitted one extra thing. I'm dying to go to the toilet. I know this isn't something that they ever mention in books or anything, and I'm only mentioning it now because it's pertinent, but I'm afraid it's true and I wanted to go before he even arrived, and then in my shock it was driven out of my head, but now I've calmed down a bit and had some cider the urge to go is overpowering me. Much as I don't want to leave him at this moment the alternative is just too awful to contemplate. I'm sure you understand. So I say in a stupid, formal way, "Will you excuse me for a moment, please?" and because I'm far too easily embarrassed I don't say where I'm going, and I don't know if maybe he thinks I'm going to do a runner or go into the bar and talk about him behind his back.

When I return he's gone. I feel like I've been kicked in the stomach, and for a weird moment I wonder if he has self destructed, after all. Despite not knowing what to say to him there were so many things I wanted to say and ask. He has left some money on the table so I know he isn't coming back.

I pick up the remains of my cider, curse my bladder roundly and take a deep breath before heading back into the bar and facing all the nosiness. I know it'll only take one person to ask one question and then they'll all start, wanting to know everything, because me having a friend who isn't Donna is such a turn up, especially as he's a man and I nearly collapsed when I saw him, and they can hardly contain themselves.

Of course it's Paulo who takes pity on me and jerks his head so I move over to the bar next to him and he talks at me for five minutes or so while I pull myself together and everyone else takes the hint. My word, I've had so many things to be grateful to Paulo for, and this is one of the biggest yet, I can assure you. Sometimes I really do wish I could love this guy, and I mean sexually as well as the way I do already, and ride off into the sunset with him and make him happy.

The next day I'm due out with the girls because it's Tuesday, and I'm in a right quandary because I don't know whether to go or not. I'm wondering if he's going to turn up at Paco's again. What will he think if I'm not there? Will he think I don't want to see him? Will he see it as a sign? But what if he *isn't* going to turn up, though? He left without a goodbye or anything, when I think about it he almost slunk off, so why would he turn up again? In which case I'll be standing there all night leaping with fright every time anyone appears at the door and having an awful time and I can't bear the thought. Better that I have my normal night out. I mean, why should he be able to reappear in my life and expect me to drop everything and come running? Or perhaps he doesn't expect that at all. Or even want it. Oh, fuck. I don't know what to think (you thought I was going to say "do", didn't you? Well, that too, to be honest).

In the end, because I'm a shameful coward, I go out with the girls to one of the local squares and a restaurant where they have a very pleasant red wine and great food, so it's good. Except that I spend most of the evening worrying that he will have arrived at Paco's and that he's wondering where I am and why I'm not there. Perhaps he's deciding at this very moment that I mustn't be interested and he might as well fly home! Perhaps he is taking it as a hint. Perhaps Paulo is telling him to fuck off. Oh, shit, I hadn't thought of that one before. I nearly throw my knife and fork down and race out of the restaurant, but I just about manage to stop myself and tell myself to get a grip. If, and it's a big if, he has come here deliberately to find me and it's taken him months and months then he's hardly going to give up at the first hurdle, is he? I mean, he doesn't know if this time it's me who's had to go to hospital, or if I had a previous appointment with someone who's really difficult to get hold of and so I couldn't miss it and risk it being another six months before he could fit me in again, or anything! Or perhaps he only wanted to see how I'd react, and oh God, he's seen that now. Aaaargh, I'm such a moron.

God knows what Lydia and Ali think is going on, because I must seem distracted. I keep losing track of the conversation and going off into trances. Or maybe I'm always like this and I didn't realise it before, because they don't say anything. I'm not sure what to make of that, to be honest, it's almost insulting. Lydia is very happy with Sergio and that makes me feel worse because now I'm worrying about Paulo as well as Scumbag. Whether they notice or not, I'm not at my best, I'm sure of that.

The evening takes forever and I'm ashamed to admit that when we finally split up I actually consider going to Paco's at this late hour to see if he's there. How desperate can you get? I don't even know if I want him, anyway. God, I really am useless and sometimes I hate myself.

The next day drags. I go swimming a lot to try to relax and it's a lovely day so I do a bit of sunning and I read to try to take my mind off everything, rather unsuccessfully. I know I'm going to go to Paco's tonight and I can't decide whether I want him to turn up or not, and if he does what I will do.

And even though Paulo hasn't kissed me or anything since February I'm worried about what he's thinking because I don't want to upset him, but I don't even know if I will. I know he likes me but I have no idea if he is harbouring any intentions of *that* nature at all, if you get my drift. Given my reaction last time he's probably been totally put off, and I can't blame him. As I mentioned before, I think he might have a secret girlfriend, so I can hardly go and ask him if he fancies me and if so will he mind if I go off with someone else, can I? Especially as I don't even know yet if I do want to go off with anyone else, because if Paulo does still want me then would I be better with him because he's so kind and considerate and makes me feel secure? Or is that unfair on Paulo, if I can't love him in the way he would like (assuming it is what he would like, that is)?

You will appreciate by now that I'm going to be flying on the seat of my pants tonight, and heaven knows what's going to happen. Or perhaps my guy won't even show and I'm putting myself through all this utter agony for nothing.

Bollocks. I know nobody ever said life was going to be easy, but quite frankly I never expected it to be like this.

Eventually seven fifteen crawls round and although it's slightly early for me I can't stand it any longer and off I go. I've made a bit of a special effort with my appearance, which is sad, isn't it? But given that I looked like Worzel Gummidge on a bad day on Monday I feel it's excusable, if shamefully vain.

When I get there it's fairly busy but there's no sign of either my guy or Paulo. I'm relieved about the latter, anyway, it's one less thing to worry about. For now, at least. I order myself a drink, resisting the urge to break all my rules and have a stiff brandy, and chat to Sue and Rick at the bar. And all the while my skin is crawling with anticipation and I am secretly watching to see if he turns up.

When he does arrive it takes all my self-control not to look like a startled rabbit, because I don't want Sue and Rick to notice and start asking questions. I can't believe he has actually turned up again and my mind is churning, trying to decipher what it might mean. Paco shoots me a bit of a look as he pours a lager and a cider, and I know the cider's for me. Once again it is placed in front of the empty chair beside Scumbag.

I try to be just a teeny bit more composed this time as I head out and sit beside him.

"Nice dress," he says, and I swear I see his lips twitch out of the corner of my eye. I just know he's referring to my unusual look on Monday, and his slightly mocking manner reminds me of how he was the night we met, and of the Chip'n'Dale show, and Madrugadas, and everything. Oh, God.

"Thanks," I say, as if it's the most natural thing in the world.

We sit for a while, and again it's peaceful, not uncomfortable. I'm starting to relax just a little bit, and I think this time it's me who should say something, so I'm racking my brains to try to think of something suitable. As in not about my past, or his life, or if he has a girlfriend or anything. In the end I say, "Are you on holiday?" and I curse myself, because he's hardly here on a conference for mysterious nameless guys, is he? In addition it makes me sound as though I want to know *why* he's here.

"Sort of," he replies, and I'm none the wiser anyway.

I sit and rack for a bit longer. A couple arrive who were here on Monday and I can feel their curiosity from where I'm sitting. Paulo hasn't turned up unless he's sneaked in invisibly somehow and I'm grateful for that.

"How long have you lived here?" he asks.

"Over three years," I reply, and I like this because it's an easy question, and then I wonder if Donna told him when the horror happened and it reminds me that he knows and he won't want me any more and I make myself push the thought away.

But although I try not to I simply can't stop myself from wondering why he's here – whether it's one of those utterly unbelievable coincidences, or curiosity, or to draw a line under our time together, or because he wants something. And the shards of silver excitement, sharper now and in danger of causing pain if allowed to go too far, are mixing with my thoughts and making them get twisted up so I can't sort them out. As you know, that's nothing new for me.

It's as if he senses my agitation - let's face it, I reckon even the fish out to sea are wondering what's upsetting me - and he sits in silence and looks out and it calms me. We finish our drinks and he must do some covert signal to Paco because two more appear, and I wonder if perhaps he is on a conference for mysterious guys after all and Paco is on it, too. Maybe they have some kind of secret code or something.

I continue to relax, and in the end I have to know so I ask, "Sort of?" and he knows to what I'm referring.

"Hmmm," he says, "Part holiday, part quest."

And now I know, and for a stupid moment I'm almost angry, because I asked him not to. "What about my note?" I demand, and I know I sound slightly accusing, and I don't want that. But then it's not as though he's going to be intimidated by me or anything, is it?

I glance sideways and see his lips press together as though he's trying not to laugh. "Was that supposed to put me off?" he asks, and I know which bit he's referring to and I go a bit red as he sniggers quietly.

I'm beginning to wonder what he means about being put off, and my body is starting to wake up and I'm trying not to think about anything like that anyway.

"How did you find me?"

I wonder if Donna has told him anything, and I'm shocked I would think such a thing of her for even a minute, because I know she wouldn't do that.

"I've visited Spain quite a bit," he replies, and I feel a shot of hot pleasure, and the silver shards are darting around more quickly now and I'm frightened they're going to get out of hand.

"I've been here before," he says, surprising me.

"Here?" I say stupidly, and again I wonder if he means the resort or the bar, and I see him nod.

"I must have missed you," he continues, "because I came in this bar, too."

Something collapses inside me as I realise he might have found me much, much earlier. I'm not sure what it means, though, because if he had found me earlier I wouldn't have been able to cope. I'm not sure I can cope now, to be honest.

"What made you come back?" I have to ask.

I see his eyes narrow slightly. "I don't know," he says, and he sighs. Oh my, suddenly I want to touch him so much, and I know I mustn't because God only knows what will happen if I do. I can feel his pent up energy and the shards are shooting around my head and starting to dash around my body, too, and I'm afraid I'm going to get hurt.

"I guessed you wouldn't live too far away from where I met you," he explains, "and this place is so peaceful. It seemed right, I suppose."

I don't know what to say. I'm taken aback by this man who has come to find me, and I don't know what he's expecting or what he wants. We haven't said much so far so perhaps he just wanted to find me and put and end to the affair. Have closure, as Donna would say. God, how I hate that word. More than ever, now.

So we sit for a while longer, and drink our drinks, and I wonder if he'll want another one or if he's had enough. I try to think of something to say, but I'm finding it difficult, and it doesn't seem to matter, somehow.

Now we've finished our drinks and as he fishes for his wallet my heart sinks, even though I know it's stupid. "I'll get these," I say, and I see a faint smile on his lips.

"Tomorrow?" he says, and relief floods through me. I nod, suddenly unable to speak, and I watch him go. Oh Christ, I'm in a mess. What the hell am I going to do now?

CHAPTER TEN

All I do for the rest of the evening and the next day is wonder what the bloody hell is going on.

I can't for the life of me decide why he has come to find me. Does he want to draw a line under our time together, or does he want more? I don't see how he can want more, not now he knows, and he hasn't exactly picked me up and run off to have his wicked way with me, has he? And it's just as well, because things are different now and I'm not sure I'd believe it if he did. I've been astonished by his apparent ability to discern my confusion and distress (I know, I know, I haven't exactly made it difficult), but more than that to do the right thing; take a step back and allow me to catch up. If he had tried to talk to me, or, heaven forbid, mention what happened to me, on Monday or even Wednesday I wouldn't have been able to deal with it, I'm sure, but his gentle silence and calm acceptance have given me the opportunity to pull myself together and think, even if I still don't really know what I should do.

And I can't understand why he's sticking around, and the tiny, hot sparks keep trying to take control and I can't let them because I can't face the disappointment if they're wrong.

Thursday evening comes and I go to Paco's. This time Paulo is there, so that's an added complication. I wonder if Paco has told him about yesterday, and of course he will have, this is a small community, and the likelihood that he hasn't is as strong as nobody being upset on Coronation Street on Christmas Day.

So I buy a cider, and stand near to Paulo because to do otherwise would seem strange, and I wait. I can tell Paulo knows I'm waiting and I feel bad about that but I don't see what I can do about it.

Then he turns up and I stay with Paulo while I finish my drink, because anything else wouldn't be fair, but all the while I know another cider is waiting for me on the table. When I finish Paulo turns away, and I don't blame him, and I go outside and sit down next to my guy. (I must stop calling him this because I don't think he is my guy any more, but Tom isn't his real name and I'm trying to get out of the habit of thinking of him as Scumbag, so please bear with me.)

I'm more composed this time. I've had plenty of time to get used to him being here and I knew he was coming back tonight, so that helped enormously. Plus he's asked nothing of me and now I'm pretty sure he can't want much. Perhaps he just wanted to see me and finish things properly, rather than me running off and disappearing in the cowardly way I did, and although I am very disappointed I can understand it, I think.

So I sit fairly calmly and sip my drink, and after a little while he says, "You took your brother's name."

This is so unexpected I nearly cry out. I swear a tiny ridiculous noise escapes me, but I hope even with his ears he doesn't hear. I suppose if he wanted to broach what happened to me it's one way to do it, it's certainly indirect.

"Yes," I reply, and I'm hoping to hell nobody else can hear our conversation. There's nobody on the next table, anyway.

"Not your sister's."

"No."

He waits patiently.

What's it to you? I start to think, but stop myself. At least these lateral questions aren't too frank, and I'm finding I can deal with it so far. I try to explain. "I didn't want to replace her," I say. "Samantha is different to Samuel. I took Amy as my middle name."

He nods. He's made me start to think about it now and I can feel a wave of intense emotion building up. It's as if he understands, because he says no more for some time. But I feel I have to say something, I feel terrible and I don't know why (or it may be that there are so many reasons I can't pick out any single one).

"I'm sorry," I say, because it's all I can think of.

His eyebrows rise slightly. "Don't be," he says, "It wasn't your fault."

Oh, God! It's so much the right thing and so much the wrong thing to say. The wave of emotion is suddenly hurtling over me and I feel tears start to slide down my face as all the guilt comes thundering back. I feel *so* guilty - guilty that I survived when my family didn't, guilty that I couldn't save them, guilty that I live in Spain in my villa when they have all gone, and even guilty that Mark had to witness what he did and couldn't deal with it.

I can't bear it. I lurch up and stumble away. As I'm dropping down onto the beach I hear my guy say, "Leave her," and I wonder who he's talking to, although I can make a good guess. I hear Paulo's furiously indignant, "Who the hell are you to tell me what to do about Sam?" He says it in Spanish, and I can just picture his incredulous face when Scumbag replies, "Probably nobody," and I'm glad his words are clearly non-aggressive.

By now I am on the beach and I walk along a little way to a discreet corner I know where I sit down under some palm trees and cry my eyes out.

After some time I start to pull myself together, and I know I have to go back up there. I can imagine how I must look – blotchy face, eyes red raw – and I'm glad that at least I had plenty of tissues with me. I learned to carry them around at the beginning when my emotions were very volatile and I've never really got out of the habit.

When I climb back up the steps I can't look at him. I feel ashamed and I know he must be revolted by what happened to me. I'm aware that Paulo will be by the bar, no doubt watching what's going on very closely and wondering what on earth it's all about. I know he will be feeling protective of me and that at the slightest provocation or sign from me he will be ready to stand up for me against this unwelcome stranger.

I sit and look down so I can avoid my guy's eyes.

"Sam," he says.

I continue looking at my hands in my lap.

"Sam, look at me, please."

Oh, God, I don't want to. Can't you understand that? I don't want to see the pity. Go away and leave me alone. Please.

He waits patiently, and of course like the feeble coward I am I finally raise my eyes to his, for the first time since he stepped into the bar on Monday. He has the strangest expression on his face, the one that always unsettles me, and this is no exception. But I see no pity, no embarrassment, and I don't understand. No change there.

"Come with me," he says, and I don't know if he means to talk undisturbed, for a walk, into his bed, or into his life. So of course I stare at him stupidly while I try to work it out. And then I shake my head, because whichever one he means, I can't do it, not now.

"The Spaniard at the bar," he says flatly.

How did you work that one out, Einstein? I think unkindly, and ridiculously I nearly start laughing. I ran out of words ages ago and so I just continue staring at him blankly, as if I'm the extra page they put in at the end of a book.

"You are with him?"

I shake my head. I don't want him to think that. "He's a good friend," I say, and it's so very true.

"You?" I ask in reply.

"I don't know him," he answers in confusion, and once more I nearly burst out laughing.

"Do you have someone?" I clarify, and his expression clears.

"Oh. No. I would hardly be here if I did."

Oh, God. That makes me wonder if really he does want something, and my body instantly starts to throb in the eager anticipation that it is what he wants. I try not to let it show as the silver shards start to appear again. I feel sick.

Suddenly there's a noise behind us and we both turn round. Paulo and Paco are arguing, and I'm aghast. I've never seen them have cross words before. Blimey, I'm already on edge and this makes me feel worse. For some stupid, vain reason I can't help thinking it's about me. I don't want to dwell on it or stare so I turn round again quickly, and Scumbag does the same because unexpectedly his face is close to mine and I can feel his pull.

For a long moment we stare into each other's eyes. I must be losing it, because I swear if he were to move an inch closer I'd rip his clothes off right here and now in front of everyone. But he doesn't, he shifts away, and murmurs something I can't quite hear.

"I can't leave here with you," I say, and I don't know if he gleans my meaning properly, because, to be honest, I'm not sure myself what I'm replying to. I realise he might think I mean I can't leave Spain, or that I can't be seen to leave the bar with him. When I think about it I know I mean both, but I don't know whether being Derren Brown's brother is enough for that one.

"I'm staying at Las Gaviotas," he says, "Apartment 802."

Gosh, I think absurdly, *I bet he has really good views,* and I wonder if I'm going insane.

"I'm here until Sunday," he continues. "I'd like to see you before I go. I won't come here again."

Once more I wonder if he means Spain, the resort or the bar and I nearly scream with frustration because I'm very worked up and could one of us please try to be a bit less ambiguous? I know I'm right now - I am going mental and no mistake.

Then I wonder if *he* thinks the argument is about me, too. Who knows? It's probably for the best that he doesn't come into the bar again while he's here, to be honest.

He meets my eyes again, and I just can't look away. "I wanted you to know that it doesn't matter," he says softly, "It doesn't matter to me."

Maybe he sees that at this I'm about to start howling again, because he gets up and I realise he's put some money on the table without me noticing. I simply can't watch him as he walks away.

I can only be thankful that tomorrow is Friday, and it'll be piss-up time.

Friday is another beautiful day – well, it's that time of year. I'm ashamed to admit that instead of going out and doing something useful, which would no doubt be good for me, I sit about the villa and mope and wonder what the bloody hell is happening. It's all I seem to do, these days. I consider ringing Donna and asking what she thinks, but I know what she'll say and it's not helpful.

Because I can't. I can't possibly put myself up for this. He thinks he understands, but it isn't that easy. I hardly know him. He hardly knows me. Even if my body is desperate to feel him touch it, it isn't enough. I can't let this guy into my life and take the risk that in a week, a month, a year, he will decide it was a bad idea. I can't face the rejection and the pain again. For heaven's sake, I don't even know if I can do the sex and emotion with one man. I'm so fucked up and it's so *fucking* unfair.

I wish I could fuse Paulo and my guy into one so I could have it all. I spend an utterly unbelievable few minutes deciding which bits I would take from whom before realising I am completely off my trolley and should be driving myself to the mental hospital by now If I'm safe to drive, that is.

I don't even know what to do that evening. I consider going somewhere different to Paco's because although I know Scumbag won't be there Paulo might be and I don't know if I can face either of them. Although Paulo might not be there. He might be on one of his mysterious nights away. Perversely, that might make me feel worse. Work that one out if you can because it's all way beyond me.

In the end I plump for Paco's because whether Paulo is there or not there will be plenty of other friends I can talk to if I want to, and anyway all I want to do is get drunk. I wonder if my guy is waiting in his apartment for me, and I wish I'd had the guts yesterday to tell him it was no use before he walked off and save him the trouble. (Underneath I know I don't wish this at all, I want him to be waiting for me because I am a selfish, self-deluding, totally stupid cow.)

So I get myself all nicely dressed up, because I need the confidence, and I slink down to Paco's a little later than usual. Paulo is there, and I'm relieved and dismayed at the same time. Another one for you to work out when you have a spare moment.

I behave in a very spineless fashion and avoid him at first. I mix with the Brits outside until I've had a few drinks and feel I can face him. When I finally say hello his face is inscrutable. He asks me nothing. He behaves as if it's just another Friday night, although I don't know if I imagine the faint sense of disapproval, or perhaps it's anxiety, emanating from him, either because of Scumbag or because once again it's Friday and I am deliberately getting myself drunk.

Anyway, he's with a few of his mates and we all chat together and it's fine. Lydia and Sergio come in, and I feel a bit bad about that, but Paulo's an adult, isn't he? He can handle most things, I know. God, if he can handle me nearly having hysterics when he tries to kiss me without rancour he can certainly put up with the sight of Lydia and Sergio happy together. In fact, if I'm honest, I think it's me who's upset by it, not him, but I don't even want to start analysing that one just at the minute if you don't mind.

The evening flies. I know I've said it before, but alcohol is a great healer - at times, anyway. I'm not advocating it as a general help-all, you understand, but now and again it does the job, numbing the senses nicely. Paco puts on some music, and having expected Paulo to be standoffish I am surprised to find he's the opposite, and we dance quite a lot and he's not standing off at all, no way. I'm not sure what I think about that, either.

It's time to go. I've had more than enough and suddenly I'm very tired. I say my goodbye's to everyone and head out. Unexpectedly I find Paulo walking beside me, and I feel a nervous frisson. However, it seems he's happy to walk in silence, I'm not getting the twenty questions I dread, and perhaps he just thinks I'm sufficiently drunk to need an escort. You know, in many ways I do love this man, he makes it very easy.

We reach my gate and I turn to say goodbye. "Can I come in for a minute, please?" he asks.

Now I'd like you to know that nobody – *nobody* - comes into my house. It's my sanctuary. I've allowed Donna in, of course, because she's from before and has been part of my life for so long, and there's been the odd electrician and so on who don't count because they don't know me, but somehow I've managed never to let anyone else past the front door, and I don't want to start now, either.

So I open the gate and allow him into the garden, and that's as far as he's getting.

"Who is he, cariña?" he asks, and it doesn't take Carol Vordeman to work out to whom he's referring, and I suppose I should have expected something like this, but I didn't. Plus I'm drunk. So I look at Paulo stupidly (it's a look I've perfected and made my own over the years) and I'm struck dumb.

"He hurt you?"

This really surprises me, but I don't know why when I think about it. He sees me nearly fall in a heap when Scumbag walks in, and then last night I burst into tears and run off down the beach. What's poor old Paulo supposed to think? I want to defend my guy but I'm afraid words are beyond me so I shake my head and hope he believes me.

"Who is he?" he repeats, and I still don't know how to start answering that one.

"You want him?" he asks, clearly thinking that I need specifics at this time of night, and he might not be far wrong. But I can't reply. Because again I don't know how to. *Physically – oh God, yes. Emotionally – I think I'm too scared.* Somehow I don't think Paulo will appreciate honesty at this stage, even if he thinks he will.

"I knew there was something," he says, finally, and once more I have to stifle an incredible urge to giggle. *No, really?* I think unkindly, and I know I'm being pushed too far and it's not his fault. I dare say he feels he's being pushed a fair old way, too.

Anyway, I grasp at the chance to have him think my previous appalling behaviour was down to an old flame. It's so very, very much easier than the truth, for both of us. I look down because I'm afraid my face will give me away, and he places his fingers under my chin and tilts it up to his.

I gulp. I think I can see sadness in his eyes, and I think, *Don't be so sure, I don't know myself yet,* but I'm glad I don't say it out loud because that wouldn't be fair.

"I'll always be here for you," he says, and I'm ashamed to say tears are forming in my eyes. For heaven's sake, that's all poor Paulo needs, more confusing mixed messages from me. "If ever you need me."

I don't know what he is thinking to say this, and to be frank I don't want to. I'm worried that he's putting two and two together and making seven hundred, and there's a note of finality in his voice that I don't like. A perverse and evil part of me is put out that he's giving up so easily – my God, after more than two years of me showing no interest, followed by me being apparently repulsed by his attentions, who can blame him? So I nod, and I feel a rush of emotion and I know I'm drunk and overwrought and I am going to snap very soon. I try *very* hard not to.

Then Paulo leans down. *Oh my God, he's going to kiss me*, I think, and his lips touch mine. It's a gentle kiss, undemanding, and somehow it's all right and I kiss him back in what I hope is a similar way. Feelings are running high and I'm aware that it won't take much for it all to get very silly indeed, and I must be very mixed up because for an idiotic moment I won't mind if it does. I have the fleeting thought that I should try with Paulo because I really trust him and know now that he loves me and he's safe.

I'm not proud to tell you this, and I can only put it down to the drink, but I lean into him a little and I might just kiss him a bit more than he kisses me. Even as I'm doing it I can't believe it. His arms creep around me and his kiss deepens, and I can feel his agitation building as he tries to decide what to do. He's a better man than me, or more probably he can't bear the thought of me suddenly having hysterics and backing off in horror again, because he pulls away and lets me go. He's breathing heavily and I feel like a wicked cow, because I am one.

"Oh, Paulo," I say very unhelpfully, but I think perhaps my emotion is clear in my voice because instead of giving me a well deserved slap for my thoughtlessness he looks at me tenderly and says, "I want you to be happy."

Oh Christ. If he had a bucket of salt to rub into the wound it couldn't be a sharper pain. I nearly collapse with it, so Lord only knows how he's feeling.

"You are too good for me," I reply, and although I know it's a corny line and usually said to get out of something without hurting anyone else, I have to tell you I truly believe it and I hope he can hear the sincerity in my voice.

"No, cariña," he says, and I'm glad to say he pulls himself together and takes a step back. You won't be surprised to learn I'm not sure what he means.

Do you know what I nearly do then? And this will tell you just how absolutely wicked and evil I am – I nearly blurt out, "I love you." (Because, in my defence, I do, just not in the way he hopes.)

How totally, incredibly and *utterly* cruel would that have been?

The next day you can't believe how terrible I feel. Or perhaps you can. I can't register properly that I was on the verge of encouraging Paulo. I can't take in that he now accepts I won't be his and so I have, in a way, lost him. And I can't face allowing Scumbag into my life, so I've lost him, too.

Didn't I do well?

I go for a swim to try to clear my head and decide what to do. It reduces my hangover but my head wouldn't be clear if it was distilled twenty times. I decide that I'll just have to put it all behind me and move forward, as per my New Year resolutions, rather than looking back. In fact, in this I am doing well:

Decide about Paulo – tick. (Even if it was taken out of my hands a bit.)

Look forward not back – tick. (I'm determined.)

Be more positive – tick. (I can hardly be less so.)

Stop thinking about Scumbag – tick. (Well, this one will be sorted tomorrow, anyway.)

I repeat: I'm doing really well. After all, what's the point of making these resolutions if you're not going to at least try to keep them?

But all the time, at the back of my mind where I don't want to hear it or even *acknowledge* it, a little voice is niggling at me and reminding me that Scumbag is going home tomorrow. And he wants to see me before he goes. To speak to me. And tiny shards of silver excitement are darting around and frightening me.

I hold out until early afternoon. I'm trying desperately to ignore the voice (honestly) and I read to take my mind off it. Then, because I finish my book, I decide to take my mind off it by shaving my legs, deep conditioning my hair and putting make up on. Finally I put on one of my favourite dresses to distract myself.

Then I am walking away from my villa towards Las Gaviotas. I am taking the lift up to the eighth floor, and finding apartment 802. I'm telling myself that it's only fair because he came all this way to find me and he only wants to talk to me, to clear things up before he goes home.

I knock on the door. Then I knock again. But there's no reply.

CHAPTER ELEVEN

I stand there like a complete idiot. For some foolish reason I hadn't imagined that he might not be in. I start to wonder if I got the day wrong and I've missed him, and my stomach twists uncertainly. Or maybe he's thought the better of it, after my obvious distress on Thursday. Maybe that brought home to him what happened to me. Or could it be because I didn't appear yesterday – I didn't come running as soon as I could? I lean my forehead against the door for a second while I pull my shredded thoughts together, and then push back and turn around.

He's standing there. He's standing a few feet from me, watching me, holding a load of supermarket shopping bags in his hands.

"You said you wanted to speak to me," I say, and I know this isn't strictly true.

"My key's in my pocket," he replies.

I look at him in confusion (perhaps he just likes easily bewildered girls and that's what he sees in me) because he's wearing cargo type shorts with lots of pockets. He indicates a pocket near his knee (thank God) and with great restraint I find his key and turn to the door. I *daren't* meet his eyes.

I open the door and walk in. His apartment is really nice and spacious; I suspect it's a penthouse. I manage to stop myself from admiring it out loud this time like a half-wit and I move well inside and turn round. He follows me in and kicks the door shut behind him.

I'm still trying *very* hard not to meet his eyes, because I know how they'll look (at least I hope I do) and that always seems to be the catalyst. Plus I'm scared that I got it all wrong and he does only want to talk. I have to remember that he knows what happened to me. How can that possibly not matter to him? Will I meet his eyes and see the pity or revulsion after all? So now I'm wishing I *had* admired the room, it would have been a nice, safe way to start. He's just standing there and giving me no help at all, *thank you very much.*

I put the key down on a table and say, "What did you want to see me about?"

He makes a snuffling sound and like a complete dipstick I look up in surprise. He's trying not to laugh, and he raises his eyebrows and I glance into his eyes by mistake.

He drops his shopping. I mean, he's tall, and it has a bit of a way to fall. Stupidly I wonder if he has any eggs in there, I hope not, and then I wonder why he is even *doing* any shopping if he's going home tomorrow. I'm completely bemused, and I must be right in thinking that's what he likes, because suddenly he's pulled me right up against him and his mouth is on mine and his fingers are sliding the straps of my dress from my shoulders.

My God, he's got a nerve, I think. *Who the hell does he think he is?* And as my mouth is otherwise engaged I use my hands to express my feelings of outrage, running them urgently under his t-shirt and pulling it off

94

him. *I didn't expect this at all*, I lie to myself, and then we are beyond hope, desperately trying to undress each other while not treading on any bread, or cheese or anything. I put my foot on a bottle of fizzy water and nearly go flying, but he catches me and lowers me to the floor.

Oh God, I think, *sex on an omelette!* and I giggle ludicrously. Then I think, *Hell! The floor's cold!* Because it is; it's tiled, and it's hard too. Don't ever believe it in the films when desire overrides comfort. Not with ice cold, marble floors, anyway. I've even seen them do it on stone steps in the movies. Christ, no, I want to enjoy this, thank you very much.

I'll never let it be said that Scumbag isn't chivalrous. Because he catches sight of my expression, and despite his obvious frenzy he picks me up and scuttles into the bedroom, almost throwing me onto the bed in his haste. God, I can see how turned on he is, his hands are stroking my skin and I'm frantic, urging him on blatantly. I can't wait to feel his hard body on mine.

He's there, and I feel him hesitate. *What now?* I think, barely able to contain myself. I nearly shout, "I'm sure, I'm really fucking sure!" How romantic would that have been? For an utterly hideous moment, too awful to even contemplate, I wonder if he's thinking of what happened to me and he can't do it. I nearly weep with an unreasonable mixture of stress and desire, and I half expect him to move away.

But he doesn't. He kisses me. Oh my God, he kisses me so tenderly, and then he moves, just like before, and I simply can't believe how lucky I am.

Some time later I'm lying staring at the ceiling. He's beside me, facing me, and I can't tell if he's asleep. We are, of course, naked, and I'm wondering where the sheet is because I prefer to be covered (for my back at least). I think it got thrown off right at the beginning and I have to say it's hot enough here in Spain now for it to be almost unwelcome. Then I ask myself why I'm bothering about a sheet when I should be wondering, for the hundred millionth time, what the hell I think I'm doing. It's all getting out of hand, and do I really want to let this man into my life? Do I really have any choice, though? I mean, he's here, isn't he? He's found me and he's here in Spain and so in effect he's put himself into my life whether I want it or not. He's certainly already had an impact on my situation at Paco's, because Paulo isn't going to hang around waiting for me any more, he'd have to be off his head to do that.

But I can't be angry with Scumbag, even though I asked him not to do this, because I'm impressed that he has come to find me for the second time, and that we can still have fantastic sex despite him knowing. I can't quite get my head around that. I don't understand how it can't affect him, not that I'm complaining, mind you. I've never known anyone who knows what happened to me not be affected by it. But then, I don't think I've ever told anyone before who didn't already know. By that I mean the people who know about it are the ones who knew me before it happened and, if you like, saw me go through it and how it changed me. They are all in

England, and nobody else knows at all, or not from me, at least, and certainly nobody in Spain. Scumbag is the only man who got to know me first, before being told. Perhaps that makes a difference. Or perhaps it's just him. I don't know, do I? I have nobody to compare him with.

Still, as I said, I'm not complaining. I have no idea how this is going to pan out. He goes home tomorrow, so perhaps this will be it. I have to admit I hope not. I guess my ideal would be that he visits every now and then and we have a brilliant time and in between I go back to my safe life undisturbed. But it's already disturbed, and I've already been through that, so there's no point going over it again. I suppose I'll have to admit that I'm not fully in control of my situation (I don't like this even though it seems to be happening more and more frequently) and see how it goes, whatever that means.

Oh God.

He moves, and leans up on his elbow to look at me. I'm smiling, of course, despite my worried thoughts, and I see his lips curl up in response.

"You're amazing," he says, surprising me.

I don't really know what he means, so for a change I don't know what to say.

"You're very brave."

"No, I'm not," I reply.

"You are."

I'm not going to get into a pantomime situation. "I haven't had much choice," I point out.

"We all have a choice."

I don't know what to make of that, either. It's not as though those evil bastards stopped to ask first, is it? This isn't something I can say out loud.

"So brave that I ran away to Spain."

"I don't blame you for that. Nobody would. There can't be much left for you in England."

Oh, thanks very much. Now I feel much better.

Once again I wonder at this man who is so unfazed by what happened to me. Unexpectedly I think of Paulo. I'm pretty sure he would be able to cope with it if I told him, but I have never wanted to and anyway I shouldn't be thinking of Paulo right now, it feels just a trifle disloyal you'll be astonished to hear.

My guy (I really am going to have to ask him his real name) kisses me, and then he gives me a gentle nudge. I realise what he's doing and I resist. Ok, so he knows, but he doesn't have to see, does he? I'm very happy just at this moment and I don't want to spoil things.

He nudges me again, and he's stroking me, too, and it's becoming harder to refuse him. He kisses my shoulder, and with a final shove I give in and allow him to turn me over. I wait for his reaction, but of course he's prepared, isn't he, so there isn't one. In fact, he kisses my shoulder again, and then works his way down until I feel his lips trace the wonky S of the big scar. I know it's a cliché, but somehow it moves me, and I shudder as I resist a sudden urge to cry. He carries on, and then he pulls me into him and surrounds me with his body, and I feel so incredibly safe.

"You are beautiful," he murmurs, and again I nearly burst into tears – perhaps you reach an age or an emotional limit beyond which even the most mindless clichés become horribly effective, who knows? I only know that his tenderness is unexpected and wonderful (or perhaps he had a few drinks while he was out) and I can hardly cope with everything that has happened this week. Oh, and I'm very, very happy.

He's stroking me again and I'm getting turned on, and I can tell that he is too, and now he's different, it's difficult to describe - more urgent, a little more demanding - but none the worse for that. In fact, I enjoy feeling his need, and knowing that what he's seen hasn't diminished his desire. Oh no. Quite the opposite, and that's another thing for me to think about later.

I've so many things to think about later (I'm not going to use the word "worry" because that would go against my New Year's resolutions, and I've already broken one so utterly and thoroughly I'm not going to risk another one yet) that my mind is now empty. It's possible that the sex has helped, too, because I feel sated and relaxed. I look up at Scumbag, and the use of this name, albeit only in thought - but it's a bad habit and increasingly there's a horrible chance that I might say it out loud – drives me to say shyly, "I don't know your real name."

He gives me a quizzical look. "Tom not good enough for you?"

"It isn't your name so I don't like using it. I keep having to think of nicknames -" I stop abruptly. That's one road I don't want to go down.

"Hmmm." He looks away for a moment, and I'm surprised, and to be honest, a bit hurt at his reluctance to tell me. Is he still wanting to leave a door open? I'm starting to worry again already, and I'm not going to say that I don't know whether to push this or not.

"I don't know *your* real name," he says.

"Yes, you do," I reply defensively, "I changed my name legally, so Sam is my real name now. I'm not the person I used to be, anyway, she doesn't exist any more."

He thinks about this, and I'm trying not to mind as he continues to hesitate. Then he looks at my face, and perhaps it's giving more away than I hope, because he sighs and narrows his eyes before saying, "It's Thor." He pronounces it "Tor".

"*Thor?*" I'm ashamed to say my eyes widen rather and I feel an inappropriate giggle rising inside me, which I struggle to suppress. No wonder he was being cagey.

He shoots me a look. "My parents were going through a Nordic phase," he explains darkly.

I know I have a wide smile plastered across my face, although at least I've managed to keep the giggles down for the moment. But it's too difficult to resist.

"What's your surname?" I ask. "Is it Mentor, or Pido, or Tellini, or Dree?" I'm afraid I do finally giggle out loud at this last one, because sadly I think it's rather clever as well as very funny.

He sighs again. "And what's your surname, then, Mosa, or Booker?"

I'm really trying to stop laughing but that last one of mine got me, and I know it's the worst form of behaviour to laugh at your own jokes. So I make a huge effort to pull myself together - I mean, it was surprise as much as anything - and he almost scowls at me. Unfortunately that only serves to make it funnier.

"Thor's the god of thunder, isn't he?" I ask in an attempt to atone for my rudeness.

"Mmm, amongst other things."

"Such as?"

"He's also associated with lightening, storms in general, oak trees, strength, the protection of mankind."

"Oh." I mull this over. He looks away, and if he was anyone else I might say he was embarrassed, but he can't be.

"I like it," I say, because I do. "It suits you."

I can tell he doesn't know what to make of this, but I find it's true. It *does* suit him, now I've got over my inappropriate surprise (because you have to admit it's an unusual one). I reach up to touch his face, and his eyes return to mine and they're a bit guarded, but presumably he can see I'm not laughing at him (well, not any more, anyway) because his face softens and I lean up and kiss him. I'm finding now that I like Thor much better than Tom, which seemed far too ordinary for him anyway.

Perhaps it explains his manner a bit, too, because I bet he came in for a certain amount of teasing at school, don't you?

I push him back onto the bed and lean over him. "I like it," I repeat firmly, and kiss him again to show that I mean it, and he kisses me back and pulls me down onto him and we lie there and I wish he didn't have to leave tomorrow.

Presently he asks me if I'm hungry and he gets up. I hear him moving the mess of shopping from the other room and offer to help. The answer's no so I lie back and grin and anticipate the rest of the time I'll spend with him. I can hear him with the frying pan and I hope he's put an apron or something on.

He comes back in with omelettes and bread and I have to stop myself from giggling as I remember my thought on the floor. So presumably some eggs were saved, or did he scrape them off rather than waste them? Ugh. Horrible thought. Now I'm inspecting mine suspiciously and he's looking at me as if I'm mental. I kind of understand, because what can possibly be suspicious about an omelette if you haven't

98

followed my train of thought right from the beginning? You can be sure I'm not going to tell him, I just know it's one of those ones which isn't remotely amusing when recounted out loud and he'll only think I'm more of an idiot than he already does.

Anyway, this makes me think and I ask him, "How come you've been shopping when you're going home tomorrow?" Perhaps he was buying stuff to take back, but bread and cheese are unlikely things, aren't they?

"Tomorrow?" he says innocuously, and raises his eyebrows at me.

"Yes. You said you were here until Sunday. That's tomorrow."

"I didn't say this Sunday. I'm here for another week."

I stare at him. I'm afraid my mouth drops open just a little, and I hate that, it's such a gormless look. "You definitely said "Sunday"," I reiterate automatically, closing my mouth firmly while my head whirls anxiously despite the silver sparks of excitement that begin to appear. Because I don't know what I think about this yet.

"You must have heard me wrong."

"No, I didn't."

I'm unsure now. It really annoys me that I can be perfectly definite one minute, but as soon as someone plants an element of doubt in my mind I'm immediately unsure, like some kind of weak-minded parrot that can only repeat what's said to it rather than have independent thought. *Did he say next Sunday?* I wonder to myself. I'm sure he didn't.

I look at him and he's gazing back at me innocently. Almost too innocently, I think. Could he have deliberately misled me to push me into coming to him sooner? Would he be so manipulative? I don't know. I'm reminded that I don't really know this man at all and I don't know what I make of this. A minute ago if you'd have offered me another week with him I'd have jumped at the chance. Now I can feel my tension building because a week is a long time. There's too much opportunity to really get to know him and like him and become close and I'm frightened again. God, I'm so mixed up and I'm beginning to feel sick. Perhaps it's something from the eggs he scraped off the floor. I almost giggle with nerves.

If he was expecting me to fling my arms around him and squeal, "How fantastic!" he's already disappointed, I realise. I struggle to dominate my alarm, it's hardly fair on him. He has that strange expression on his face, and that's no help.

"Gosh," I say inanely, and I know I sound unenthusiastic, and I know it's stupid but I'm scared. I don't know what to do. My half eaten omelette is still in front of me and I decide to stare at it in the hope of inspiration. For God's sake, what inspiration do I think an omelette's going to give me?

He's quiet. He isn't eating his omelette either, I notice. I know I'm being really ungracious and probably giving him the wrong message because once I get my head around this I'll be pleased, I *know* I will. Oh God, another day or two wouldn't have fazed me, but a *week*. How am I going to explain this at Paco's? What will everyone think? What if I grow to really like him and then he leaves forever? I can't cope and I'm starting to panic. I don't know what the hell to do and every second that passes makes it worse. *Why am I not jumping for joy?* I wonder uneasily, and I feel very disturbed – ok, ok, I know, I'm already disturbed. That's an old one, thank you very much.

"Sam," he says, and I look up hesitantly. "You can walk away at any time you like, you know."

Well! I don't know what to make of *that* at all. Is he saying he won't care if I do? Is he telling me he has no hold on me? Is he saying that the fact he came to find me doesn't put any pressure on me? Or is he really Derren Brown's brother and he knows exactly how I'm feeling? That's the most frightening thought of all.

"I don't want to walk away."

I don't know where that comes from, I honestly don't, and I think I must look bewildered for a moment because he gives me a hot look. If all I need to do to turn him on is look confused I'm in for the busiest sex life since Silvio Berlusconi. I giggle out loud and God only knows what he makes of that.

"Would you like to stay here tonight?" he asks, and I look at him with relief. It's so the right thing to say. I can handle one more night, manageable chunks of time.

"Yes, please," I reply, and for an awful minute I think I'm going to cry. That would really help the atmosphere, wouldn't it? What on earth is wrong with me?

"Only you don't have a change of clothes with you." His face is deadpan.

I look back at him. "I don't suppose I'll need any," I reply coolly, and I feel a frisson as I remember and anticipate. *Anyway, I was only coming for a chat, wasn't I?* I think, and have to suppress another giggle. Honestly, I can't keep up with myself. But he's done it again – said exactly the right thing – and I feel much better.

He leans over to me, across our abandoned omelettes, and kisses me, and I feel even better still.

"Do you still want that?" he asks, eyeing my plate dubiously, "or should we go out later?"

If he'd asked this before, when I'd thought I only had one night with him, no way would I have wanted to go out. But as it is, dinner sounds good. A proper date. I giggle. "Are you asking me out?" I ask.

"I suppose I am. For tonight." He grins.

"About time," I say.

"And whose fault would that be, then?" He gives me a dark look, which I guess I deserve, and removes our plates. Then he heads for the shower and I smile widely. This time I have no hesitation in joining him – after all he's seen my back now – and I'm pretty sure (going by experience to date) that he won't want sex in there and so I needn't spoil things by worrying about falling over.

I enjoy the evening. I pick one of the nearby restaurants because neither of us wants to drive and the food is good there. I am self conscious as we go in, because I'm known there (as I am more or less everywhere in this quiet resort) and I know that me appearing with a man will cause a spark of interest. However, nobody makes a big deal of it and we are left to get on with our meal in peace. As I look across at him I have to keep reminding myself to call him Thor, I'm trying to implant it in my head. I'm sure I'll slip up occasionally internally but as long as I don't say anything stupid out loud I should be fine.

The wine flows and as before we talk about nothing personal and we are both relaxed. After dinner we go for a couple of drinks in one of the Spanish bars, and I'm pleased to be able to show him how different my resort is to the one where we met. I don't know why, it doesn't really matter, but I can still remember how he picked Madrugadas for our drink and I want to show him that we have lots of places like that here.

After our drinks we go back to his apartment with the inevitable result. I lie awake for some time trying to get my head around everything that's happened. Even though I first saw him on Monday and it's now Saturday everything seems to have happened quickly. I'm very pleased that he is here and that he made the effort to find me, and I'm trying to convince myself that there's nothing wrong with another full week together. Assuming that he wants to be with me all week, and come to think of it I'm being a bit presumptuous and perhaps he will want some time alone to do other things. I know little about him and maybe he likes being alone, from what I've seen so far I could believe that. This makes me feel better, and it just shows how confused I am because the silver glitter is still flurrying inside me at the thought of a week of him, and underneath I know that if I'm not overfaced I will want to spend the whole time with him and I won't want him to leave at the end of it. And that won't do at all.

If anyone out there knows a good analyst perhaps this would be a good time for them to get in touch.

CHAPTER TWELVE

The next few days follow a similar pattern, divided between bed, the sun terrace (I was right, his is a penthouse), eating, talking, swimming and going out. Both the penthouse and the sun terrace are very private, not overlooked at all. It feels odd not having to worry about anyone seeing my back and it takes a while for me to relax about it. Eventually though, like him, I'm hardly bothering with clothes and it feels liberating. I can't believe I spend quite a bit of my time lying naked on the sun terrace, not self conscious at all, it's not like me and it feels weird, even though I like it. I like the side effect even more.

Although we do a lot of talking we don't touch on anything too personal. These are the things he doesn't tell me about:

His family.

His work.

Any previous relationships he may have had.

His life in England in general.

These are the things I don't tell him about:

My life before I came to Spain.

Ok, so that's only one thing but it covers a lot. Oh, and I don't talk about Paulo, either.

These are examples of what we do talk about:

Films.

Books.

Music.

Religion.

Politics.

Places we've visited.

So we learn quite a bit about each other in a way, likes and dislikes and so on, but nothing too intimate. He has clearly done a lot more travelling than me, but whether through work or in his spare time I don't know and I don't ask. I have no idea if he has any brothers or sisters, what he does for a living, or anything. It's great. The less I know the less involved I can get. I don't even know where he lives, for heaven's sake.

Yet we are never at a loss for conversation. We have plenty of comfortable silences, but when we are out or want to chat there's no problem.

We take each day as it comes, there's no forward planning. Therefore every day I head back to my villa for a change of clothes. I can't determine whether he keeps things like this deliberately, I think I have said before he can be very astute, or whether it simply follows the natural flow, but it gives me a bit of space and psychologically I know it helps me to cope, keeping each day as a separate chunk of time. I find I have no doubt that I want to return to him each day, and he makes it clear that I'm welcome to. I don't allow him anywhere near my villa.

I know he spends most of this time on his laptop keeping up to date with his business and goodness knows what else, so I'm not made to feel as though going off each day is a problem, and I can take as long as I like. Perhaps because of this I find I don't want to take very long at all.

On Tuesday I decide to walk back to his apartment along the beach for a change. It isn't a long walk, less than ten minutes, and it's very pleasant. Up until now I have avoided walking this way because it takes me past Paco's and for some reason I don't want to see anyone from there. It's like I'm in a parallel world for the moment and I want to keep it that way. So even though I walk along the beach today I take a detour before Paco's and walk around the roads until I have gone past. You are forgiven for considering me a complete idiot for doing this, I know it sounds pathetic.

As I'm heading back towards the beach I hear Paulo's voice. I'm surprised as I would have expected him to still be at work. I can't make out what he's saying but he sounds agitated. His voice is coming from the beach ahead of me. There's a wall between us and from where I am, still a bit away from it, I can't see over. Then I hear another, cool voice, and my blood runs cold. Because it's my guy's voice, and he's clearly talking to Paulo. Why this would upset me so much I don't know, but it does. Oh Lord, how on earth have those two ended up on the beach talking? Is it a coincidence? Because if it is, it's exponential that I would also end up here right now. So have they arranged to meet? How can they, they don't know each other? It must be a coincidence, one hell of a coincidence. Oh, God, this is all I need. What should I do? Like a completely underhand sneak I stay behind the wall and my ears are flapping. It's only to make sure things don't get ugly, you understand, and so that if they do I can step in and intervene.

Someone nearby is playing music and it's the kind that keeps changing tempo and volume (oh, like nearly all music, I hear you say), so although I can hear some of what's being said there are moments when the voices are drowned out. I can't begin to tell you how frustrating it is, because obviously it's better for me to be able to hear everything to enable me to judge whether any intervention may be necessary or not.

"...what it's got to do with you," my guy growls.

"Enough, Sam's my friend." This is Paulo, and his voice is hard and tight.

I feel sick. Although I'd guessed they might be talking about me, having it confirmed chills me. I have to look, I just have to, and so I creep up to the wall and peer carefully over.

They are standing side on to me, facing each other, and they are bristling. *Bristling.* I've never properly understood what that meant before, but now it's perfectly clear because it's the only word for it. If they were dogs their hackles would be up and the hair along their backs would be standing on end (or is that the same thing, I've never been sure?) I can sense my guy's pent up energy from here; he's like a coiled spring. Paulo looks furious, he's standing very upright and seems about six inches taller than usual, he's really quite imposing, although still the smaller of the two. They are glaring at each other and it seems there's no danger of either of them spotting me. Even so, I'm far too much of a coward to risk it so I crouch down behind the wall. Then I realise how suspicious I look if someone sees me so I sit down as though I am keeping out of the sun for a bit. If Paulo or my guy sound like they're coming my way I'll have to make a run for it or pretend I've fainted with heat stroke or something. Because although I know it's wrong, and I really shouldn't listen, wild horses couldn't drag me away at this point. You know I've never said I was perfect.

"...just walk into our lives. Who the *hell* do you think you are?"

This is Paulo. Even I think *our* lives? So goodness knows what Scumba-, sorry, Thor is thinking.

"I'm not aware that I have walked into *your* life," Thor snarls rather predictably. "What the fuck are you trying to say?"

Oh, God, this isn't going well.

"Fuck you," says Paulo, and I'm shocked because I don't think I've ever heard him swear like that before. *Shit.* I've never thought of Paulo as the aggressive type, but I know the Spanish can be very hot blooded if pushed too far.

I can't hear the next bit for the music, although I strain for all I'm worth.

"... face when she saw you ... beach ... upset..." You might have guessed this is Paulo again. For heaven's sake, I can only hear bits and it's *really* frustrating.

"Oh, and you know all there is to know about her, do you?"

Oh my God! My heart stops and I draw in a sharp breath.

"More than you ... nearly three years ... long time ... *ever* hurt her I ..."

At this point I nearly give my self away by jumping up and screaming to whoever it is to turn their bloody music down. That would be a good move, wouldn't it? And it would certainly allow me to carry on eavesdropping - not.

"... no intention ... adult, isn't she? ... own mind ... hurt *me*?"

Bloody hell. If my guy's said what I think he might have I'm desperate to look over the wall and see Paulo's face. He's quiet, and it has certainly taken the wind out of his sails, and no mistake, and perhaps that was the intention.

I can't hear anything for a while. I'm very worried that they are going to start fighting and I'm getting into a proper tizz. Or perhaps they are fighting now! Perhaps it isn't the music drowning their words but the fact that they are no longer talking, communicating with their fists instead! I can't bear the thought of the two men I like most in all the world fighting and I don't know what to do. God, I thought I'd got over that, it's been at least two days. Should I walk around the wall innocently and stop them before it goes too far? Should I walk off and leave them to it (because I can hardly stand the tension) – they're both adults and although I know my guy is good in a tight spot I don't think he would look for violence? Or should I stay hiding here and carry on listening to their conversation ready to rush out if necessary? Yes, I think that's the most sensible option, really, let them have it out but be ready to intervene if I have to. Keep an eye on things, or rather an ear. Definitely.

"… keep her away from Paco's because … everything she's … here in Spain … we're all family here."

The current track is coming to an end and I'm praying that the next one is quieter.

"I'm not keeping her away from Paco's. Christ, it's only been a few days." This is Thor and he sounds a bit bewildered for some reason. It seems that having taken the wind out of Paulo's sails they have both calmed down a bit.

Oh for God's sake, the music's getting louder again. I wonder how far away the source of it is and if I could achieve anything with a well-aimed stone. I can't hear anything for a good few seconds.

"… you are. You're just too fucking stupid to see it." I can tell Paulo's getting worked up again, perhaps it's that Spanish temperament getting to work after all. *Christ, please don't push my guy too far*, I think, *you don't know what he's capable of.*

"… Oh, right … very likely if … like this, *Scumbag*."

I jump at Thor's use of his own name for Paulo and for a terrible moment I think I'm going to guffaw out loud. It's only nerves, but nothing would be less welcome at this point in time, of that there's no doubt. I do some ridiculous jerking for a moment or two as I try to control myself, and I hope to hell that nobody's watching; they'll have me taken away.

The voices are still raised and getting louder – at least Paulo's is loud and my guy's is hard and controlled, but the music is also loud and I can't make out what they're saying. Oh God, I think they're going to come to blows after all and I'm cursing them, I mean, I'm just not *worth* it, and it's so ridiculous. I'm thinking I'm going to have to jump up and wave my arms and distract them after all, and I'm trying to think of an excuse I can give for being here just at this particular moment by coincidence. I don't want to admit to being such a pathetic coward that I have taken a detour to avoid Paco's (especially after what Paulo seems to have said) and I'm not sure how to make it clear that I've only just turned up, honestly I have.

Then suddenly the music stops and I can't hear anything. *Anything*. I'm thinking definitely they must be fighting and I'm about to peep over the wall (having decided against the arm waving scenario) when I hear them, and thank goodness their voices are lower. I can't make out what they are saying, but at least they appear to have calmed down a bit. I didn't think they were *that* stupid. Now I'm starting to worry that one of them is going to come round the wall when they finish and I'm dithering about whether to sneak off before that can happen. God, the last thing I want is to get caught listening in on them, how utterly shameful would that be? Ok, I know, if it's so shameful I shouldn't be doing it in the first place, but I challenge you to have walked off when you realised what was going on. I'm only human.

The voices continue and although my ears are nearly reaching over the wall by themselves I can't make out the words. Then all of a sudden it goes completely quiet again and I think they must have finished and I panic wildly that one of them is going to appear at any second and I gather up my things, scraping my hand on the wall as I do so, my heart hammering in my chest in my fear. I nearly fall over my feet in my haste as I gallop up the path in a most ungainly fashion, only daring to look back at the top and nearly fainting with relief when I can't see either of them behind me. I decide I've played my luck for long enough and hurry back to the apartment so I can be cool and relaxed as though nothing has happened by the time Thor walks in.

So I dump my things and I stare round the apartment trying to decide where would be the most innocuous place to be. Up on the roof terrace? No, unlikely at this time. On the settee? Perhaps I could be reading my book. Making a cup of coffee? What am I thinking – I hardly ever drink coffee in this weather, that would look decidedly odd. In the end I collapse on the settee with my book, and just in time because I hear the key in the door (we have one each, in case you are wondering) and in he walks. I'm hiding behind my book trying to look innocent, although as I'm behind my book he can't see me and I don't know why I bother.

After what I hope is a cool minute I lower my book to look at him. He's staring at me with the strangest expression on his face, and I nearly give a pathetic little whimper because I'm so unnerved. Could he have seen me after all? I'm trying hard to keep my face impassive and I'm relieved to see there's no sign of blood or bruising or anything, not that I really thought there would be. So I get a grip and smile lazily (or at least I hope I don't look like some kind of garish Halloween turnip lantern) and say hi in my best drawl.

He says nothing and he still has a funny look on his face and I can't make it out. I must be starting to look bewildered because suddenly his eyes are smouldering (I'd forgotten how effective that is) and his whole demeanour is changing. I feel my pounding nervousness turn into something completely different as he advances on me, and for the first time in a while I'm reminded of the leopard.

He takes my book and drops it on the floor. *Oh, do you mind if I interrupt you?* I think irreverently, *fancy a bit of hanky panky? By the way, did anything interesting happen on the way back from your villa?* (I don't know where these thoughts come from because I don't encourage them.) I snigger. I can only guess it's the stress of wondering what the hell he and Paulo have said to each other and how things were left between them. He pauses and gives me another look, but now the funny look is mixed with desire and it's not so off-putting, in fact it's amusing and I snigger again. God, I can't help it even though I know it's inappropriate.

He smiles briefly, Lord knows what he's thinking, and then the next second his face is wiped clean and he pulls me up and strides into the bedroom. *Oh, don't mind me.* He's undressing me and whatever has gone on it's wound him up nicely, because he's not messing around and I'm left in no doubt as to where he stands. Or should that be where I stand? Or at least I would be in no doubt if I knew what had gone on with Paulo, but of course I don't, do I? Anyway, I'm not complaining, not at all, we all like to feel wanted sometimes, don't we?

Afterwards I'm lying next to him trying to enjoy the after-sex glow and not worry about Paulo. He has his arm across my waist and it feels lovely. We are going out for dinner tonight and I have brought one of my smarter dresses with me because I felt like it and I try to concentrate on that rather than what I tried so desperately to overhear over the wall. Really, they should ban music on the beach, people can be very inconsiderate.

We shower, and I feel very close to him, and then we laze about before getting ready to go out. My dress is long and it fastens by the way of buttons all down one side, although I only do them up to my mid thigh. When he sees it I'm glad to say it has the desired effect, as I can see from his face that he's deciding whether he'll start at the top or the bottom when we get back. I give a little shiver of delighted anticipation, and I know that however good dinner is I am going to enjoy the desert.

We go for steaks, and as usual my appearance with a man causes some interest. However, Domingo is not a nosey person and I can see he is pleased to see me. He looks after us very well, and the steaks are excellent. We chat about generic things and I steal secret looks at this man who has done so much for me. He is being cool and sardonic tonight. I like him like this, it reminds me of when I met him. I can hardly wait to get back to the apartment.

He starts from the bottom, working his way up. All worries are banished from my mind as I give myself to the moment and the exquisite pleasure that he offers.

He surprises me the next day by suggesting we take a drive out to one of the rural towns. It's a good idea and will make a change. I know a few of the towns in the hills about an hour from here and the difference from the coast is considerable. For example, the paella changes from seafood to rabbit and snail (luckily the snails are in their shells so I can pick them out). Perhaps that's not the example you are looking for but it's the best I can do at short notice and I think it sums it up nicely, thank you. If you want some more, the bars are far more rustic. Tapas are eaten at the counter and all the rubbish thrown onto the floor as is traditional, allowing it to be swept up regularly as the day progresses. The towns are scruffy but friendly with interesting churches and squares and local industries. The countryside is covered mainly with trees – olive and almond to name just two – replacing the vegetables, oranges and lemons we have on the more fertile plains by the coast.

Anyway, we have a fun day exploring and trying the local dishes and don't set off back to the resort until early evening. I haven't been for my change of clothes but it doesn't seem to matter, and I'm taken off guard when, on the way back, my guy asks if I want to call into Paco's for a drink. I wonder where that has sprung from, nudge, nudge, and I like the fact that he can argue with Paulo but perhaps also think about what he said, too. Always supposing what I think was said actually was said, if you understand me. I might be quite wrong.

Oh heck, we're only five minutes or so away so I don't have long to think about it. Maybe it's just as well. I was quite happy keeping my two worlds separate, but overhearing what I think Paulo might have said has affected me, too, (never let it be said that I'm easily led – or weak, if you prefer to be more blunt) because I don't want to upset him more than I have to.

But going in with Thor, rather than simply joining him at the table outside, is going to be noticed and my life at Paco's will change even more because people will associate me with him and ask after him (especially as I've never been seen with another man before) and if it all goes horribly wrong it'll be awful. Oh God, I just don't know what to do. Aaaargh.

Suddenly I realise that going in while Thor is here could be the best option, because much as I would love to leave it, if I do so it could look like either I am ashamed of Paco's or ashamed of him. Ashamed might be a bit too strong a word, but I hope you know what I mean. So on the spur of this thought I say yes and instantly regret it, but I'm not going to make a fool of myself by changing my mind now and making it obvious how utterly hopeless I am. Anyway, if people meet him and see him for themselves it might stop a load of nosiness later on. This thought makes me feel better.

We are pulling up now so it's too late to change my mind. We park nearby where we can leave the car until tomorrow if we like.

I turn to him. "How shall I introduce you?" I ask shyly.

He looks at me blankly.

"I mean, what do you want me to call you?"

His eyebrows rise slightly. "I think Thor would be best, wouldn't it?" he says sardonically.

"Only you called yourself Tom at first, so I don't know whether you prefer that." My voice tails off because even as I'm saying it I know I sound like an imbecile.

He looks away. "Thor's fine," he says, "Unless you'd rather not."

I don't know what this means at all. What on earth's he getting at? You won't be surprised to learn that I'm starting to worry and wondering what he's thinking. I must give him a bewildered look because he narrows his eyes and gazes forwards again. "If I'm going to meet people it's easier if they use my real name – it'll avoid future complications."

Oh. Now I see. Or I think I do. I feel such a berk and I don't know what to say. It seems he's thinking of me, and the word "future" starts a weird bubbling in my stomach that unnerves me, even though he may only be referring to tomorrow. Let's face it, it wouldn't be the same if something didn't unnerve me. Anyway, I realise I prefer to introduce him as Thor, too, because it's his name and I'm so useless that if I called him something else I would be bound to slip up at some time. I don't know how on earth I've managed to avoid calling him Scumbag all this time. In fact, I don't even know why I asked what I should call him and I'm squirmingly embarrassed. Does he think I didn't want to take him into Paco's to meet my friends? Have I made him think that I don't want to give his real name in case I don't want to see him again? But what difference would his name make to me? Plus it was him who started the whole "Tom" thing and I thought it was him who wanted to keep a door open. God, I'm really mixed up now and worried I've upset him or something.

I look at him as he's looking out of the window and I can't help wondering if he thinks I'm some kind of deranged half-wit. *Perhaps he was a naughty boy last year and he thinks he should take on some kind of charity case to make up for it*, I can't help thinking, and the idea of calling him a naughty boy makes a giggle rise inside me which I do my best to suppress, without that much success, to be honest. Oh God, I bet now he thinks I'm laughing at him, too, and I'm not, or at least not in the way he thinks. Shit, I'm so clueless sometimes even I think I should be locked up.

I reach out and touch his arm because I can't think of anything else to do. He turns to look at me then, and I know I still have the remnants of my giggle on my face, which doesn't help my composure. Suddenly he smiles, and his whole face changes, and I'm so relieved I almost clap my hands like a two year old. My word, I really know how to impress people. I wonder at myself sometimes, I mean, is it just me?

We climb out of the car and he takes my hand. This makes me feel much better although I wonder if he just thinks I'm not capable of crossing the road on my own.

When we walk into Paco's it's quite busy and I swear there's a momentary hush and I want to giggle. It might be because I was almost expecting it, but I don't think so. I dare say we have been the subject of many a conversation in here over the last week or so, no doubt from when Thor first walked in and I nearly fainted with shock. After all, it's a small community. It makes him seem like my mystery guy again and for some reason this pleases me. I bet they are all dying to know who he is and how come I knew him and why he surprised me and everything. I'm not usually one for being in the limelight, but maybe because it's reflected limelight this time I don't mind. As we walk to the bar I can feel numerous pairs of eyes swivelling and following our progress.

God, I wonder what Thor is making of this, it's like the moment when they walk into the country pub in *American Werewolf in London*. (I know it's an old film but I saw it again recently.) At least in this case it's friendly curiosity. Well, on the whole – Paulo is standing by the bar with Pepe and Sergio.

Uh-oh. This could be fun.

CHAPTER THIRTEEN

I order the drinks, although I suspect Paco already knows what we're having, and for some reason I enjoy waiting for them while everyone stews. I glance at Thor and I can see his lips are pressed together. I almost snigger myself, but that would be so rude. Actually, it wouldn't be much ruder than all the obvious nosiness that is surrounding us.

Because Paulo has always been so good to me I know I am going to introduce him first, even though secretly I know they've already met. I bet they didn't get round to names and favourite foods at the time, though. So I turn to him and he turns to me and his face is unreadable.

"Hola, Paulo," I say, and he leans forward and gives me the standard two kisses, one on each cheek. As he pulls away I see a flicker of something cross his face, but I can't make out what it is. Oh God, I hope this isn't all going to go horribly wrong. From what I heard on the beach I think Paulo should be pleased we've come in, but you never know.

I introduce Thor to all three of them. The bar is very quiet as I do this and I just know everyone is listening in. I see a few eyes widen when they hear his name and I know how they feel. If he notices he doesn't let it show.

He speaks to them for a minute or two in Spanish, and I know that will help things along because so few Brits bother to learn even the basics and it's always appreciated when somebody does. His Spanish is very good considering he doesn't live here. I've been here for three years and I still wouldn't say I was fluent, although I can say most of what I want to and understand nearly everything said back to me. But there are always some words I don't know and I get caught out now and again.

Of course this frustrates the Brits because they can't understand what's being said and I start to grin. I know the minute we finish one of them will ask a question and everyone will be glued to the answer. Honestly, you might think it's sad to be so interested in someone else's business, but very little happens here, and a lot of the interest is friendly, because as I may have mentioned we are all a bit like one big family we look out for each other. So already I can see a lot of weighing up being done, and it's going to get much worse once the conversation starts in English.

Paulo and Thor both make an effort, it appears there must be some kind of truce, and I'm really relieved, but it doesn't take long before Paulo turns away and we face the sea of eyes. For a ridiculous minute I consider climbing onto a chair and making an announcement just to get it over with and keep everybody happy. I wonder how much detail I should go into, and I realise there would be no such thing as too much information for this lot at this stage. Then I realise I'm being unfair and they're looking out for me and me having a man is such a turn up that I can't blame them.

As it happens John and Val are next to us and Val asks me how I am, thus opening the door to the interrogation. I consider asking everyone to gather round to save them having to strain their ears so hard, and I almost giggle. I realise I know very little about Thor really, and I don't want to know much more, so I hope the questioning will be limited to how we met and so on, and not what he does and how big his family is and where he lives and all the other things that people ask. Please. Anyway, they are more interested in how we met, and I cut him off at the pass, saying he's from England, because I don't want Paulo to know I met him on Donna's hen weekend. Although he still has his back to us I'm sure Paulo's ears are waggling, I can practically see them from where I'm standing.

Thor takes the hint and doesn't contradict me. I wonder what he's going to say about him walking in on Monday, because many of this lot saw my reaction so saying I invited him isn't going to wash. I didn't exactly throw my arms around him in welcome, either. I'm getting nervous as I wait for this inevitable question and I'm starting to fidget. I can see him eyeing me surreptitiously and I'm probably putting him on edge, which isn't fair. Really he should have given me more than five minutes notice for this and we could have sat down and come up with an acceptable story. God, that makes me sound like a complete cow as if I'm ashamed of him or something, so I probably couldn't have done it, but it isn't that. I don't want to hurt Paulo's feelings, but I'm not sure I could have said that to Thor, either.

So I wait and fidget and when the question comes Thor says that he hadn't seen me for some time and he wanted to surprise me. That manages to be true, and it doesn't raise any eyebrows, you won't be even mildly astonished to hear. I think everyone saw that I was most definitely surprised when I clapped eyes on him. There is a lot of appraising going on as we're talking and I can't help wondering what everyone thinks of him and hoping they like him. If anyone is curious about why I had that particular reaction to his appearance (as if), they nobly put a lid on it. It seems some things *are* too nosy, and I'm relieved.

In the end we mix with quite a few people and everyone's friendly, asking easy questions like what he thinks of the resort, and I start to relax. We handle the questions with aplomb (I love that word) and nobody asks anything too personal. Someone does ask what he does, but he simply replies that he works for himself, and something about the way he says it discourages further prying in that direction. I wish I could do that.

Then Paulo turns back to us. I'm sure he's been listening the whole time. Don't even start me on Paco, he's been polishing the same glass only a few feet away from us for about half an hour, openly lapping it all up.

Paulo gives my guy a long look and says, "So how well did you know Sam before?"

He asks it blandly, and I appreciate that it can be taken as an innocent question, but I'm wondering what he's getting at. Is he fishing, because he doesn't know how well we know each other now, never mind before? Thor hasn't been outwardly affectionate to me in the bar, but then he's not normally a touchy feely person in public anyway, and that suits me fine. Even so, to my mind he's been tactful in here, especially considering what happened on the beach yesterday. Paulo must have a good idea of what's going on anyway, after seeing what he has so far, so I don't know why he's asking now, but the way he's deliberately avoiding my eyes tells me he knows it might be an unwelcome question and that annoys me. Thor doesn't bat an eyelid and replies, "Pretty well, I suppose."

Gosh, that's a good answer, not exactly a lie but not exactly the whole truth, either. For a moment I remember the time when I'd thought Paulo was going to ask *me* this and I'd thought I could say, "more intimately than you could ever imagine," and "I've only met him twice," and both answers would be true. For an insane minute I almost say it out loud, because it would be funny and it would just about serve Paulo right if I did.

Anyway, I let out a slow breath of relief at Thor's much more considered reply, but Paulo hasn't finished yet. I'm cringing because the whole bar is listening with glee now as they sense something is going down. "She didn't seem too pleased to see you," he remarks, and he does this ingenuous grin to make it seem like a joke. But I suspect it isn't and I want to slap him. This is a side to him I haven't seen before.

"Perhaps you don't know how Sam looks when she's pleased to see you," Thor retorts dryly with a mocking smile, and he's certainly getting his own back. I'm getting very worried that this is going to get out of hand and I don't know how to stop it. Oh God, if them kicking off on the beach would have been bad enough, open antagonism in the bar isn't far away and will be much worse. I'm racking my brains to think of a way to stop them, and for a change I don't know what to do. I mean, it's not an everyday situation, is it? I'm furious with Paulo because although he's hiding it behind a veneer of innocent amusement I'm almost sure this normally mild mannered man is being aggressive, although I guess he would say he's been provoked. But he has no hold over me, so to me he is pushing it too far. Plus we're in his local and he knows everyone and that puts him at an advantage.

I consider walking off and dragging my guy with me, but if I do I won't be able to come in again and I don't want that. Also, he's done nothing wrong so he shouldn't be made to leave, and he probably wouldn't come with me anyway. Shit, shit and triple shit. I'm glaring at Paulo so hard it's giving me a headache, but still he won't look at me and it's doing no good. I'm almost having palpitations I'm getting so worked up.

"I know Sam better than you think," Paulo says with a cheeky grin, and I think, *what on earth does he mean by that?* There's a clear insinuation there and I'm getting really angry with him but I don't want us to fall out. Christ, this is awful. First he suggests we come in to Paco's (at least I think he does) and then he uses it to have an underhand go at Thor. I'm beginning to think that open aggression would actually be better because then they could have it out properly rather than using these sneaky digs and implications. What on *earth* is wrong with Paulo? I know he must be disappointed and everything but this isn't like him. I won't admit it to myself but what's really upsetting me is that in effect he's having a go at me, too, and I'm dreadfully hurt. Can't he see that?

"I doubt it," says my guy with an indolent smile, and he half turns away. I realise he's trying to diffuse the situation but I think Paulo sees it as a dismissal and I can see he's incensed. Fucketty fuck – and still I stand there like Stan Laurel on a hopeless day, how bloody useless am I? I have to do something but I don't know what. I want to defend my guy, but it's all been so surreptitious that it's difficult to. Not to mention that I think he can stick up for himself more than adequately and I don't want it to look like he can't. Plus despite everything Paulo is still my friend and although I think he's bang out of order I know he's upset and probably not thinking straight.

We have finished our drinks and I don't even want to ask Thor if he'd like another and put him on the spot, but he beats me to it. I feel his eyes rest on me for a second, and then he orders and turns to Paulo. Christ, I wonder if he's going to pour his beer over his head, I wouldn't blame him. For a split second I see it in my mind's eye, and I see Paulo do the same to my guy, and I think, it's a shame I don't like beer because I would enjoy cleaning him up. Then I know I'm losing it with the stress and I should go home and lock myself in a dark room.

Thor says, "Would you like a drink?" and I'm gobsmacked. I can see Paulo is, too, and for a moment I think I see shame on his face. I've known Thor isn't a fool to pride since we left Simon in the bar that time, but I didn't expect this. Or perhaps it's simply clever management of the situation, because I can see that for once it's Paulo who doesn't know what to do, and I almost give a triumphant grin, and that would be so unkind.

The whole bar is listening - honestly, you could hear a pin drop - and I know Thor has backed Paulo into a corner because if anyone has heard the antagonism behind Paulo's words they will only admire Thor for rising above it. And if they haven't I reckon most people are aware that Paulo has a soft spot for me and it will still look bad if he refuses with bad grace.

Now, finally, Paulo meets my eyes and I see chagrin. So I should. I try to give nothing away, and I think for once I achieve it. Paulo accepts a beer and I know he's calmed down now and he's regretting his words, and he's sorry, to me at least. He's forced to be polite to Thor and I think it isn't only me who heaves a huge sigh of relief.

We don't hang around for much longer and when we finish our drinks we head off. I'm silent; I don't know what to say. Good Lord, I hear you exclaim, really? I feel I should apologise for Paulo, and yet I don't have the words. I'm very impressed by how Thor handled the situation, and I wonder if he's a politician or something. Then I think *no politician could have done that, not from what I've seen, perhaps he's an ambassador.*

Then he breaks my reverie and I jump as he says, "Did I say that was a friendly bar?"

My eyes snap up to his in distress but I can see his lips are twitching and he's totally unfazed. Sometimes this guy is amazing. I want to laugh but I'm still upset, even though I can see Paulo must have been having a funny turn and is now sorry, because these are my two favourite men in the world and I'd like them to be friends. Or at least not enemies. Who am I kidding? But at the very least I want to be able to take Thor into Paco's without worrying about it, and surely that's not unreasonable?

Shit. I'm sorry, I know I seem to be saying that a lot recently.

We reach the apartment and go in. I'm still kind of on edge but Thor seems perfectly relaxed and suggests a drink on the balcony. I wonder if he's going to ask about Paulo, I can't say I'd blame him if he did, but he doesn't. He sits quietly for some time, and like before at Paco's when we sat outside, gradually I calm down. The view from up here is impressive, even in the dark, somehow you can tell you are looking out over the sea and can see for miles. It makes me and my troubles seem more insignificant - again, like before.

Finally he says, "I think I'll have a shower," and it's so not what I expected him to say on any level. I know what he means, now he mentions it I feel a bit grubby after our long day out and about. So I want a shower too but I'm worried that he might prefer to be alone, it didn't exactly sound like an invitation, and he might have had enough of me and my issues for one night. So I sit and dither and try to stay relaxed and not mind, and I leap with fright when he suddenly appears next to me. He takes my hand and leads me to the bathroom, and everything is all right again and by the time we've finished all stress has left my body.

As I lie next to him in bed I'm wondering at myself. I've turned out to be different to how I expected. By this I mean I've always considered sex to be an important but secondary part of a relationship. Obviously you have to enjoy sex with your partner, that goes without saying, but the main thing for me has always been the relationship itself, the emotional and mental bond. Now I find I'm in a relationship (if that's the right word) where I suspect that sex is the main component, with the rest coming second, and I'm not sure what I think about that. I suspect that part of it is down to Mark, and that forging that bond is too frightening for me, so I'm glad to hide behind the sex. But part of it is definitely down to my guy, I'm so ridiculously attracted to him and I don't know why.

What I mean is I can't help wondering why, after three years, I found him so attractive that I didn't run a mile when he came near me. Christ, after what happened to me I thought I'd never be able to enjoy sex again. And yet here I am, I mean, I hardly knew him, so how come I found it so easy to jump into bed with him? God, not just easy – I was desperate to, I'm embarrassed to say. I've never done anything like that before, even before what happened to me. I can't think of anything much that could have made me feel that way. But then again, how can I say that when he rescued me from the Chip'n'Dale hell, not to mention his impressive defence of me against Simon. Perhaps that was it, being exactly the opposite of the horror which has inhibited me for so long. Even, and I know this is a shameful thought even as I think it, being the opposite of what Mark did (or rather didn't) do, although I know utterly and categorically that Mark couldn't do anything. Neither of us could. Although he didn't have to turn me away afterwards. Oh, God, I don't know, I only know that I find him almost impossible to resist, and when he gives me his hot look I'm gone.

He's got an incredible sex drive and perhaps that adds to it. I'm embarrassed to say the sex is so good it's overshadowing everything else and making it secondary by default. I'm even more concerned to find I don't mind, not in the slightest. But I'm also worried that the sex won't be enough in the long term in just the same way that I'm too scared to get more involved so work that one out if you can. If, by now, you are shouting, "Just enjoy yourself and stop bloody worrying for once!" I can understand your reaction, because to some extent I am thinking this, too.

Dear me, sometimes I don't know whether I'm coming or going.

Also, and I know I should shut up now, but I can't help wondering what *he* thinks, as in how he feels. He clearly enjoys the physical side, there's no doubt about that, and I'm not sure if there's any more to it than that for him. But he made the effort to come and find me, didn't he? I still can't get my head around that. Even so, he has shown no interest in my life before here, and he hasn't enlightened me as to his life at all (although this might be in response to my distinct lack of interest and forthcomingness), so perhaps this is all he wants, too. I can't help worrying that he won't be celibate when he returns to England - anyone who has his sex drive can't be, surely? - and I don't want to think about that because although I don't think I can handle more than this I don't want to think of him with anyone else, either. How unfair is that? Have I ever mentioned that I might be a bit mixed up and that I like spoiling my own good time by self-torture? Because I know I hide it well.

Oh, God.

For all I know he will leave on Sunday and I will never see him again so why should I worry about what he does when he goes back? And now everything is ruined with Paulo and I'll be worse off than I ever was. Except that before Thor I didn't think I'd ever be able to cope with sex again, and after the time we've had how can I possibly suggest I could be worse off? I start to smile at this thought and it's a good one to finish on, so I try very hard to go to sleep. About time, I hear you cry with relief.

The next day I wake up in a far more positive state of mind, you'll be glad to hear. It appears my final thought has stayed with me and I'm smiling to myself at the great time I'm having, and that does actually include the company as well as the sex. I've been so used to being on my own I'd forgotten how nice it can be to spend time with someone, so although it's a bit scary it's also a bit of an eye opener, and I'm glad.

I wait for Thor to wake up. He was restless in the night so I guess he might be catching up now. I think he actually got up for a while, but I can't be sure.

Eventually he moves. He turns towards me and his eyes are still closed. I feel that rush of gratitude again for all he has given me and the fact that he has asked for nothing in return. God, I'd be a thankless cow if I resented just one single thing about him, I realise, and my heart seems to swell. I reach out for him almost without thinking because I'll be disturbing him, but he doesn't seem to mind, and I find myself snuggling closer, with the inevitable result. I didn't know you could have this much sex and not go blind (or is that something else?) and I feel guilty because somehow I should be feeling more guilty about the pleasure I get from him than I do.

Thursday follows a now-familiar pattern. I go back to my villa for some things and I stay away for a bit longer than usual, partly because he had no time on his own yesterday and partly because I know he will be going soon and I will have to get used to being on my own again. So why not spoil the time now in anticipation of it being spoiled next week? I'm good at that. In fact I go for a leisurely swim on my own, I always find it easy to relax and let my mind wander in the water, and it refreshes me, so it isn't a bad thing.

Friday progresses along similar lines although I don't stay away for as long. I'm beginning to be uncomfortably aware that we only have a couple of days left and it's making me feel closer to him. In the evening he suggests Paco's and I'm really surprised, perhaps I'm not the only one who enjoys a bit of self-torture. It takes me a while to make up my mind, but that's nothing new. Friday is always a good night in Paco's, and on balance I decide it might be better to go in again before he leaves. I'm saying this on the assumption he might come back here one day, although I know that might not happen. I certainly don't want to spend my last night with him in there worrying about what might go on, so in that respect tonight is best. Anyway, if it's awful we can always leave, can't we? I guess I also reckon that he wouldn't have suggested it if he wasn't up for it himself.

So we go. I wear my button-up dress again because I like the way he looked at me when I wore it the last time and it gives me confidence. We stop on the way for something to eat, so by the time we reach Paco's it's busy and I'm pleased. I notice Paulo is there with his mates, and Lydia is with Sergio, and Ali is also with them. There are other Spanish and plenty of Brits, and it's noisy and buzzing and should be easy to enjoy ourselves without the attention we received last time. In this respect coming in again is a good thing as we are more part of the furniture than we were before, if you know what I mean. At least, I'm hoping that's a good thing.

It turns out to be one of those evenings where everything just gels. The number of people, some of them holidaymakers and up for a good time, together with that additional *je ne sais quoi* creates a party

117

atmosphere and before long we are all standing round the bar and Paco is putting music on and everyone is letting their hair down.

Lydia and Ali haven't seen Thor before so I introduce them, and I feel a little shy for some reason. I can see Lydia is impressed, and that pleases me, but Ali, as usual, is giving nothing away. Sensible girl.

The music starts in earnest and those of us who are inclined to start dancing. I've had enough to drink not to be too self-conscious and I dance with Lydia and a couple of the Brits. I don't ask Thor, once again for some reason feeling slightly shy, and he doesn't offer. Then Paulo's song comes on (I always think of it as that, it's the one we always dance to together) and I wonder what he's going to do. Oh hell, if he asks me should I dance with him? It will look very odd if I don't, and might spoil the effect of Thor's peace offering or whatever it was on Wednesday. But what if Thor minds or takes it personally? God, it's only moments but I'm getting myself all worked up before I even know if Paulo is going to ask me. I'm not even supposed to know about their argument on the beach, anyway, so I shouldn't let that affect me. Then that perverse, and in my opinion not so nice, side of me (and I try not to let it influence me but sometimes I can't help it) suddenly thinks *what if Paulo doesn't ask you, or even worse, dances it with someone else?* You know, I've never said I was perfect and this thought makes me go cold because despite everything I don't want to lose my friendship with Paulo although I know I'm being horribly self centred.

Then Paulo approaches me, and I'm panic-stricken. Honestly, it's only been about two seconds because all this has rushed through my head in the most disjointed and jumbled up fashion and I'm still confused. I'm incredibly relieved because it appears he is going to ask me to dance but I am also at a total loss to know how to react. I glance over to Thor but he isn't even looking, then for a split second he meets my eyes but I'm no wiser. Poker faced isn't in it. God, what should I do? I only have a nano second to decide and as usual I'm dithering like Mavis Riley. Then I think, for God's sake, it's only a dance, why are you making such a song and dance about it, and this thought almost makes me laugh out loud. Then Paulo's in front of me and I have to do something.

CHAPTER FOURTEEN

So I'm standing there dithering, and I swear that if he had just gone ahead, making that assumption that I was going to dance, I might actually have turned him down because the memory of his behaviour on Wednesday is still with me. But at the last minute I see him hesitate, and for a second he's looking for reassurance in my eyes, and so I dance with him. Because in many ways I do love this man, and you don't override nearly three years of care and friendship with one day of confused bad behaviour. At least not in my book. I don't look at Thor again, coward that I am, I'll just have to deal with any fall out later.

Paulo dances with me just like normal, the spinning and twisting makes me giggle as usual and his hand only lands on my waist as much as I would expect. Perhaps at the end he pulls me in just a little closer for the finish, but it's in no way too much, I don't think. Then he gives me a mock bow, and there's a twinkle in his eye, and I hope it's not because he thinks he might have caused some trouble. It just shows you how unjust you can be, and it's a lesson to me, because in fact to my surprise he takes my hand and leads me back to where Thor is standing. It makes me feel a bit like a chattel, to be honest, and I don't know quite what to think about that, but I guess I appreciate the sentiment and it's about the least incendiary thing he could do under the circumstances.

Paulo turns away and I glance at Thor. His face is inscrutable and I can't tell what he's thinking at all. But I've had a couple of beers and I'm happy to be in Paco's on such a night as this and so I push any concerns away to worry about later. You will appreciate that's quite an achievement for me. I love Paco's when the impromptu party starts, and one of the things I like about it is that you can dance with anyone without worries or undercurrents because we are all friends, and I don't want that to stop now because of my guy. That wouldn't be fair on either of us.

The music changes from Spanish to English (by this I mean it's in English, it's a mixture of British, American and so on) and more people get up to dance, it's getting quite crowded. I'm dancing with Joe, and out of the corner of my eye I see Lydia pull Thor in. I'm pleased, because I want him to join in, and I don't really know why I didn't do it myself. Perhaps I should have done. Have I done the wrong thing and was he waiting for me to ask, being that this is my drinking place? Especially after me dancing with Paulo? Now I'm worrying about it and wondering if I should ask Thor for the next dance or something. Or he might be annoyed with me in which case should I wait for him to show he wants to?

Bloody hell. I'm doing it again.

In the end another couple of dances go by and we are separated anyway and dancing with other people. Apart from everything else I'm very glad that he's accepted, it's what I had hoped for and I hope he's having a good time. Then I think I really should go to him (not that he isn't perfectly capable of looking after himself) and by chance we end up next to each other and by silent agreement move over to the bar. He seems his usual self and I'm beginning to relax. Honestly, I do work myself up about nothing sometimes, it does my head in.

We get some more drinks and I say, "Cheers," and clink glasses with him. I'm feeling lighter now because it seems everything is ok and I giggle because I'm happy (it might have something to do with the booze too) and I look into his eyes. He leans in to me, putting his mouth close to my ear. "I want you right now," he breathes huskily, and I nearly dissolve right there on the spot. It's so unexpected and I can feel myself *melting*. I have to stop myself from taking his hand and racing out of the bar, but then he smiles at me and I know, despite what he said, it will wait. I have such an urge to kiss him but I don't know if that will be welcome because he isn't very demonstrable in public, and neither am I for that matter, and anyway, you don't do that sort of thing in Paco's, he'll tell you to get a room. So I'm left with blushing furiously and smiling back almost shyly, and I swear that must be the next best thing to being confused, because the look he gives me would melt an iceberg. Oh, God.

I turn away to try to cool myself down and like when Thor first walked into Paco's I'm not paying attention to where I'm looking because I stare straight into Paulo's eyes. Fuck! I'm so startled and I can't bear to see the look on his face. Why didn't I pay more attention? Why don't I just massage a bucket load of salt into the wound? Christ, talk about rubbing someone's nose in it. Shit. I can't believe I just did that.

Paulo holds my eyes for a horribly long moment and then turns away. I turn back to my guy and he's seen what's happened. He shrugs. "He's a big boy," he says, "he'll live."

I know Thor's right and I don't know what I expected, but I feel really bad and something about it all's making me uneasy. I look away, avoiding both Thor and Paulo. God, I was having such a good time, too. For heaven's sake, if *I* don't spoil my own fun it appears there's always someone else ready to step in.

Thor takes my hand and pulls it gently. Reluctantly I swing my eyes back round to his. I don't know why I feel quite so bad and I don't really want him to see it; it isn't his problem, after all.

"Sam," he says, "do you want to leave?"

"No," I reply.

"Do you want me to go?" He has that strange expression on his face.

"No!" I'm aghast that he would think this and that I must have made him think it. "Don't think that!" *Shit.* I'm such a *useless* cow sometimes. Once more I want to kiss him but I can't bring myself to.

"I don't want to make your life difficult," he continues, "I know it's been hard enough so far."

I almost burst into tears at this. I'm scared he's implying that he won't be coming back, and I'm scared that this thought scares me. Christ, I *knew* I was starting to get attached and I didn't stop myself. I'm *such* a dickhead. I'm also moved by his understanding and concern, and I don't know what to do. Fucketty fuck, I *never* know what to do.

I stand there gulping like a goldfish, and out of the corner of my eye I can see Paulo watching us. He's bound to think Thor's upsetting me again. Dear God, this can't get any worse, can it? I try to pull myself together, I'm made of sterner stuff than this.

"I don't want you to go," I say with more composure. "Believe me," and he nods, satisfied.

"Unless you want to go, that is." I suddenly have the thought that this can't be an entirely comfortable situation for him, either, and perhaps he's looking for the excuse to get out of here. I wouldn't blame him. Perhaps he's looking for the excuse to get out altogether.

I see his eyes flicker to Paulo. "I don't want to go," he replies, and for some reason this doesn't reassure me, so help me God, and I don't know why.

Well, if I'm not going to go, and he's not going to go, we had better stay and enjoy ourselves, hadn't we? Otherwise there's no point. I take his hand. "Dance?" I say. It's something we can do together that doesn't involve talking and doesn't involve thinking, because my mind is full for the minute, thank you very much. I've exhausted myself with wondering what's going on and what he's thinking and what Paulo's thinking and what kind of dickhead I think I am and I just want to relax. It appears he's in agreement, (with the dancing rather than me being a dickhead, I hope), at least he doesn't demur, and as we dance I begin to relax again. I do have a tendency to get my knickers in a twist, I know that, and although sometimes I think I have my reasons I do try to do better, or at least not let it show too much. I never know whether I hide it well and everyone thinks I'm a really cool customer (somehow I doubt it) or whether everyone is well aware that I'm a dithering pathetic freak who can't cope with the slightest turmoil. If you remember Frank Spencer you'll know where I'm coming from.

A bit later on I dance with Paulo again because it appears that it's ok to do so, and he takes his opportunity and asks if everything is ok.

I'm a bit taken aback, but I suppose I prefer him asking to harbouring his concerns, and I warm to him because it reminds me that he *is* concerned for me. So I smile and say, "Yes, thanks," and hope he believes me. Because on so many levels everything is ok, as long as I ignore the thousand or so worries I keep putting on one side to worry about later. By definition that means I'm not worrying about them now, doesn't it? So everything is ok.

He gives me a searching look. "I want you to be happy," he says. *Oh really?* I think for an ungracious moment, *you were hiding it well the other night.* I remember he's said this before and I don't know how to reply. "I'm ecstatic," seems a bit tactless, but "I suppose I'm not unhappy," hardly covers it. I am happy, so how do I tell him without rubbing his nose in it even further?

He reads my expression, and it seems that's enough. Thank goodness. I've had enough soul searching for one night. He pulls me to him briefly – it's one of the most outward signs of affection he's ever shown me and stupidly I think he's taking a risk in here because if I freak out everyone will see – but I'm moved and I don't mind. I'm sure Thor will be watching and I hope to hell he can see the spirit in which it's intended, and as he doesn't come over or punch anyone I guess it's ok.

God. I'm *exhausted*. Really, I am.

The rest of the evening passes in a blur. Everyone seems to have finally relaxed (I think by this I mean me, mainly) and there's dancing and drinking and talking and laughing and by the time Thor and I fall out of there we've had a brilliant night (or at least I have) and we're giggling to each other as we head for his apartment. I feel very happy and it's like in the beginning, we go up in the lift standing opposite each other and staring. I'm starting to feel the silver sparks of excitement and I'm glad I wore this dress.

I wake up very early, it's still night really. It's one of those sudden awakenings I experience sometimes after a few drinks where I'm awake with a bang and I know there's absolutely no chance at all of going back to sleep. I feel restless and I know I will disturb him if I stay in bed so I slip out and grab his shirt to pull over me. It's a good choice because it's quite long on me and it holds his scent.

I decide to sit on the balcony. His shirt keeps the chill and any stray mosquitoes at bay, and I choose a recliner and gaze out to sea. It's beautiful. Dawn is just beginning to show and tendrils of light are creeping across the sky in subtle shades of pink, turquoise and blue. The sea is very calm and the reflection on its surface is almost perfect. It takes my breath away.

I sit for some time watching the gradual progression as the sky lightens before me. I feel very tranquil and my mind starts to wander.

I can't believe today is Thor's last day, and he will be leaving tomorrow. I've gone from wondering how I will cope with a full week of him to not wanting him to go. Although we don't know much about each other I do feel close to him (assuming I'm not deluding myself, of course, it wouldn't be the first time). I've grown used to his company and to not being alone and I'll miss him when he's gone. *God*, I suddenly think, *I'm not sure that's true. How awful*. I realise that when he goes I will return to the sanctuary of my life and it will be as if he'd never been here. That's the reason I didn't let him near my villa. I think I must be quite a cold hearted bitch underneath.

All the same, even if I don't miss him, I can't help hoping that he will come back. I see this as a completely different issue. I've had such a brilliant time with him and I'd love to do it again. But I have no idea how he feels. At times he's made me think that this is a one off and he has no intention of coming back, but at other times I've wondered. I don't want to ask him and put him on the spot, and after all I hardly live five minutes away. Perhaps he often does this – goes away and finds a girl to be with for a while – and he just used me as a focal point for his travels. Perhaps he has someone at home, but he said not and I'm inclined to believe him, although to be honest he would be unlikely to say anything else, wouldn't he? But if he had someone I can't see why he would bother with me, so that kind of puts my mind at rest. I know it sounds stupid but I want to invite him back but I'm nervous of doing it in case he doesn't want to. I don't know what he'll think. God, I wish I was one of those people who had the confidence to just do what they wanted and not worry about how it looks and what other people think, I really do. But I'm not and I never will be. So I guess I'll be my usual pathetic self and wait for him to take the lead.

A silent part of me knows I've grown to like him and I'm frightened to ask him back in case he says no. Even if I don't miss him when he isn't here (and I might be kidding myself with that – I'll find out soon enough) I definitely want him to come back. And I want him to want to come back, too. So I'm scared to ask and lay myself open to the rejection.

Then I have an unexpected thought. What if *he* is waiting for *me* to ask? He always seems so self-assured to me, but who knows? After all, I'm the one who ran off without telling him where to find me - I put him off for months. It's he who has stuck his neck out so far, and when he got here God knows what he thought with my reaction to seeing him and Paulo and everything. God knows what he still thinks, to be honest. He might think I don't want him here interrupting my life and my friends and he might even think that I want Paulo underneath and can't wait for him to leave. No, he can't think that, he isn't stupid, but now I think about it I could understand him wondering where he stands. So perhaps I should say something. But I don't dare. Oh, for heaven's sake, what kind of lily livered cretin am I? What's the worst that can happen? Worst case scenario is I say something and he's not interested and I'll be disappointed and that will be that. End of story. However, if I don't say anything I will end up sitting here in the weeks to come wondering if I should have said something. Bloody hell, that would be awful. So now I am going to have to say something, I know I am. That's my peace shattered.

I watch the sky for a while longer hoping to recapture the tranquillity I enjoyed before, and I do to some extent because there's no point worrying about how to broach the subject, I'll think of something. Despite what I said about not missing him I feel a pang of regret that we have only one full day left, and I'll be sad when he leaves. If I was prepared to admit it to myself I'll be very sad, but I'm not, so there. Simply sad is sad enough for me, thank you very much.

I'm feeling a bit drowsy now so I head back into the bedroom. I take off his shirt, and a for a daft moment I consider stuffing it into my bag so I can have something of his to keep, better than that, something on which his scent might linger. Then I pull myself together (what kind of deranged stalker would I look like?) and slide carefully into bed beside him.

Despite my efforts I must disturb him because he reaches out to me and mumbles, "Cold." But instead of cringing away like most people would (I would, anyway) he pulls me to him and surrounds me with his warmth. God, it feels wonderful and I drift off to sleep with a smile on my face.

The next day seems to rush by. We don't do much, I don't even go to my villa. He asks me what I would like to do for dinner and I suggest staying in. I don't want to share him tonight. He seems happy enough with this and we do venture out to the supermarket before going for a swim.

We share the cooking and it's good fun, and we open a decent bottle of wine to go with our meal. Despite not nosing into each other's business we chat easily, and I'm determined not to allow the black cloud of his impending departure shadow our last evening together. We eat on the balcony, and it's very pleasant and I feel very close to him. He's difficult to read, but he seems happy enough and gives me intimate glances every now and then that make my stomach curl with pleasure. Once again I almost feel as though we are a normal couple and I don't know what to think about that.

You know, I was so determined not to allow myself to get too fond of this guy, but I can feel it's happening and I can't seem to stop it. I never expected him to turn up here, and then to stay for two weeks, so what was I supposed to do? Maybe I should have stayed away more, but I've been having such a good time so why should I? I might be good at torturing myself sometimes, but I'm well aware that it had been three years since I'd been with anyone, and he's been amazing, and I'd have been mental to turn it down. So I'm telling myself it's a good job he's leaving tomorrow, but I'm going to enjoy myself tonight and not let anything get in the way. Except for wondering how I'm going to invite him back - or perhaps just let him know he's welcome back - and when I should do it, and what he'll say, of course. But in the scheme of things that's nothing.

Sometimes I wish I could just be with someone and not feel the fear that seems to go with any kind of emotional (and before him, physical) intimacy. But there you go.

I have a lovely evening and I hope he does too. We chat endlessly, goodness knows what about, but there's no awkwardness at all. We both ignore the fact that he's leaving tomorrow, and I wonder if, were he not leaving, I would feel the same about him anyway. Maybe part of it's been down to the excitement and the knowledge that it will only be a brief affair.

See, sometimes I *can* look on the bright side and not worry about anything!

We stay up late talking, and when we go to bed we undress each other slowly, making the most of it. I'm beginning to have that *last time* feeling, but I don't suppose there are fire alarms in these apartments so I'll have to get on with it. Like it's a problem, or anything (or the last time, yet).

Surprisingly I sleep well, and when I wake I'm in his arms. It's a very indulgent place to be, and a wonderful place to wake up, believe me.

He isn't moving but somehow I know he's awake too. I realise that this is the best moment I'm going to get, my face is against his chest and he can't see it. So I fumble around my brain for the right words, but as usual I don't do very well, and in the end I simply say, "I'm glad you found me." I say it very quietly and my voice mumbles into his chest but I know he has bionic ears so hearing me won't be a problem.

He stays still and says nothing. This is in no way helpful. So I continue, "I've had a great time."

His arms tighten slightly around me. "So have I," he replies gruffly, and I was right, he is awake, but he's giving very little away. God, how can I kind of invite him back without it being awkward and also without him thinking he's welcome at my villa? Because I'm not ready to go that far yet. Hell. I'm scrabbling around frantically for the right thing to say, and I have to say it soon before the moment's lost.

"If you ever want to come back, and you might not want to, and that's ok, it would be nice to see you," I say, and even as I'm saying it I'm thinking *Goodness, you've left him in no doubt there, have you?* But I'm stumped for anything further.

He's quiet for a few moments, and I'm starting to panic, thinking that I've put him on the spot and he's trying to find a nice way to say *I never, ever want to come here or see you ever again!* and then he says, "Good."

Oh, thanks, Mr Ambiguous, I'm in no doubt as to what that means, I think. *I'm glad you're glad I'd like to see you again. That's my mind put at rest.*

We lie in silence and I'm wondering what he's thinking. He's very still and perhaps he's gone back to sleep, but somehow I don't think so. It still feels quite early, and his flight isn't until late afternoon, so we have plenty of time. I'm glad I've said something, anyway, whatever he made of it at least he knows he's welcome if he wants to return. Without getting out our diaries and making a date it's the best I can do. Or perhaps he's not bothered at all and this has simply been time out for him. Maybe he'll walk away and return to his life without a backward glance. In many ways it's easier for him because he has been away from home in a different place altogether and there'll be no reminders lying in wait for him when he goes back.

So I lie there dozing lazily and my mind is wandering over the time we've had together, and I still wonder what else went on with Paulo on the beach and wish I could ask because it's my last chance. But of course I can't, and he obviously has no intention of telling me, and why should he? He doesn't even know I know.

My mind moves on to all the nice things we've done and I'm very happy in my little bubble of reverie. I feel him move and I know he's awake, and I turn my face into his chest and kiss him. He runs his hand slowly over my back and I realise I don't even think about my scars any more when I am with him. Now he's stroking me and kissing me and his face is above mine. He kisses me again, and then I hear him whisper, "Sam," and it's so very quiet I wonder if I imagined it. And then other things take precedence as very gently he begins to move.

Neither of us is in any rush to get up. He goes to make coffee and toast for breakfast, which we have in bed. Eventually we go for our shower and I keep thinking, *last time, last time*, like I'm one of those annoying dolls with a string coming out of it's back which someone is repeatedly pulling, and I can't help it. But I'm not unhappy, and I have a quiet acceptance of the fact he is leaving, probably because I always knew he would.

I make us some lunch while he starts to pack his things. We eat on the balcony again, and it's lovely with the view over the sea and the warmth of the late May day. Despite the fact that he's leaving in an hour or so there are no uncomfortable silences and I could almost believe that it's just another day.

Then, all too soon, it's time for me to go. I pull my things together and head for the door. He follows me and puts his arms around me. Now, for the first time, I feel awkward and I don't know what to say. "See you later," is rather inappropriate, but I can't help thinking that "Goodbye, my lover, for what may be forever!" would be a bit dramatic. So I reach up and touch his face above his eye, on that spot where he was cut the first time and which I seem to have made mine for moments such as this. He drops his head for one last kiss, and I cling to him for a small moment, before he pulls back and fixes me with his eye.

"Call me," he says, and there's that hint of mockery, and I guess I deserve it because it probably is about time I made some of the running, isn't it? I want to reply but he has that strange expression on his face and suddenly my throat is constricted, so I merely nod, and smile my best smile, and turn and walk away.

CHAPTER FIFTEEN

When I return to my villa I don't unpack my things, for some reason I can't face it. I go for a swim and it soothes me and as I lie in the water I picture him driving to the airport, boarding the plane and flying out of my life. I'm not sad as I do it, perhaps a touch wistful but that's all, and it helps me to draw a line under my time with him.

I wonder if I'll ring him, knowing full well that I will. If not because I want to, then because after running out on him last time and all the trouble he went to to find me it would be a bit out of order to let him down again. I'm assuming that he asked me to call him because he wants me to, and although he left it a bit late (that bothers me a bit) he didn't have to say it at all. So now I'm wondering when I should call him. Not today – far too desperate – and not tomorrow either, I don't think. Let him get settled in and give him a call in a few days, that's best. God, I don't know what I'll say when I ring anyway, I can hardly ask him about his work/family/friends, so what will we talk about? Bloody hell, it's a bit early to be worrying about that, even for me, I'm sure it will be fine.

I don't go out that evening, I'm enjoying my solitude. The next day I've promised to take Mavis shopping (and I can stock up at the same time so it's worked out well) and to call in on Val and translate a letter for her. I don't know if I mentioned that although I don't have to work or anything I like to help people when I can, be it running them around, translating at the doctors, even helping with their computers since I am interested in that type of thing. I enjoy helping out, it fills a bit of my time and makes me feel useful, and I can generally fit it in when it's convenient for me (doctor's appointments excepted). I rarely charge anything for my time, but people generally like to give me something as a thank you and I like this, it gives me a bit of what I call treat money to spend frivolously if I wish.

Donna rings on Monday evening and tells me she's been trying to get hold of me. She's curious as to why I have been out so much and when I tell her she's stunned into silence, and that takes some doing, I can tell you. She's amazed that Thor came to find me, and understands my reaction as much as anyone ever will. I know she's pleased for me and predictably she's asking when I'm going to see him again and I tell her I don't know.

"Didn't you arrange anything?"

"No."

"Nothing at all?" She sounds incredulous.

"Well, he asked me to call him."

"So have you?"

"Not yet, no."

"Why not?"

"He only left yesterday. I thought I'd give him a bit of space, allow him to settle back in at home first."

"So when are you going to ring him?"

"I don't know." I'm beginning to get a little annoyed because although I want to speak to Thor for some reason I don't want to do it too soon. We had a pretty intense time, spending most of the week together, and I just think he might be glad of a break. I can't explain this to Donna, though, she's mad keen for me to ring him so he doesn't think I'm not interested. I don't think it's like that, but now she's making me doubt it and I don't want to be swayed.

She hears my tone and backs off a bit. "Well, you know best," she says doubtfully.

"Yes," I say, "I think on this one I do."

She's coming to visit me a week on Friday for the weekend, and we move on to that. We're both excited. She couldn't take time off work the following week, which would have been the anniversary of her hen party, but it hardly matters. We discuss what we'll do when she's here and finish our call on a good note.

On Tuesday I'm out with Lydia and Ali. I cried off last week so it is good to catch up with them. Lydia plies me with questions and it reminds me that I know very little about my guy, really. I try to fob her off without making it obvious, avoiding questions about what he does for a living (he has his own business – don't ask any more please) and his home life (I don't even know where he lives, for God's sake) and trying to keep her happy by telling her what kind of films he likes. Honestly, how pathetic, I dread to think what she's thinking but really it's none of her business, is it? I can tell she likes him, though, and that pleases me. Ali, as usual, is more quiet and mainly listens.

It's Wednesday. I have a few things to do during the day and I'm becoming agitated as it goes on because inside myself I've decided that this is the day I'm going to call him. I'm distracted and wondering what I'm going to say. I won't say I'm actually worrying, but I'm definitely having a good old think about it. I've decided I'm going to go to Paco's tonight (the first time since he left) and somehow I want to know where I stand with him before I go. Always assuming I'll be any the wiser anyway. The day drags and then suddenly it's seven o'clock (six in England) and I think I will ring soon because he should have finished work by now. I'm starting to procrastinate, I'm very nervous, and I see my bag still sitting in the corner from when I came back on Sunday. It's a nice little diversion as I decide that I had better empty it and put what I need to in the wash because after three days it suddenly can't wait any longer. So I tip the bag out....and I freeze. Because out falls a note with "Sam" written on it.

Well, I'm not kidding, my heart stops and my blood runs cold at the same time. Actually, I'm not sure if this is strictly possible because one depends on the other, doesn't it, but that's how it feels. I stare at the note in horror. *He's doing it to me.* It's going to say that he doesn't want to see me again. Oh, God, all at once I realise how much I've been wanting to ring him and hear his voice, and now I can't. I shudder as I realise I could have rung before finding this note, and how excruciating would that have been?

I don't know what to do. I stare at the note, unable to move for a few moments, but I know I have to read it. But I don't want to. My washing is forgotten once more as I reach out with trembling fingers and open the piece of paper.

On it is written his mobile number (which I already have) and a landline number (so now I know the area he lives in). Underneath are simply two words: "Call me."

I nearly faint with relief. Oh, *God*, I nearly died back there. My blood thunders in my ears as my heart hammers in my chest and I clutch the piece of paper like a moron, almost in tears. Heaven help me, I must be in deeper than I thought.

Well, now I'm desperate to ring him, I can't stand it any longer. It's good of him to leave me his landline because it will be a lot cheaper to ring. I wonder if it's his home or his work number. Or does he work from home – he might do? Then I have a horrible thought – what if a woman answers the phone? This is something I hadn't thought of before (only having his mobile number), and it chills me. Should I slam the phone down (thereby possibly making things awkward for him) or be cool and ask for him and pretend that I'm a casual acquaintance? Oh, God. I'm winding myself up nicely, and then I think, don't be so bloody stupid, he'd hardly leave you a number if that was likely to happen, would he? Get a grip. So I reach for the phone and dial.

"Hello?" His voice is cool and terse and for a moment, despite my relief that he isn't a woman (well of course he isn't a woman but you know what I mean) I nearly drop the phone with fright. Have I rung at a bad time? Shit. I hesitate, and he says, "Hello?" again, sounding impatient.

""Hello," I say, "it's Sam." I'm cringingly uncomfortable by now, and almost wishing I hadn't rung.

"Sam?" he says, and I swear if he was in front of me I'd slap him. What does he mean, "Sam?" Was I so insignificant that he's forgotten already? My stomach is contracting into a tiny ball as I wonder what I should do.

"From Spain," I say, feeling like a complete idiot, and a worthless fool, as well. *Please let the ground open up and swallow me,* I think.

"Ah, *Sam*," he says, and his voice has changed. "Sam from Spain," and I can hear that mockery again, but I'm not sure he was teasing me, all the same.

"Did you get back all right?" I ask, not knowing what else to say.

"Apparently," he replies, and he's putting me all on edge.

"Good." I search my mind for some inspiration, and I think how can we possibly have a relationship when I can't even think what to say to him? I'm so stupid.

"How are you?" he asks, and I tell him I'm fine.

"How's everyone down at Paco's?"

I tell him I haven't been yet, I'm planning to go tonight, and he's quiet. I wonder why.

"Is everything ok with you?" I ask, "Business ok?"

"Yes, thanks."

God, this is awful, so stilted. I wish I could think of something to make it better.

I hear him sigh. Oh God, I shouldn't have rung, I'm such an idiot. Then I start to get a bit angry. Why did he leave the note if he didn't want me to ring? I can feel my anger building even though it can only be a split second.

"Well," I say, "I won't keep you, you're obviously busy. It was nice to catch up." My tone is designed to convey the opposite of my words and I'm dying inside.

"Wait," he says, "give me a second, will you?"

I hear the phone go down and some moving and rustling. For an insane moment I wonder if he has a woman with him – surely not? I'm getting really upset and I don't know whether to hang up or not. Before I can pluck up the courage he picks up the phone again.

"That's better," he says. *What's better?* I wonder, and I can't imagine what's going on, and he's made me feel awkward so I don't ask.

"Sorry," he adds. Bloody hell, I'm totally confused and it's a good job he can't see it. "It's good to hear from you." His voice is completely different now, warm and welcoming and I can't keep up.

"Is it?" I ask.

"Of course," he says, "I was just - it doesn't matter – sorry. How's sunny Spain?" I can tell he's relaxing now and so I start to relax too. I'm so easily led.

"Fine, thanks," I say, and I tell him a bit about what I've been doing because he knows something of my life here and I can. In the end we have a good chat, mainly about me, to be honest, whatever was the matter when I first called has disappeared and it's good to hear his voice. He does seem genuinely pleased to hear from me and I'm glad I rang. He tells me he's been very busy, the usual back to work situation after a holiday. I get the impression that he has an office and some staff, but I can't be sure, and being the stupid idiot that I am I don't like to be nosey. Like it would be some big secret or something, but having kept out of it for so long it's not so easy to broach.

Our conversation draws to a close, and just as I'm going he says, "Sam?"

"Uh-huh?"

"Do you think I could have your landline number so I can call you? If it's ok with you," and he's mocking me again.

"Oh, yes, of course." God, I'm stupid. I'd forgotten he didn't have it and of course it will be much cheaper for him, too. He shouldn't have had to ask but I'm glad he has. He says he'll call at the weekend and we ring off.

I get changed and go down to Paco's. It's fairly busy and a few people ask me if Thor got off ok. Then Paulo comes in, and I feel awkward. It seems to be my permanent state at present. He comes and stands near to me at the bar.

"Has he gone?" he asks.

"Yes," I reply.

He nods. He's giving me a bit of a look and I can't work it out. Perhaps he's trying to see if I'm sad, I don't know.

"Is he going to visit again?" he asks.

I guess I should be honest so I say, "I don't know." Paulo raises his eyebrows but says nothing, and just for a change I don't know what else to say.

"Will you be in on Friday?" he asks.

"I guess so."

"Good."

I don't know what this means and I don't ask. It appears we are ok and I'm grateful for that so I don't push it. Paulo starts to chat and the awkwardness disappears and all in all I have a pleasant evening.

It turns out it's Pepe's birthday on Friday and the Spanish bring food in later on and it's party time again. Paulo dances with me a lot, and I don't mind, quite the opposite. I'd been worried that he might be put off by Thor (from being friends, I mean, nothing more) but it appears not. In fact, I begin to wonder if seeing me with Thor has given him ideas, if you know what I mean. I hope not, or at least, I hope he isn't planning on acting on any ideas he might have in the near future because I don't yet know if Thor might come to Spain again and anyway I don't think I could handle Paulo so soon after, if at all.

He walks home with me and we're both a bit drunk but he's quiet, and when we say goodbye I receive the standard two kisses and no more, and I'm relieved. Paulo's not stupid, and if he is still interested I don't think he'd rush in, certainly not while he can still remember my previous reaction to him. I wonder what he thinks about that now. Of course he doesn't know the extent of my relationship with Thor but he must wonder.

Thor rings on Saturday as promised and while we are chatting I tell him Donna's coming next weekend.

"Oh," he says, "that'll be nice."

"Mmm, I'm looking forward to it."

"She's a good friend."

Don't I know it? I'm glad he can appreciate it, too.

"Will she be staying with you?" he asks.

"Uh-huh."

"Good."

I wonder if he's getting at anything but I can't tell. He asks about Paco's and I tell him about Pepe's party. I ask him if he's busy and other non-nosey things and after a while he rings off. I guess it will be my turn to ring next.

The next week flies. For some reason a lot of people have asked me to help them with things and I'm busy. All of a sudden it's Thursday, Donna's arriving tomorrow and I ring Thor while I'm still alone. There's not an awful lot to say and he wishes me a good weekend with Donna and I wish him a good weekend and I wonder what he will be doing and who he will be with, but I don't ask. He says he won't ring while Donna's here. It seems we might be slipping into a casual friendship and I'm not sure what I think about that. I wonder if I should ask him if he has any plans but I can't bring myself to.

Donna arrives on Friday and we go out for dinner. The resort is getting a bit busier now. We catch up on all our news and it's not long before she asks about my guy. I'm not surprised when she is aghast that I haven't specifically invited him back, and I find it difficult to explain.

"You couldn't blame him for waiting to be asked," she says, "I mean, he's had to do all the running up to now."

"I know. I did tell him I'd like to see him if he wanted to come back."

"When he was here two weeks ago? Gosh, I bet he's been bowled over by your enthusiasm. Don't you think you should be a bit more definite?"

"I don't know what he wants. I still don't know much about him and he might not want to come back, I don't know."

"Surely if he didn't want to come back he wouldn't stay in contact with you?"

"I suppose."

She gives me a searching look. "What is it?" she asks.

I look away.

"You like him," she says softly. "You're scared."

I look back at her and she can see it's true. I tell her about his note and what I had thought when I saw it, and she nods. "You don't want him to say no," she adds.

"I'm so pathetic," I say.

"No, you're not. Not under the circumstances, I can understand it."

"I'm not sure how I feel, really. I just know I like the possibility that he might come back."

"Leave it a while longer, then. After all, he has his business and I dare say he can't run off and leave it every five minutes. Take it as it comes."

Once again I'm not sure what this means, but I nod. "I know he came to find me and everything, and we had a brilliant time – or, at least, I did - but I don't know if he wants much more than that. I can't make him out."

"I dare say he's having the same problem," Donna remarks dryly, but I don't know if she's right. To me Thor has the confidence to say if he wants to come to Spain again, so if he isn't saying it I can't help thinking that he doesn't want to. I try to explain this and I think she gets it.

132

"What about Paulo?" she asks.

I tell her everything that happened, because she's my best friend and the only person I can tell, and I trust her.

"So what now?" she asks.

"What do you mean?"

"With Paulo?"

"God, I have no idea. I don't know what he thinks."

"What do you think?"

"What do you mean?" I know I'm sounding a bit thick, but I'm not sure what she's getting at.

"Do you like him?"

"You know I like him." I'm beginning to get defensive.

"Who do you like best?"

I'm totally taken aback. "It's not like that. It's not a competition. You know I like Paulo but not in that way."

"Not before. But before you were different. Things have changed."

"Not like that. God, don't get me worrying about Paulo, too. I want to know where I stand with Thor before starting on him."

"So Thor comes first?"

"I guess so. I don't know. Paulo's different."

"How do you think you'd feel now if he tried to kiss you?"

God, she's being a bit nosey, albeit I invited this by telling all. She's also pushing me to think about things I'm not comfortable with at present.

"I don't know. I've never really fancied Paulo in that way. We've always been friends."

"Are you sure it's not that before you didn't feel you could handle it with anyone?"

"What are you getting at? You sound as though you'd prefer me to go with Paulo." I'm getting a bit annoyed.

"No. I suppose I know Paulo better, that's all. I have no idea what Thor is like. I can see how Paulo feels about you. If you're scared of rejection he would be the better bet."

"It's not that easy." Once again a seed of doubt has been planted and I'm so hopeless I'm beginning to wonder if Donna's right. Heaven help me I might ever stick to my guns.

"Take no notice of me." Donna backs off. "I don't know Thor and I don't know how you feel. You know best."

God, I wish this was true and perversely it makes me even more unsure. I understand where she's coming from, I really do, but as I said, it isn't that easy.

She changes the subject and I'm relieved. She's given me enough to worry about for a good while now, and I wonder if, if time goes on and Thor doesn't mention coming to Spain again, I will be brave enough to ask him myself, or if I will start to look towards Paulo, or just give up altogether.

I mean, it would be so unfair to accept Paulo as second best, but Donna has made me think and perhaps I *am* different now so things might have changed. I might feel differently to before.

Oh, God. I can do without this, I really can.

The next night we go to Paco's so Donna has a chance to see for herself because Paulo's there. I knew he would be because he knew we'd be coming in. He likes Donna, and they have a good chat, and I can't help wondering what they are talking about. My skin is crawling a bit, even though I know I can trust Donna and they are both my friends.

Anyway, we have a good night. It's not a wild one, but it's fun. Paulo walks back with us and I can't sense any undercurrents and I guess everything is ok.

The rest of the weekend flies and all too soon I'm driving Donna back to the airport. She hasn't said much more about my guy and I'm not sorry, she's done enough to make me even more unsure of myself than I was before.

Except that when she's gone and I'm driving home I have a surprising blast of self-assurance. I'm finally (or at least at this moment) tired of worrying about what other people think and being swayed by them, even my best friend. I'm tired of being scared, too, I don't want to live my life like this. I decide that when I speak to Thor I'm going to ask him if he'd like to visit (only not in my villa, I hope he won't mind that). Even if he says no I will know where I stand and be able to move on (I hate that expression but it's the best I can think of). Donna is right on one thing – he has had to make all the running so far and it's only fair that I stick my neck out now and again.

For once I'm determined.

So I ring him the next night – Tuesday. He asks me about my weekend and I tell him, and I'm trying to think how I can ask him without making it difficult for him to say no and without giving him the impression he can stay at my villa. It's not easy, I can tell you. So I ask if he's busy, and he says not too bad, he's on top of things. So then I ask him if he manages to take many holidays, with it being his business, and he says it depends. Sometimes it's easier because you can give yourself time off, and sometimes you have to be there.

"And how is it now?" I ask.

"Not too bad," he repeats, "this week's a bit quieter."

I'm just trying to form the right words to say that he could come to Spain, when he says:

"In fact, I reckon I could take a couple of days to make a long weekend."

"Oh, that's nice," I say, and I'm still struggling and heaven knows why because he's making it easy for me, really. "Do you have any plans?"

"I thought I could get away, find some sun."

"Would you like to come here?" I say. Dear me, I have to say more than that, if I'm not careful I might give him the impression I'd like to see him. So I add, "It would be nice to see you." And I'm holding my breath.

"I thought you'd never ask."

Oh, God, he must think I'm really pathetic. "I didn't want to put you on the spot," I explain.

"I'd like to come."

I feel the silver sparks of excitement, and my stomach is starting to fizz.

"When do you think you could get here?"

"Thursday to Sunday, I hope."

"Do you want me to pick you up from the airport? It seems silly you hiring a car."

"No, that's fine. I'll hire a car and I'll see if I can book the same apartment. I liked it."

I'm quiet. Part of me thinks I should offer to have him stay with me, but I don't want to. Not yet.

"I'll give you a call when I have it all booked."

"Ok." I can't help feeling ungracious, so I add, "I'm really glad you're coming."

"So am I. If it fits in with you ok."

"Of course it does. I was going to ask you if you wanted to visit anyway. I didn't expect it to be so soon, but I'm really pleased."

"Good. I'll let you know."

We talk for a bit longer and then ring off. I can't believe it – he'll be here in a couple of days. I'm very happy. Oh, God.

CHAPTER SIXTEEN

The next night I go to Paco's. I often go on a Wednesday. Paulo isn't there and I'm a bit surprised but also relieved. I kind of wanted to warn him about Thor visiting again, but I was also dreading it and not sure how to, so now I'm off the hook. I'm talking to some of the Brits for a while and then one of them asks about Thor and if he's going to come to Spain again.

"He's coming tomorrow," I tell them, "for a long weekend." I can't help grinning, and I turn away because I don't want them to see how pleased I am (goodness knows why) and as seems to be my excruciating habit I end up staring at Paulo. He must have come in at some point and I hadn't seen him as I had my back to the entrance. Oh Lord. I catch a glimpse of his face before he turns away to pick up his pint.

I know it sounds really horrible but in a way I'm relieved he knows and I didn't have to tell him directly. Have I ever mentioned that I'm a bit of a coward? Anyway, there's nothing I can do now so I continue my conversation and decide to let him get on with it and catch up with him in a while. However, when I turn round he's gone. Perhaps he was going to go early all along, I don't know. Well done, Sam.

Now it's Thursday and I'm on hot bricks waiting for my guy to text me and tell me he's here. I've had a long shower and pampered myself and put on one of my prettiest skirts with a colourful vest and I'm finding it impossible to relax. Time is dragging. I've been imagining the plane coming in. Now he'll be picking up his car. Now he'll be on his way. Any time now he'll be here. I consider starting to make my way over and wonder if I'll look an itsy bit too keen if he texts and I knock on his door within thirty seconds. I snigger at this thought and stop myself from going because for all I know his flight is delayed and I'll be waiting outside his door for hours and look like a complete loony.

Then my mobile goes off and I nearly have a heart attack. It's him and he's here. I faff around for a minute or two trying to persuade myself that it doesn't do to appear too eager before telling myself off for being such a twerp because what's the problem with that and anyway I can't wait and I'm only torturing myself. The next thing I'm picking up my bag (because I'm assuming I'll be staying) and practically galloping out of the house and down the path.

Within ten minutes I'm going up in the lift and then I'm knocking on the door.

It swings open in front of me and I'm inside. He appears from the bedroom and I nearly collapse with desire when I see the expression on his face. He walks over to me and kisses me. Oh God, he tastes so good. He feels fantastic, and we slowly and deliberately begin to undress each other.

Then we're both down to underwear and the final stages are a sensuous rediscovery. Oh my God, he's even better than I remember, and that takes some doing, believe me. I never want him to stop.

Later I'm lying next to him, relaxed and happy, and I realise we haven't said one word to each other. I'm shocked at myself. I lean up to look at him and he smiles lazily.

"Hello," I say.

His eyes widen slightly. "Oh," he responds, "hello."

I kiss him. Even though I'm a bit disturbed by my behaviour in a way I like the fact that we don't need words. It almost seems a shame to have started it now, but I have, and it's not often I act before I think, you can be sure of that. "Good journey?" I ask, and he nods. "Ok."

That's enough for now. I settle down again with my arm resting over his chest. We lie peacefully and think our own thoughts. I'm very happy, and in the end I have to say something.

"I'm glad you're here."

"Me too."

I snuggle a bit closer and he pulls me on top of him. I'd forgotten how insatiable he is. No, that's a lie, I hadn't forgotten at all. No way. And I'm still not complaining, either.

Later we shower and go out to a local tapas bar for something to eat. It's fairly quiet and I'm grateful that we don't bump into anyone I know – quite an achievement for this place. We talk and catch up on each other's news as much as we are prepared to without prying too much and we share a bottle of wine and it's great. I can't believe how comfortable I feel with him, and I hope he feels the same.

We go back to his apartment and drink some more wine on the balcony before falling into bed. I want every day to be like this one.

The next morning I wake up and I've no idea what time it is. It doesn't matter. I think he's awake but I can't be sure so I lie still so as not to disturb him and go over the previous evening, and I'm smiling. Presently he moves and turns to me and I'm lying in his arms with my face in his chest. It's a place I like to be. My mind is wandering and without thinking I say, "It was Donna's hen party this weekend last year."

"I know," he replies, and I'm surprised. I feel his body tremble slightly and he mutters, "I'll kick you in the shins." Then he's sniggering properly and for a moment I am back there with the Chip'n'Dale hulk in front of me and the sniggering behind. "You were so funny," he adds.

"Oh, thanks." I remember turning round and seeing him for the first time, and how gorgeous I thought he was. "You made that clear at the time."

"It was difficult not to."

"At least you got me out of there. I was surprised at Madrugada's."

"You fitted right in." He's sniggering again.

"God, what must I have looked like?"

He says nothing for a moment, he simply carries on quietly laughing while I cringe to myself. "Sexy," he says finally, "Dishevelled, ridiculous, uncomfortable and extremely sexy."

There's no answer to that. "God, I thought you were gay," I say, and I start to giggle.

"You really thought that?"

"Uh-huh."

"I told you I wasn't. Didn't you believe me?"

"I wasn't sure."

"Oh, thanks. When did you make up your mind?"

"The next night."

He pulls back slightly to look at my face. "The next night?"

"When you punched Simon."

His face turns dark as he remembers, and like at the time he brushes my breast softly with the back of his hand.

"And then when you kissed me," I add.

"You were terrified. I understand why, now."

I'm silent. It's the first time we've referred to what happened to me since he first came here. I put my face back into his chest so he can't see me.

"He might have had a knife," I whisper, and I can hardly form the words. Fear grips my body as it remembers and I'm rigid. My head's telling my body that it's safe, but it won't listen. He's still, and then he moves his arm away casually. It gives me room to escape if I want to, and perhaps because he does it I don't want to. He knows, and I have to get used to that and the fact that he can handle it, so I have to try to handle it too. He says nothing, and does nothing. He doesn't try to soothe me or tell me it's all right (because it isn't) and gradually I relax until finally I let out a deep breath as the last of my tension leaves me. I look up at his face and he kisses me, and as casually as before replaces his arm.

"And yet you tried to help. You were amazing." He continues as if there was no pause.

"I was angry."

"You were brave. And funny, too."

"No, I wasn't. I was scared."

"But still, you got on with it."

"I surprised myself. I think the anger was winning at first."

"Jesus, Sam, I wanted you. I wanted you so much. But I couldn't make you out at all."

"I thought I was fairly obvious."

"In the end, yes, but for a while I had no idea. I couldn't tell if it was shock, or if you didn't like me, or what."

"I shocked myself. I hadn't let anyone near me for three years. I couldn't." I'm surprised I'm telling him this, and he doesn't say anything. I realise that now he knows for sure there's been nothing between Paulo and me. Nothing physical, anyway, and up until then, at least. I wonder if it matters.

His arms tighten around me slightly and I wonder what he's thinking. Maybe I shouldn't have said it, but it's too late now.

"God, Sam, you *were* brave," he says eventually, and I'm not sure exactly what he means, so I don't reply. We're quiet for a while, and once more I wonder what he's thinking. Perhaps I'm better off not knowing.

"I'm glad you let *me* near you," he adds after some time.

"Let you near me? I couldn't resist, and you were fantastic."

Hell's fire, I hope I'm not saying too much. All of a sudden we are baring our souls and I'm not sure if it's wise. "A year ago this weekend," I say, to try to distract us a bit.

"Mmmm. We haven't exactly made the most of it."

"I'm sorry."

"I don't blame you. Not now. Christ, Sam, when I found your note I couldn't believe it. I simply couldn't believe it. After I'd tracked you down at Donna's wedding and you'd stayed that extra night and everything.

"I know I only turned up to explain - I hated the thought of you standing there waiting and thinking I was so heartless that I hadn't even bothered to text - and then when I saw you, and you were so hurt and angry, God, it was awful. Then when you realised what had happened you could see you change. Christ, and then your note. I didn't understand. I simply didn't understand and I wanted to know why. Perhaps I shouldn't have done, but I had to."

"Donna's such a good friend."

"Yes, she is. It can't have been easy."

"It was Donna who persuaded me to let her tell you. I didn't want to."

"I know. She told me why."

"She wasn't supposed to. She was only supposed to tell you the bare facts, but she said she felt she had to explain why I hadn't wanted you to know."

"If she hadn't I wouldn't have come looking for you. I'd have thought you couldn't handle it, or you didn't want me. But when she said it was because you thought *I* wouldn't be able to handle it, that was different. I had to find you, I had to tell you that it didn't matter to me."

"You could have told Donna that."

"No. I had to tell you to your face. You wouldn't have believed it otherwise. If I'm honest, I think I had to see you to be absolutely certain I was right and you were wrong. If, then, you had still wanted me to go I wouldn't have bothered you again."

We are back to the soul baring and I'm not sure I like it. "Well, you found me," I say, moving the conversation on slightly.

"Your face. Your face when I walked into Paco's."

"Well, you *knew* you might see me. I had no idea. It was such a shock."

"Really? You hid it well." He's sniggering again now, and I feel better for it. "Not to mention Paulo," he adds.

I'm quiet. Poor Paulo. If it was bad enough for me, it must have been ten times worse for him.

"Does *he* know?" Thor's voice is low.

"No! Nobody here knows, nobody!"

He's silent.

"You mustn't say anything!"

"I won't."

"Even if we fall out, whatever happens. I couldn't face having to start again."

"I won't, I wouldn't do that, I'm not vindictive."

I take a deep breath. "I know. Sorry.

"Hardly anyone knows. Anyone who knew me before doesn't know where I am or that I changed my name. I couldn't cope with them, so I vanished and came here. Only Donna knows, and her parents, and Mike too, I think. And now you."

His arms tighten around me again. I keep my face turned into his chest.

"Thank you for letting Donna tell me. I know it can't have been easy."

"You should thank her."

"It was your decision in the end."

"I liked you, and you had given me so much. I felt if you wanted to know so badly it was only fair. I'm glad now, very glad."

He's quiet, and I'm relieved. All this openness is making me nervous.

We lie there for some time and I wonder what he's thinking. I'm not ready to go over what we've said in my head yet and I'm trying to divert my thoughts. I know none of it was exactly earth shattering, but I'll only start to worry that I've said too much. Perhaps he's doing that too.

"Coffee?" he says, and I start at the sound of his voice.

"Mmmm," I say, but I don't want him to move yet so I push him back and lie across his chest so he can't go. He puts his arms around me again and it feels so good. Whether he understands or not he seems happy to follow my lead and I feel him relax as he realises he isn't going anywhere for a while. What a guy. I smile to myself and enjoy being close to him - physically at least.

We spend most of the day around the apartment and beach. In the evening he suggests going to Paco's, and I agree because I would normally go on a Friday, and like before, I'd rather not spend our last night there. People know about him now and so there's no point trying to stay away.

When we get there it's fairly quiet for a Friday, and I guess we have hit a lull between the early drinkers (mainly Brits) and the late drinkers (mainly Spanish). Paulo doesn't appear and I'm relieved, and I

140

wonder whether it's because he has another one of his mysterious nights away or because he guesses we'll come in and doesn't want to be there. We chat to a few Brits for a while then sit outside looking over the sea while we have another drink, but we don't stay very long. We head off for something to eat and end up at Domingo's for steaks.

We keep the conversation light; perhaps we've both had enough for now. I understand that if we are going to carry on seeing each other we can't keep ourselves in separate bubbles and I will inevitably learn about his home life and family and so on, and he will learn more about me. But right now I don't know if we are going to carry on seeing each other, and there's no rush, because the more I know of him and the more I let him in, the closer to him and the more vulnerable I will feel.

Sometimes I get very tired of feeling vulnerable and scared, but I just can't seem to help it.

Domingo tells us there's a Spanish music concert on in one of the local squares tonight, starting at around ten. I'm surprised I didn't already know. We decide to wander down and take a look.

We get there at about eleven and it's in progress. There's quite a big crowd but we find ourselves a bit of space and watch and listen. At least he watches, as usual I'm too short to see over to the stage very well, but I'm used to that and listening's the main thing, isn't it?

After about an hour there's a break and we head to one of the bars for a drink. It's while Thor is at the bar that I see Paulo. I don't know if he's been in here all night or if he has done the same as us, but he's with a group of Spanish people and he doesn't see me. I decide not to disturb him (especially as I'm with Thor) but while I'm waiting I find myself glancing over. There are a few girls in the group and I can't help noticing that Paulo seems to be very friendly with one of them, but I might be imagining it. My stomach twists uncomfortably and I don't know why.

Thor brings the drinks and I suggest we take them outside because I don't want to watch Paulo and while I'm inside I can't seem to stop myself. In addition, I don't want Paulo to see us.

We finally head home at around three o'clock. It's been a really good night, we've both enjoyed the music and once I got Paulo out of my sight and out of my head I relaxed and it was fun. We have a last drink on the balcony and crash into bed.

The next morning is a late one – no surprises there. We're in no rush to get up and I, for one, enjoy lazing in bed with him. I can't believe he's going home tomorrow. Eventually we get up and go for a swim before lunch. We spend the afternoon between the sun terrace (which thankfully has a shaded area too) and the beach, reading, chatting, and generally chilling out. It's great. We go shopping as we've decided to eat in – once more I don't want to share him on his last night.

As before we cook together and open some decent wine. We eat on the balcony. It's still light and the view is impressive. We discuss the night before and I wonder if he's going to want to visit again and if I should ask him. God, I spend half the time worrying that I'm saying too much and the other half worrying that I'm not saying enough and he might go off thinking I'm not bothered. I'm such a dickhead. After all, he came to find me twice, and if I do want to say something coming clean should be a good thing. Why can't I just relax and enjoy it? Why can't I, for once, be sure of what I want? Stupid cow.

I push my worry away and decide to deal with it tomorrow. No change there.

But as the evening progresses (and it might have something to do with the amount of wine I drink, too) I start to nag myself that I should say something and to feel a bit braver about it. He's made the effort to fly here for a second time, surely that means something, and it shouldn't be so difficult to admit that I want to see him again, and by implication that I might like it to be an ongoing thing. I can't bring myself to say the word "relationship" to myself, I'm such a pathetic fool. So now I'm really worrying and spoiling my good time for a change by wondering how to bring it up.

Did I mention that he can be quite astute at times? He's watching me, and it's that strange expression of his and it's making me even more unnerved, heaven help me.

"What's up?" he asks.

Well, I'm really on the spot now and if I don't say something I don't think I'll ever be able to forgive myself for being so bloody useless. I flounder around for the best way to put it and like before my thoughts and worries are racing around my head and making it difficult for me to think straight. I look at him cluelessly and he stares back at me, not helping at all. Oh, thanks. So I take a deep breath and say, "The weekend seems to have gone very quickly." God help me, it's the best I can do.

"Mmmm," he says, and still he isn't helping. I wonder if it's deliberate and if so what it means, but I plough on because for once I know I have to.

"I've enjoyed having you here," I say, and I see his lips twitch slightly. *Oh, very funny*, I think sarcastically, because I'm very wound up, but at least I don't say it out loud.

"Me too," he replies, and perhaps he's feeling sorry for me.

"I'd like it if you wanted to come again," I say, and it sounds like it's all one word because it comes out in a nervous rush. This time he can't help grinning and I think, *Stupid cow, why am I speaking in double entendres?* Normally I can't be deliberately amusing if I try.

He nods, probably because if he opens his mouth he'll start to laugh at how ridiculous I am, and I'm starting to cringe as I say, "I mean, I know it's you having to do all the travelling and you might think I should come to England and I understand that, but it's difficult for me - it's hard to explain - you must think I'm pathetic, I'm sorry. But if you don't mind doing it I'd like to see you again. If you want to see me, that is." My voice is tailing away as I'm losing my nerve. He's looking solemn now and my stomach squirms as I wonder what he's thinking. Oh God, perhaps he's trying to think of how to let me down gently. I look down at the table, away from his face, and try to compose myself.

"Sam." He says it earnestly and I'm waiting for the blow as he deliberates over his words. For Gods sake, I don't know what on earth is wrong with me, I'm all in a tizz and it's not as though I've spent that much time with him. He must think I'm some kind of deranged moron, going all serious on him all of a sudden when all he wants is a good time.

When he finally speaks I nearly leap with fright. "I don't think you're pathetic, you already know that," he says, and I feel even more stupid than I did before. Maybe he sees this because he smiles, and the change is dramatic and I'm confused, and suddenly his eyes are smouldering, it's just as effective as before and I can feel my body start to pound. Dear God, I'm totally bewildered by this - I was trying to compose myself for heaven's sake - it's like I have no control over myself, and although I've had more than a few instances of feeling like this in the past year I'm none the wiser for it. I thought we were supposed to learn from our experiences, but I seem to be woefully incapable of doing so, now more than ever.

I continue to stare at him like some kind of vacant shop dummy and he must take pity on me because he says, "I don't mind coming here, it makes it more of a break for me."

I guess he means because he is away from his work, and I realise he is in effect saying that he wants to see me again, too, and for a moment I'm overcome. Sometimes I don't understand myself, so I appreciate nobody else can have a cat in hell's chance. For a change I don't know what else to say, however he must read my expression because he walks around the table and pulls me up to him. His eyes are hot and I'm lost, unable to resist. I still don't know how he does this. It's a good job I don't mind.

So the morning comes and I wake first, or at least I think I do. I lie there and go over the weekend and the things that have been said. Although I wanted to ask him back to Spain and God knows I'm happy to know that he wants to come, I also expected it to make me uneasy because I would feel more vulnerable and I am so used to spoiling things for myself. So it's with amazement that I realise I don't feel uneasy at all, and this makes me anxious. Bloody hell, sometimes I just think I should top myself and put myself out of my misery.

However, as I remember our weekend I'm smiling a silly smile, and it seems he's awake because he puts his arm across me and pulls me nearer. He knows that smile, and he's not stupid or even slightly reticent. It's one of the things I like about him, but then you already know that, don't you?

CHAPTER SEVENTEEN

Oh, God, so here I am. I'm not going to say I'm in a relationship, but it appears we might both want to go on seeing each other. I'm happy and anxious at the same time, and I'm not sure how I've managed it. Still, it's nice to know he wants to come back even before he leaves, and oddly it makes saying goodbye harder. Work that one out if you can.

He comes to Spain when he can, usually every three weeks or so for a long weekend of up to five days. I know it might sound crazy, but although I hate saying goodbye to him I slip back into my old life very easily when he's gone and I'm glad he lives in England. It makes me feel less vulnerable in that I'm used to being on my own as well as being with him. I mean, I do miss him, and so I should, it means he's important to me and I like it, but because he goes back to England I still have my own life here to fall back on if I need it, and this makes me feel better. I still don't let him near my villa. I feel a bit bad about this, but I would feel too exposed. Once he's been here I will feel his presence when he's gone and miss him so much more, I know I will. So I never invite him, and to be fair he makes it clear that he likes his penthouse apartment and the privacy it offers. I can't argue with that, and I still wonder sometimes if he's Derren Brown's brother and he can read my mind.

However, it makes me feel bad that it's always him who does the travelling, hires the car (he never accepts my offer to pick him up from the airport) and rents the apartment. I can't help wondering how he manages to book the apartment for odd weekends through the summer, but it's none of my business and I put it out of my mind. It suits me so why question it? I offer to pay for his flights a couple of times but he won't have it. He never asks me to go to England, and I'm relieved about that. I wonder if, perhaps, he likes the distance too, and if I've never been to his house or met his friends then he's unlikely to miss me when he's there. I'm not sure what I make of that, to be honest, so I push the thought away.

I love it when he's here in Spain. He still manages to be both cool and funny; and to respect my boundaries without me having to point them out, as I try to do with him. But we are growing closer, I can tell, talking endlessly and easily about anything (but nothing *too* personal) and I enjoy being with him very much. I still find him ridiculously attractive, and when he gives me his look I'm gone. And I wouldn't want it any other way.

I slip back into my old relationship with Paulo. If he still has any feelings for me or feels bad about my continuing to see Thor he doesn't let it show, and I'm glad. He still looks out for me when I'm in Paco's and I'm always pleased to see his face at the bar. He and Thor tolerate each other without rancour but I don't suppose they'll ever be best buddies. Paulo goes missing a bit more than he did before, and I hope he has a girlfriend somewhere, and if so I wonder if he'll ever bring her in to Paco's to meet everyone.

It's late September. Thor has just gone back to the UK and I'm sad to see him go. I suddenly realise that I do miss him when he's not here, I miss him a lot actually, he's on my mind much of the time now - I know, I know, I should get out more - and perhaps it's about time I invited him to my villa. This thought takes me by surprise, but after all if I'm missing him when he isn't here anyway it can't do any harm, and it will assuage my increasing guilt at him having to do all the travelling to see me. I feel a nervous frisson as I think this, but for once I am fairly sure (you will understand that I could never be absolutely certain) or perhaps it is simply that the guilt is overpowering the apprehension.

So when he calls to confirm his dates for coming over I say hesitantly, "Would you like to stay here, at the villa?" and for some reason my heart is in my mouth. I mean - why? What do I think is going to happen? That he's going to laugh at me or have hysterics at how forward I'm being? Actually I think a part of me is wondering if he has preferred the emotional distance staying in the penthouse offers, too, and perhaps staying with me might be too much. Or perhaps, as usual, I'm making a meal out of nothing. I'm good at that.

Anyway, he's quiet for a moment or two and I'm stewing nicely as I wonder what he's thinking. Then he says, "Are you sure? I'm quite happy in the penthouse," and I don't know what this means.

"Of course if you prefer the penthouse that's fine," I say, pussyfooting around shamefully, "but it might not be so pleasant once the weather changes." I know this is true. He might like it there now but the weather will change soon and it won't be so nice when he's stuck up there with a force ten gale blowing and no proper heating. "And it would save you some money," I add weakly. I know this sounds feeble and I squirm.

"I can afford it," he says, "especially off season." Oh, God, now he sounds slightly mocking and maybe he's thinking, *Oh, thanks, make the offer now the penthouse is cheap anyway. Very helpful, Miss Generous.*

I'm stung, and so I say without thinking, "It's not just that. I'd like you to stay here." I'm surprised at myself, and I suddenly realise it's true and that was why I was prevaricating because I was dreading he might say no. I hold my breath.

"I thought you'd never ask."

Oh, *good*. Oh, *God*, he must think I'm awful. I should have asked earlier, but he always said he liked the penthouse, and I believed him. Or at least I told myself that I did. Oh, God.

"I can pick you up from the airport, too," I say, scrabbling to make up for my previous reticence.

"Ok, thanks," he replies.

Oh God, I hope I've done the right thing, I really do.

So now I'm driving to the airport to pick him up. I'm mindlessly excited to be seeing him, it's three weeks since he was here, and I'm horribly apprehensive, too. I hope I'm not going to regret this. He's staying for five days this time, so I guess I'll find out soon enough. I wonder what he makes of me finally inviting him to my villa, and my toes curl slightly.

I'm waiting at arrivals and I can hardly keep still. Normally I'm at home until he texts so I can attempt to busy myself while I wait, but now I'm standing staring at the double doors on pins willing him to come through. I know he'll have a suitcase because I told him he could leave some clothes and things at the villa if he likes to save carrying them each way all the time, so he won't be the first through. That was another offer I made when I was feeling bad about how long it had taken me to ask him to stay with me. We've gone from never arranging another visit until he's back in England (he's been very clever about that) to me suggesting he leaves things at mine with all that implies. Oh, God.

There he is! He has a big case and I think, *It's a good job he isn't flying Ryanair*, before my thought is wiped from my head by the wide smile that breaks over his face when he sees me. I realise it mirrors my own as my apprehension has fled at the sight of him. He strides up to me and murmurs hello, and I don't know what to do. Is he expecting me to fling my arms around him in welcome? Because we are in a public place and that might be too much. My uncertainty must show on my face because he gives me that hot look and it's far more intimate than any big hug could be, and I'm practically melting. I take his hand and lead him to the car.

We catch up on general things while I'm driving and all too soon (why do I think that?) we arrive at my villa and I'm parking on the drive. All of a sudden I feel anxious and shy as he pulls his case from the boot and waits for me to open the door. Oh my God, apart from Donna (and the odd electrician and so on as I said before - and by odd I mean occasional, not weird) nobody has ever been in my villa. For a stupid second I'm actually frightened, and then I tell myself to get a grip and open the door. He follows me in and puts his case down.

Normally the first thing we would do is jump on each other (I'm sure you're not surprised to hear that) but then normally we are alone when we first see each other, not in an airport. Jumping on him just didn't seem right at the time. Plus we are usually on his territory, or before that neutral territory. Now we are on my patch, the initial surge of excitement from seeing him has passed, and for a change I don't know what to do. Perhaps he's reacting to my behaviour, because he keeps his hands off me and waits.

This makes me feel even worse so, of course, I procrastinate like the lily livered imbecile I am and I make a big deal of showing him around the villa, taking him into the kitchen, the living room, the bathroom and so on. I wonder what he thinks of the place - in a way he's learning more about me now than he ever has before. We reach my spare bedroom and I suggest he puts his things in there, because there's more room and they will be out of the way when he isn't here. His face is inscrutable as he moves his case and I still don't know what he's thinking. Finally I can't put it off any longer (unless I show him the empty garage, and how interesting would that be?) and I show him into my bedroom. For some reason I'm horribly embarrassed and I feel very self-conscious. He's quiet, and I'm not surprised, I'm not exactly inviting comment. He glances around the room, and if he notices the photograph of my family by my bed (it's the only photograph in the house) he doesn't mention it. I like to say goodnight to them every night before I go to sleep.

I turn to look at him and he's giving nothing away. God, we should have done our usual straight away, because now I feel awkward and don't have a clue as to how to approach him. What's wrong with me? I hesitate for a second and I'm about to move past him back into the hall but he stops me. He takes my face in his hands and he kisses me softly, and then he says, "I like your villa. Thank you."

Once more he's managed to say exactly the right thing. I look at him gratefully as my stress starts to dissipate and he slides his hands down from my face and undresses me with great tenderness. He's very gentle; and he introduces his presence into my space with astonishing sensitivity; and I'm moved.

Honestly, I knew I'd done the right thing, asking him here.

Later on I light the stove as the evenings are becoming chilly now and it takes the edge of it as well as being cosy and welcoming. We eat in and lie on the sofa, watching telly and chatting. Like a normal couple. Uh-oh.

The days pass quickly. I find I like having him here in my villa. It feels different, but it's nice. I needn't have worried about it at all - silly me. We spend more time than usual around the house, partly because the weather isn't so good and partly, I think, because we are both very comfortable here. At least I know I am, but then it's my villa, isn't it? Of course, I now have no reason to leave him every day for my change of clothes, but I suggest he sets his laptop up in my study and he can go in there if he needs to do anything for work and so on. He does so, but either his work is quiet or it's running smoothly, because he hardly goes in there at all. We do have one day out, but otherwise we stay local and chill and enjoy being together (or at least I do) and spend a couple of relaxed evenings in front of the fire. Like a normal couple. Gulp.

It's one of those evenings in front of the fire. I'm lying next to him on the sofa and he has his arms around me. Having him here feels right and I'm relieved and I feel very close to him. He kisses the top of my head and he says, "Sam?"

He sounds almost hesitant, and this is unusual to say the least. My worry radar switches to 'alert' as I say, "Mmmm?" in what I hope is a lazy, unconcerned tone.

"Do you think you'd ever go to England again?"

He probably feels me tense slightly. Oh God, why's he asking? In some respects I've been expecting him to ask at some point, but I've been more than happy to accept his silence and assume (or rather hope) that it means he isn't bothered about having to come to Spain all the time. I wonder what to say. He saw me in England for Donna's wedding and I don't suppose he knows that's the only, single instance I've been there since I moved to Spain, and I dare say I appeared happy enough at the time. Well, apart from nearly breaking down when Donna's father gave his speech, and nearly fainting with fright when that girl thought she knew me and so on. Hmmm - come to think of it, maybe I didn't seem so relaxed after all, and I remember thinking at the reception that he must have had me down as a half-witted lunatic by the way I behaved. So how can I explain to him that I was all right (well, sort of) while I was with him, but he didn't see me locked and bolted in the hotel fearful as hell the night before, or buying sandwiches at the airport so I wouldn't have to leave my room until it was absolutely necessary?

I *did* cope with being in England, it's true, but I'm sure a lot of that was down to him, and I don't want to sound like a needy, hopeless idiot. I rack my brains and I say, "I don't know."

It was well worth the rack, wasn't it? How helpful am I?

He doesn't say anything for a little while, no doubt he's trying to digest the huge amount of information I've given him. I know I should say more. He has every right to ask and he must wonder, I can't blame him.

Needless to say it's him who speaks up, not me.

"I can't imagine," he says, and I know he's trying to be sympathetic and let me off the hook but I can't help thinking unkindly, *No, you bloody well can't, not even for a minute.*

This makes me feel mean, so I try again.

"I find the thought of going to England very frightening," I say in a small voice. Admitting this is doing me no good at all, I can tell you, "It's difficult to explain."

Once more he's quiet, and that puts more pressure on me than if he were to question me further. Perhaps he knows this, he's not stupid.

"This part of Spain is very quiet and I feel safe here," I continue eventually. "I know in my head it's unlikely that anything bad will happen to me in England, but that's where it happened before and there's so much more aggression there, I can't help being scared. I think I'd be ok if I was with someone I trust - you or Donna, say - but I would find it extremely difficult to be on my own."

I'm glad I thought to put Donna in so it doesn't sound like I'm too reliant on him, and I'm trying to tell him that I could face it if he were with me but if he's thinking he could go off to work and leave me alone all day I would find that very difficult. Actually, I think I would find it virtually impossible, but I can't say so because even to me it sounds so very pathetic.

Again he's quiet as he mulls this over, and I wonder what he makes of it and if I've explained well enough. In the end I can't stand it, so I say, "I know you have been doing all the travelling. I'm sorry."

"It's not that," he says, surprising me.

What on earth is it, then? I can't imagine. He must be able to tell how difficult I'm finding talking about this, so surely he wouldn't ask me without good reason?

This time it's me who's quiet and in the end, and somewhat reluctantly I think, and I have the distinct impression that he's totally regretting starting this conversation, he says, "My sister's going to get married."

This really surprises me. I didn't even know he had a sister, for some reason I've always imagined him to be an only child. Why is he telling me now? Oh no! Is he asking me to go to the wedding with him? Shit! It would mean meeting all his family! How much more involved than that can you get? *Shit.* I'm not sure I can face that. I *can't* face that. I *so* shouldn't have invited him into my home, I'm so stupid.

"It might not be for ages," he says quickly, "she's only just got engaged." I think he's back-pedalling frantically and I feel wretched for making him do so. Now I'm sure he's regretting bringing it up and really it was my fault for lulling him into a false sense of security. I mean, I've been so happy to have him here. I'm such a thoughtless cow.

I force my body to relax. If it might not be for ages perhaps I can ignore it if I try very hard. "That's nice," I say, and I realise that doesn't sound right. "I mean, your sister getting engaged, not that the wedding might not be for ages." (Although to be honest it possibly not being for ages *is* nice, very nice indeed, thank you very much.)

Now I think he might be thinking *I* think getting engaged is a good thing, and I feel sick. No, he's not that thick, I'm sure. It's my turn to back-peddle as I hurriedly add, "I'm sure they must have been together for a very long time."

I feel his body tremble slightly and I realise he's trying not to laugh. How dare he? How *dare* he find this funny when it's so excruciating for me? For a moment I'm furious at being put on the spot like this and having to explain my innermost feelings and then being laughed at.

I raise my head to glare at him and he says innocently, "At least fifty years," in his best mocking tone. All of a sudden it *is* funny, or perhaps it's simply relief, and I start to giggle helplessly. I do worry too much sometimes. Honestly - and please don't try to argue with me - I do.

Later that night I think over what he's said and how I've felt having him here, and I realise it's futile and ridiculous to try to keep our relationship static in the way I do, even though it's often only subconsciously. I'm moved that he would mention his sister's wedding, even if I suspect he didn't start off intending to, and I berate myself for reacting so badly to it. God, I wonder if there's anything else he dare not mention - how awful. I mean, if I can't face it why can't I just say so clearly and discuss it calmly, instead of panicking wildly to myself and making a complete mess of trying to look as if it doesn't bother me? He knows what happened to me, so he's not going to be terribly surprised if I find such things a bit difficult, is he? He probably even expects it - hence his initial

149

reluctance to broach the subject. In fact, I realise I'm doing him a great disfavour in behaving as though he wouldn't appreciate how I feel or be able to deal with it. In many ways he's shown himself to be better at dealing with it than I am. But then, when I think about it, that's not surprising, is it? Oh God, I'm tying myself in knots. Anyway, he didn't actually invite me to the wedding in the end, did he, (what a surprise, I hear you say), so perhaps I'm jumping the gun and overreacting a little bit.

As if I would do such a thing.

I realise I didn't even ask him anything about his sister, I was so thrown off kilter by the thought of the wedding, and how ungracious is that? I must remember to do so in the morning, or he'll think I don't care.

I look at him, lying next to me in my bed, and I know that I do care, I care very much. In fact, I care more than I'd ever admit to anyone, even to myself (even though I'm doing it now). I really am a self deluding, spineless fool at times, I hate myself.

It's his last morning; he flies out today. I'm lying in bed and I think he's awake. I've so enjoyed him being here with me, and I hope he has, too. I open my eyes to find he's looking at me. He smiles and puts his arm over my waist. I feel such a rush of emotion it almost knocks me for six, and I think he sees it because his face changes and he pulls me to him. He kisses me, and he's taking no nonsense. Perhaps he does want to make his impression on the place before he leaves, after all. I giggle at this thought and he draws back to look at me enquiringly. It's not exactly something I can say out loud, but luckily I can be determined too, occasionally, and I take hold of him and pull him back to me, and he needs no further encouragement. For the first time in a while I get that *last time* feeling, but we haven't had our shower yet, so who am I kidding?

So time goes on. I'm very happy with my two little worlds which I still see as separate even though they are based in the same place. Thor manages to spend a bit more time here as he gets himself organised for it, and it helps that he can leave things here in my villa, and that pleases me.

Then one day Donna rings, and her voice is strained.

"What is it?" I ask, and I can feel my insides tighten cruelly.

"Is Thor there?" she asks.

"No," I reply. Actually, I thought she knew that, we speak often enough, and I wonder why she's asking. I'm starting to feel cold as the bad vibes get worse. "What is it?" I repeat.

"Bradley," she says, and my blood turns to ice. Bradley is one of the evil bastards. I can't speak.

"They're letting him out of prison this week," she says, and I drop the phone.

CHAPTER EIGHTEEN

I can't speak. The shock is too much. Tears are streaming down my face as I am forced to remember. I can hear Donna calling my name down the phone but it sounds like it's miles away. I can see the four of them as the sentences are given. I can hear them, too, telling me what they are going to do to me when they are released, and how much I'll wish they'd finished me off the first time. I sink to the floor – I cannot take this. I can still hear Donna, and I hang up the phone. I can't face her yet.

How can he be being released? *How?* It can't be right, she must be mistaken. I try to pull myself together. He got six years, and only four have passed. It must be a mistake, it's the only explanation. The only explanation I can cope with.

Mark didn't give evidence at the trial, he was too traumatised, so they blamed me for being found guilty, even though they left enough evidence behind to be caught anyway, I know that. I'll never forget their faces and their chilling threats, too awful to describe. I sit on the floor, for how long I don't know, as the tears flow down my face and I shake and shudder.

Eventually I calm down. You have to, in the end. God knows how long I've kept Donna waiting, she must be worried sick. I pick up the phone and dial her number.

"Oh, God, Sam, are you all right? I'm sorry, I'm so sorry."

"It must be a mistake."

"No, it isn't. I've checked and double checked."

Of course she has. Donna loves me. She wouldn't be telling me this unless she was absolutely certain. Poor Donna, she gets caught up in all this far more than is fair.

"But how come?" I say. "He got six years."

"Good behaviour," she replies.

Oh, *God. Good behaviour!* They murder my family and torture Mark and I, and Bradley gets out early for *good behaviour.* I can't believe it. The horror returns, together with the feeling of utter, utter degradation that my family's lives and all our pain and suffering are only worth six years. Now four.

"I'm so sorry," Donna repeats.

"It's not your fault," I reply automatically.

She's quiet.

"When?" I ask.

"Tuesday," she says.

Today is Sunday, so I have one more day of peace before the fear starts again. Except it won't be even slightly peaceful, I'll never feel at peace ever again.

"When's Thor back?" she asks.

"Friday."

"Can you ring him, ask him to come earlier?"

"No."

"Why not? He'd want you to, I'm sure." She knows Thor a bit better now. She and Mike came to stay one weekend when he was here. We had a brilliant time and it was so lovely for me having the people I love most in all the world here with me. For a moment I remember how happy I was, before realising I will never feel like that again, not once Bradley is out.

"No." I repeat. This isn't his problem. What happened to me has affected him enough, I'm not going to add to it by making him come running the minute everything isn't all right. I know he's working away all week and I'm not going to distract him from that. In fact I know I won't even tell him about it until he gets here. I don't say this to Donna, she wouldn't understand.

"Do you want me to come over?" she asks, "I could try to take some time off."

Oh God, Donna is so good to me. I don't deserve her.

"No. Thank you so much for offering. Nobody knows I'm in Spain. I don't see how Bradley could find me now." I say this with far more certainty than I feel. After all, Thor found me in the end, didn't he? At the time I thought that was a good thing. How naïve can you be?

"I don't mind."

She wants to come, I can tell, but there's no point. Even if she's here this week, what about next week, and the one after that, and the one after that? I have to deal with this, and I have to start now or it will only become more difficult. I try to explain and although she doesn't like it one little bit she accepts my decision.

"Promise me if you change your mind you'll tell me," she says, "I'll sound work out anyway."

"I promise. And thank you, Donna. Really."

There isn't much more to say. Small talk isn't going to wash on top the conversation we've just had. She makes me promise again and then rings off.

I go round my villa and make sure every shutter, lock and bolt is secure - and I have plenty of them to check, I can assure you.

I decide to go to Paco's, and I'm hoping like hell Paulo is going to be there. There's no point staying in and worrying, and Bradley won't be out until Tuesday so I am safe for now. I must try to be normal, and I have to try to take my mind off it because it's already torturing me. Oh, God, please let Paulo be there. I know he probably has another woman and doesn't want me in that way any more, but that doesn't matter, I need his unquestioning affection tonight.

I get there at about seven and there's a few in. One or two have been in since lunchtime and are well on the way. There's no sign of Paulo and I'm unreasonably disappointed, but I distract myself and mix as usual. Then he comes in, and I think he must see the look on my face, because he comes straight over and gives me the two kisses before pulling back and looking at me earnestly. I do my best nonchalant impression, but I've never been good at impressions and I can see that this time is no different. But he can tell that I'm very pleased to see him, I know, even if he can also see that I am drinking rather more quickly than usual. Still, he's used to mixed messages from me.

He stays by me, and when there's a quiet moment with no-one else around he gives me a look. "Are you all right?" he asks.

I nod, and smile a too-bright smile.

"Is Thor all right?"

I nod again and his face is inscrutable.

"Then what is it?" he asks.

"Nothing, I'm fine," I lie, and once again try to look cool and unconcerned.

He gives me another dark look, but he's not the nosey type and he lets it drop. Even so, he doesn't wander far from me the whole evening, and when I'm ready to go and rather more drunk than I'll admit I find him beside me and walking with me. In fact, I'm surprised to find I'm a bit wobbly and he takes my arm as we go. I like the contact, it soothes me.

We reach my villa and stop. Paulo drops my arm. I look at him and say goodbye, and we do the two kisses. His face is a picture of concern but he doesn't press me to tell him what's bothering me. I love him for that, and perhaps because of it, for an unbalanced minute I almost decide to tell him. Christ, I must be more drunk and far more wound up than I realised. Thank God I don't do it. I know I can trust him totally but it wouldn't be fair to burden him with it, really it wouldn't. My eyes are on the verge of tears and I know I'm losing it so I repeat my goodbye quickly and hurry into the house leaving him standing on the pavement watching me go.

When I wake up the next morning I have a fleeting moment of normality before the feeling of dread that something is wrong worms its way into my brain. Then I remember, and I'm afraid I burst into tears and it's not a good day. What's more, I know that tomorrow will be worse, and that knowledge doesn't help in the slightest.

Donna rings me later on because she's worried about me. Luckily I've pulled myself together by then and I think I reassure her, at least I hope I do. At any rate she isn't jumping onto a plane and dashing out here whether I like it or not, so I must be partly successful.

I decide to go to Paco's again. I can't stand sitting and worrying in the house any longer and it's my last chance. So I get there at about eight and I'm surprised to see Paulo is there again. It's unusual, to say the least. He raises his eyebrows when he sees me, but he doesn't look very surprised and I wonder if he guessed I'd come in tonight. I try to be a bit more composed, and I think I manage it, because the initial shock has worn off and I feel more weary than anything. I suppose it's hardly surprising with the amount I drank last night, the tears today and the knowledge that this feeling is never going to go away. Gosh, I'm going to be a barrel of laughs tonight if I'm not careful.

I make sure I don't drink too much or too quickly, partly because I don't want to and partly because I don't want to worry Paulo any more than I already have. If he notices he doesn't let it show, but then he's like that. Once again he stays close all evening, although we are not always talking together, and I'm very grateful for his thoughtfulness and care. When I leave he accompanies me although he doesn't take my arm this time, I guess because he doesn't feel he needs to. We reach my gate and he says goodbye. I can't stop myself from reaching up and touching his face, and he turns into my hand and kisses it tenderly. It's one of the most touching gestures I can imagine, and I feel humbled because I know now that he still has feelings for me, despite everything.

I drop my hand and say, "Thank you," and I don't know if he knows what for, because I don't really, there are too many things for me to be able to pick any single one out. "I'm always here for you," he says very quietly, before turning and walking away.

So now it's Tuesday and he's being let out today. I'm taking Mavis shopping in the morning and this distracts me a bit, but I can't help wondering what time he'll be free, and I feel full of vitriolic bile that he is going to be free when my family are all dead and I know I will never be free again.

In the afternoon I go to the phone to ring Lydia and tell her I won't be out that evening. As I reach out I hesitate. Is this what my life is going to become? Am I going to let him beat me? More practically - and more in keeping with my actual cowardly self - is he really likely to know where I am and race here on his first night of freedom, and aren't I safer now than tomorrow and the next day and the one after that? Although this thought doesn't cheer me (what a surprise) it does give me a certain resolve and I decide to go out with the girls as usual.

Thor rings me before I go. We don't normally speak every day, and particularly when he is staying away I don't like to disturb him as he's often busy. God, it's good to hear his voice and I might be a bit more gushing than usual, and I think I sound agitated even to myself, but he doesn't seem to notice and I'm relieved. The last thing I want is any awkward questions because as you know I find it very difficult to lie to this man. He tells me that everything is going well at his client's and he should finish on Thursday as planned and be home in the evening to pack so that he can go into his office on Friday morning and carry on to the airport straight from there. Christ, I can't wait to see him, I really can't.

So I go out with the girls and try not to think about Bradley or imagine him being reunited with his family as I never will be again. I try very hard not to be distracted and not to worry that he is standing outside the restaurant waiting for me, or hiding in the bushes around my villa, and I think I succeed to some extent and it's good to have the diversion the girls offer.

But the fear's still there, underneath. I might be easier to find than I think. As far as I know, apart from Thor, nobody has ever *tried* to find me so how do I know how easy it could be? Especially as Bradley knows my original name, so there may be a trail he can follow. Oh, God, I'm winding myself up like an Olympic champion and when we finish I hurry home and I'm so nervous it's untrue, and I fumble with the front door clumsily and heave a sigh of relief once I'm in. Honestly, whatever else I might think he'd have to be Superman to find me and get here in one day, but then fear isn't always logical, is it?

I'm even worse on Wednesday but I try really, really hard not to be. I can't carry on like this. I know I'll feel much better once Thor is here and I can discuss it with him and he will manage to say something to make me feel better. I know he will. I just have to get through today and Thursday and then he'll be here. I keep the villa totally locked up and I don't go out all day.

In the evening Donna rings me and I'm not surprised. She sounds strange, and this is a surprise. Once again, fear immediately grips me as I hear the tone of her voice.

"Have you seen the papers today?" she asks.

"No," I reply warily. "Why?"

"Oh Sam," she says, "he's dead."

I drop the phone. Once again my legs give way, it appears this doesn't only happen in films. I slide down onto the floor as I see Thor in my minds eye, firstly lying in bed beside me - God, for a second I can even feel his presence - and then lying on a mortuary slab. I know how somebody looks lying on a mortuary slab. I have no tears, I feel numb, but I can hear my voice sounding like it's a million miles away, saying, "Oh no, no, no." My mind is blocking everything else out.

Then I hear Donna. She's shouting down the phone but I don't want to listen, I don't want to hear any more. I nearly hang up, but her words are permeating into my brain against my will.

"Sam! SAM! Listen to me! *SAM!* Not Thor! Do you hear me? NOT THOR! Bradley! *Bradley's* dead."

I have the presence of mind to say something - I don't know what I say actually, but something that will tell Donna I've heard her - and then I do hang up the phone. I can hardly breathe as the relief overwhelms me and once again I'm shaking and nearly throwing up. I start to laugh hysterically. What is it about me that makes me always imagine the worst? Well, you know the answer to that one now, don't you?

I redial Donna pretty quickly because I know she'll be worrying and although I'm still shaking I'm ok because what I thought had happened is wrong.

"Oh Christ, Sam, I'm so sorry! I didn't think. I thought you'd know I meant Bradley and I just didn't think."

"It's ok," I say, because it is.

"I'm so sorry, I'm so sorry."

"It's ok. It's not your fault. You know me, always look on the bright side." I try to make a joke of it because I'm feeling light headed and she's feeling bad enough, and it isn't her fault, no way. "What happened?" I ask to distract us both.

"Well, it seems he got out yesterday and went home to his family. Then he met up with some mates and they were drinking all evening. He walked home along the side of the canal and fell in. He couldn't get out - either too drunk or too difficult for him. He drowned and someone found his body very early this morning."

Good, I think, and for a fleeting minute I'm ashamed of myself, and then, and I'm not terribly proud of this (although in fact I'm not sure it's so bad under the circumstances) I think, *Why shouldn't I be glad? After what he did to me and my family, why shouldn't I be glad that he got his just desserts? He had it coming.* Then I realise I can stop being afraid and have my life back and my throat is constricted and I can't speak.

Donna understands. She waits while I sort myself out.

"I'm glad," I finally admit.

"So am I," she responds, and this makes me feel better. "He deserved it."

"Thank you for telling me."

"I could have made a better job of it."

"No. That doesn't matter. Thanks."

We ring off soon after, once again small talk isn't going to make much impact after that news.

Now I'm desperate to see Thor. Even though I know he's fine, thinking he wasn't for that split second has given me a stupid feeling of dread and I need to see him to reassure myself that he's ok. I know it's not logical, but there you are. I can't wait until Friday.

But for now it's still Wednesday, I've been shut in my villa in fear all day and I need to get out. It's still only eight thirty so I decide to go to Paco's. I know I'm hoping Paulo will be there - only so I can reassure him that I'm ok.

He is there, and when he sees I'm quite clearly over whatever was bothering me I feel his mood lighten and we have a few drinks and a good time together. Once again he asks no questions, he merely seems happy to see that I'm fine. He walks me home and says goodbye as normal. I don't touch his face (even I'm not that stupid) but he takes my hand and squeezes it before I go in, and I'm not offended (how on earth could I be?) because I know what he means. Or at least I think I do.

Finally Friday arrives and I'm on pins waiting to go and meet Thor off his plane. It seems like forever before I see him walking towards me and I'm afraid I clutch hold of him and cling for a second or two even though I try to stop myself. He hugs me back for a few moments then gently extricates himself and I say, "It's good to see you," which is so much the truth plus I hope it might deflect any thoughts he might be thinking as to why I've acted like that.

"Me too," he says, and we make our way to the car.

If he does have any curiosity he keeps his questions to himself and allows me to concentrate on my driving. I am still a bit agitated and I wonder if that's why I seem to be able to feel that pent up energy of his so strongly, perhaps he's reacting to me, and once more he seems to be like a coiled spring.

We reach the villa and he's hardly put his bag down before he's dragging me into the bedroom and his face is so intent I nearly pass out. God, he's determined, and for that matter so am I (I must still be reacting to thinking I'd lost him) and finally I'm able to relax in the knowledge that Bradley's gone, Thor's here (oh boy) and everything is all right.

What a week. *Fuck me.*

We're lying in bed and I'm exhausted - emotionally, physically and mentally. I'm trying to turn my mind off and give myself some peace, so I jump when Thor suddenly says, "What's up?"

What makes you think something's up? I think with an internal giggle, and it's going to be so much easier to tell him now that Bradley's gone. Even so, I pause for a minute to pick my words, because it's going to be unexpected for him, to say the least.

Of course, being me, no amount of pausing or picking helps and in the end all I can think to say is, "Bradley got out this week." I wonder if he'll remember who Bradley is - after all, it must be a year since Donna told him.

"Bradley?" he says absently, and then he must put two and two together because he's very still.

"One of the evil bastards," I clarify.

I half expect him to cry out, or jump up, but he doesn't. He turns carefully to look at me and says, "But I thought he got six years," and his voice is very controlled.

"Good behaviour," I say, and I titter nervously like a mental case. I watch his face as he goes through the thought process.

"Can he find you?" he asks.

"Not now," I reply, and I titter again. God knows what Thor makes of this.

"Good," he says, and he slides his arm under me and pulls me to him.

"He's dead," I add, and wait for his reaction.

I'm not disappointed, something strange definitely flickers across his face - something unpleasant - and then he looks at me again and says, "Dead?"

I explain what happened, and I'm uneasy. Thor isn't really reacting as I would expect. Then I remember how Donna said he was when she told him about the horror, sitting impassively and showing no emotion, and I guess this must be how Thor is when he's shocked.

"When did you find out?" he asks.

"Donna told me on Sunday," I reply, "and then he got out on Tuesday."

Now I see some emotion. That cold, contained anger I've seen before. "You found out on Sunday?" he says. "Why didn't you tell me?"

Well, I'm taken aback by this and not sure what to say. "You were going away for the week. I didn't want to worry you." All of a sudden this sounds so feeble.

"You didn't want to worry me. You find out that Bradley's going free and you didn't want to *worry* me."

"I didn't want to disrupt your work. It's important."

"I think it's for me to decide which is the more important, not you."

Shit. I guess I hadn't looked at it from his point of view before. His face is tight and he looks away.

"I knew you'd be here on Friday," I try to explain further. "He didn't get out until Tuesday and I only had to last until Friday and then I would see you and could tell you. In the end I knew he was dead on Wednesday anyway."

"You must have been terrified." Still he won't look at me and I feel hideous. Now I look down. "Yes," I say in a small voice, because to say anything else would be ridiculous.

I start to move away because I feel so stupid and I can't stand his disapproval any longer, but he stops me. "Don't exclude me, Sam, and don't make my decisions for me. You should have told me. You should have let me help."

There's not much you could have done, I think to myself, but I can't say it. I know now that he's right, and I should have told him, at the very least he could have reassured me to help me through until he was here.

"I'm sorry," I say, "I didn't want to put it on you. It's my problem and I didn't want to make it yours, too."

He gives me the strangest look, and although I don't like it at least the anger has gone. Then he pulls me to him. "That's what I'm here for," he mutters under his breath, "Idiot."

I'm so relieved I could jump up and run around the room, but even I'm not that daft, I'm glad to say.

So time goes on and Christmas is coming. Thor is going to be in Spain for nearly two weeks and I'm very excited. I'm very happy, and I think he is, too.

Christmas is great, and although it goes without saying that I miss my family it's wonderful to be with someone. I made it clear to Thor that if he wanted to be with his family I didn't mind, but he was fine about being in Spain. I guess if your family is alive and well you feel differently about not being with them. I'm not complaining. It reminds me of his sister and her engagement. He hasn't mentioned it again, and I'm not sorry, perhaps they're in no hurry, but I make a mental note to ask about it at some time, I don't want to appear uninterested.

So now New Year is approaching and my mind turns to my resolutions and the ones I made last year and how I got on with them in the end. I'm thinking I didn't do so badly after all:

1. Look forward not back - well, perhaps not doing brilliantly but Thor definitely makes it easier.
2. Have a purpose - I'll come back to this one.
3. Stop thinking about Scumbag - ok, so this one is thoroughly trashed (except he's not Scumbag any more - does that count?)
4. Stop worrying about everything and especially about what everyone else thinks - check, I've tried very hard.
5. Make a decision about Paulo - I suppose I've had to.
6. Be more positive - I must be, by definition. As I said before, I could hardly be less so.

Hmmm, so maybe not one hundred percent, but nobody's perfect. I don't think I'll bother this year.

New Year's eve is at Paco's, of course. I can't help remembering last year, and how Paulo kissed me and I first believed he really did have feelings for me, and I can't believe it was only a year ago. So much has happened since then and my life has changed drastically (even though for more than half the time I still have my old life, too, and I like it like that). We have a great night, and at the stroke of midnight I can't believe I'm kissing Scumbag as he wraps his arms around me and holds me close. "Happy New Year, Sam," he says softly. "Happy New Year," I respond, and without thinking I reach up and touch his face above his eyebrow where he was cut fighting Simon. His eyes are warm as I trail my fingers down the side of his face, and he turns into my hand and kisses it. I feel a moment of swirling confusion and I kiss him again to push the feeling away.

Then everyone is kissing everyone and Paulo is there and he meets my eyes for a moment before he bends his head and I know what he's thinking and he knows what I'm thinking before he wipes all expression off his face and kisses my cheek. "Feliz Año Nuevo, cariña," he murmurs, before turning away. "Happy New Year," I say, and I watch him go.

It's a fantastic party, the bar is rocking with Spanish and Brits and music and laughter. We finally leave the stragglers well after six o'clock and walk home arm in arm, and I'm very happy.

And now it's a new year. Dear me, so much happened in the last one I wouldn't mind a bit of peace and quiet this time, please. If it's all the same to you, that is.

CHAPTER NINETEEN

I seem to get my wish at first. The first half of the year is uneventful in the main. Thor spends as much time as he can here with me, and I'm blissfully happy and I can't believe I've been so lucky as to find this man and this life after what happened to me.

At times I can't help worrying about Wayne, the one who got seven years, and wondering how good his behaviour has been. After all, it's a new year now so I'm allowed to worry, aren't I? But I try not to think about it. It serves no purpose and I know Donna will be on top of it and will let me know soon enough if he's going to get out. Until then I'm better off not knowing.

Occasionally I think I really should offer to go to England again, but Thor never mentions it and the coward in me is happy to let it drift. I keep meaning to ask after his sister and her wedding, too, but every time I remember Thor is in England, and whenever he's here or on the phone I'm distracted and I forget. Is it just me this happens to? I can't believe I keep forgetting as the months pass, I really am hopeless.

Then one morning in late July when we are lying in bed and my mind is wandering aimlessly as it always seems to when I'm relaxed and happy, I remember. Hallelujah! It's only taken six months, I deserve a medal.

"I keep meaning to ask you about Astrid's wedding," I say, (it appears his parent's Nordic phase lasted some time), "Have they decided when they are going to get married yet?"

"Yes," Thor replies, and something about his voice puts me on edge.

I hesitate, then say, "When?"

"The first of September."

I'm silent. That's only about six weeks away. I lean up to look at him. "You haven't mentioned it," I say.

"You clearly didn't want to go." He's avoiding my eyes and I can't read his face at all.

"I didn't say that," I point out, and my stomach is churning because I don't like his expression. I'm starting to feel sick and wondering what he's thinking, because whatever it is, it isn't welcoming.

He's quiet. *Shit.* I'm trying desperately to remember exactly what I did say, but it was ages ago, and that doesn't help because I know I haven't mentioned it since, so in a way I can't blame him for thinking I don't care. Bollocks.

"I said I'd be frightened to go back to England and be on my own," I say, and I hope this is right, because he's bound to remember if not. "That's not the same thing."

Still he says nothing. It's awful. His face has closed off and I'm beginning to think I might even have hurt his feelings, and this makes me want to curl up into a tiny ball and die.

"Anyway, I don't remember you actually inviting me," I say, a trifle defensively.

"How surprising," he replies, and his tone is sarcastic rather than mocking. I'd go for mocking now, if I had the choice. God, what have I done?

"Thor." My voice is pleading.

He looks at me now and his eyes are guarded.

"I'd like to go to the wedding," I say, "if you'd like me to go with you." *Bloody hell*, I suddenly think, *have I got this wrong and he didn't mention it because he doesn't want me to go?* Shit! It's too late now.

"You don't have to," he says, and that's no help at all.

"I know I don't have to," I say quietly, and I throw caution to the wind - it must be a leap year or something - "I want to."

I realise this is true. I'm so used to not wanting to get involved, but for heaven's sake, we've been seeing each other for a year now and I'm already involved, whether I like it or not. Now I realise that not only do I not mind going, but I'd like to get to know more about him and meet his family, and if I have to go to England to do so I'm willing to. He'll be with me, it's two years since the last time, and I've changed, too.

I lower myself onto his chest and I can't help whispering to myself, "I'd do anything for you."

His arms move around me and I remember his bionic ears. Oh well, I can't do anything about it now. And it's true, anyway.

After he's gone back to England I wonder what would have happened if I hadn't asked. Would he really not have mentioned it at all and gone to the wedding without me? I have a cold feeling, because I think he would. Not because of pride, I already know he isn't a fool to pride, so presumably because he genuinely thought I didn't want to go and he didn't want to push me. It's a lesson to me, I can tell you. I can't begin to imagine how I would have felt if I'd found out about it afterwards. I mean, imagine if I'd asked in September and he'd said, "It was two weeks ago." I'd have felt awful. That was a close thing, and no mistake. Can I please learn from one of these mistakes one of these days? It would be nice.

The following week I'm taking Don and Jill to a town about an hour up the coast because they have a meeting with their bank manager there. Don't ask me why they have to go all that way, it's none of my business, but I don't mind the trip out, it's a nice town and I can have a walk along the front while they do whatever they have to do. I leave them outside the bank and we agree to meet in a nearby café in an hour.

I'm glad I brought my hat because it's very hot now and it shades me a bit. It's a still day and even though it's early there's no breeze and I feel like I'm baking. Nevertheless, I have a pleasant walk, and arrive back at the café at the appointed time. Don and Jill walk in just after me and we have a coffee together. I keep my hat on because I know my hair will be plastered against my head in the most unattractive fashion. Really, I'm not usually so vain.

We finish and are just getting up to go so I put my sunglasses on ready for the glare. A man comes in and speaks to the barman and he's showing him something.

No! I nearly drop down dead on the spot. I can't believe it. The man is Wayne. Oh my God, oh my God, it's *Wayne!* He's a few years older but I'll never forget that face or his voice. Fuck! He's only a few feet away from me. *Christ Almighty!* My body goes into spasms as it's desperate to run away as quickly and as far as possible, but my feet seem to be nailed to the floor and I can't move. I'm frozen to the spot. My heart is hammering in my chest and I can't breathe. Don and Jill are oblivious, and they head out past him.

He shoves a photo in their faces. "Do you know this girl?" he asks, "She's missing."

Well, I'm no relation of Derren Brown but I know straight away who he's referring to. No prizes for guessing. Don and Jill peer at the photo while I try to be invisible. I think I'm going to be sick. Perhaps I should be, I could aim it at the photo. Thank God I have my hat and glasses on. Wayne has hardly glanced at me so far but if he were to give me a proper look I think I'd get away with it, with luck he won't recognise me or see the stricken expression on my face. Fuck and shit, I desperately hope so. I don't know whether to try to sneak out unobtrusively, risking him looking at me and stopping me, or to continue trying to hide. Christ, I'm almost gibbering to myself as I try to think what best to do, and I wait for an exclamation of surprise from Don or Jill as they twig who it is they're looking at.

Now Wayne does look at me, and to stop him I inch forward (this takes all my willpower) and look at the photo. I see myself and nearly pass out with fear. The photo is an old one, from before it happened, and despite myself I note with interest my darker, short hair and the bump in my nose which I hated so much, but which I am now so grateful to have had. God, I look so very happy and as if I don't have a care in the world. When I think about it, I suppose I didn't. Then I take in the rest of the photo and I nearly start howling. That wouldn't give anything away, would it? I actually jerk slightly as I stop myself and force myself to keep looking. Because there is an arm around me, and Mark is next to me, looking at me. I haven't seen Mark's face for five years, and the sight of his tender expression nearly sends me over the edge. Then, for a fleeting, stupid moment (or perhaps my brain simply can't handle any more) I find myself wondering where he is now and what he's doing. *Like that's the main thing which should be occupying me just at this moment.*

Anyway, to my relief (and I don't have a word emphatic enough to express the extent of this relief) Don and Jill look at the photo and say, "No," and I manage to shake my head before we all head out. I nearly collapse as we walk away and Wayne doesn't shout out or come running after me. I have to put a mental gun to my head to stop myself from taking hold of my friends and sprinting to the car.

If they notice anything wrong on the way back they don't mention it. I drop them off and when I pull up at my villa I realise I can't remember the drive at all. It worries me when I do that. I mean, was I paying attention? (This time I think the answer's almost definitely no.) Did I go through any red lights or drive on the pavement at all? If someone were to tell me I had I wouldn't be able to argue.

I feel horribly exposed as I dash out of the car and into the villa. I race around every room and lock and bolt every single door, window and shutter until I am standing in the dark. I'm shaking now as I have time to think properly. *What am I going to do?* He's out! Why didn't anyone warn me? He's coming for me! Christ, if he finds me I'll be better off being dead. I can't think straight and I'm trembling and rigid, if that's possible, like a statue teetering on the edge of a cliff. I try to tell myself that he hasn't found me yet and obviously it will take him time to ask around where he is, and then he has to decide to come to this resort and ask here, and his photo is old and if Don and Jill don't recognise me when I'm standing right next to them then surely nobody else will. But none of this attempt at logic does any good and I'm almost sobbing with distress and I know I'm falling to pieces.

Thor! I'll ring Thor. Last time I didn't want to tell him, this time suddenly I'm desperate to. He'll know what to do. He'll know what to say. Christ, I can hardly work my fingers as I pick up the phone and find his number. *Oh my God, oh my God,* I can hardly function.

"Sam!" he says, "What is it?" Me ringing him during his working day is unusual to say the least.

"Hi, Thor," I say in what I hope is a light tone.

Quite clearly I'm fooling nobody. "What *is* it?" he repeats.

"Wayne. It's Wayne. He's out, I've seen him. He's here in Spain, looking for me. He's out, Wayne's out and he's here. He's here in Spain. I saw him today." I realise I'm gibbering and force myself to stop. I wonder if Thor even remembers who Wayne is.

"He can't be," Thor says, and I think, *What does that mean?*

"He *is*. I saw him when I took Don and Jill to the bank. I *saw* him. He's looking for me." I am sobbing now.

"He can't be there," Thor repeats, "He's supposed to be here, I -" He stops abruptly.

"What do you mean? *What's going on?*" Fear grips me even harder as I say this.

"Did you say you saw him this morning?"

"Yes." I'm so easily distracted.

"How far away from you was he?"

"Right next to me! He asked us if we knew me! Oh my God, he *spoke* to me! Thank God I had my hat and sunglasses on, otherwise..."

"I mean how far was he from your villa?" Thor says this slowly and clearly, realising that I'm losing it and need simplicity at this point. His cool voice helps to calm me.

"About fifty miles or so up the coast."

"So he doesn't know the resort you live in, never mind where the villa is?"

"He can't do."

"Ok, so he isn't about to come knocking on your door for a while yet."

"I don't know. I don't *know*." I can't think straight and my mind is jumping about all over the place.

"Why didn't Donna warn me?" I say. "I don't understand."

"I told her not to. After Bradley was released and you were so scared I told her if anyone else got out to tell me and not you. I told her I'd deal with it."

Oh my God! My mind is still jumping and I remember his earlier remark.

"What did you mean *he's supposed to be here?*" I ask, "Where are you?"

Thor hesitates for a second, and I think he makes a decision. "In Leeds," he replies.

"Leeds? *Leeds?* You're supposed to be in Warrington. *What's going on?*" A cold feeling of dread is coming over me. Thor's silent. "*What are you doing in Leeds?*" I demand.

"Wasting my time, obviously," comes the reply.

"What do you mean?" I'm almost hysterical. "What are you doing there?"

"Making sure he can never hurt you again."

I hang up the phone. I stare at it as though it's a lethal snake about to strike and almost throw it into its stand. I'm shaking and horrified and I don't know what to do. Wayne is in Spain, he knows I'm here and he's looking for me, and all of a sudden I don't know Thor at all.

God knows how long I stand there. I'm completely stupefied. I can't believe this is happening. The phone rings and I nearly fall over in fright. I don't answer it. I don't know what to say to him; he isn't the person I thought he was at all. Oh, God, I'm so confused and I don't have a clue as to what to do. I'm so frightened.

The phone rings again and I reject the call and disconnect it at the wall. My mobile rings and I reject that call too, but I don't turn my mobile off, I can't bring myself to. I don't want to talk to him but I don't want to be completely cut off either. Work that one out if you can. Oh God, oh God, what should I do - where should I go? *Fuck!*

My mobile sounds again and this time it's a text. Ok, I think I can handle a text. I have a look.

"Lock all the doors and windows," it says.

Oh, really? I think, *Thanks, I'd never have thought of that.* I'm losing my mind.

"Your villa is as secure as anywhere I know." Well, that's true, there's no doubt.

"Don't let anyone in." *What, not even you?*

"I'm on my way."

Christ, I don't know what to think. What was he going to do in Leeds? Threaten Wayne? Maim him? I'm too scared to think this thought, but I can't help it - *kill* him? Oh God, that makes Thor almost as bad! My mind suddenly leaps to Bradley. Was his death an accident? *Oh fuck!* Somehow now I think not. I can't cope with this. I don't know what to think. I don't know who to trust.

It seems he's still Derren Brown's brother even from a thousand miles away. A second text comes through.

"Call Paulo if you need to. He'll help you. If you need someone with you ask him to come to the villa. Don't talk to anyone else. I'll be there soon. Wait for me, Sam, please."

He's right. I can trust Paulo. I glance at the clock. Oh, God, is it only half past one? It seems like years since I saw Wayne. I can't drag Paulo out of work. Thor's right, Wayne doesn't know where I live, he won't find me yet. I can wait until Paulo finishes work. Of course I can. I'll have to. Oh, *God*.

I don't know how I do it, really I don't, but somehow I manage to occupy myself and distract myself from worrying too much about how long it will take Wayne to find me, what he will do to me when he does, where I can go to escape him and what to do about Thor. Because I have no idea who *he* is any more at all.

I last out until five and then I text Paulo. I'm not going to ring him at work and I know that even receiving a text will be unusual enough to set his alarm bells ringing. I deliberate for a moment as to what to put, but I'm beyond anything clever so in the end I just text:

"Hi Paulo. It's Sam." (I know he knows it's me but I can't help spelling it out for some reason.) "Are you busy tonight? Can you come to my villa after work please?"

He doesn't reply at first, no doubt he's busy, and I start to worry that he's changed his mobile or turned it off or forgotten to take it to work or something. I'm getting myself into a proper mess because now I've texted him I can't wait, but he doesn't reply. Then my mobile goes off and I get such a scare (why do these things always startle me more when I'm waiting for them? I mean, I'm actually expecting my mobile to go off but it gives me more of a fright than if I wasn't. What's that all about?)

The text says:

"Are you ok? I finish at seven but I'll try to get off earlier."

I reply:

"I'm fine." (I cross my fingers for this bit as it's such a blatant lie.) "C u then. Thx."

Only an hour and a half to wait. I don't want to put the TV on because if it's audible from outside Wayne will know there's someone in. *Don't be stupid*, I think, *you needn't put it on loud. He won't find you yet, and anyway lots of people leave the TV on when they're out to scare off burglars.* This thought winds me up again and I'm in for a fine and dandy wait, I can tell you.

The time absolutely drags as I try to read the paper, then to do the crossword, and then to make a paper aeroplane. It's a dismal failure. When I finally hear a car pull up I give myself a nice little paper cut in my fright. God, I hate them, they're so painful. Oh Christ, not as painful as Wayne's going to be. Once again, I'm almost sobbing as I go to the door and peer through the security spy glass or peep hole or whatever the bloody thing's called. Thank God! It's Paulo, and I unbolt the door and drag him in while he looks at me as if I'm a complete and utter nutcase, before gazing around him with interest (because he's never been in here before, if you remember).

I'm trying to calm myself and breathe evenly, and I'm succeeding to some extent because he's here and already I feel better, and I don't want to alarm him any more than I already have, and I don't want him to ask too much because I don't know how much I want to tell him. Oh bollocks, I don't know how to handle this at all.

He gives me a steady look and says, "What's up?"

I stare at him gormlessly while my brain whirls and I try to think of something suitable to explain my obvious distress without going too far. You will not be surprised to learn I can't think of anything.

"Are you ok?" he persists.

"I'm frightened," I say, because I'm so het up I can only think of the truth to tell.

I think he's already worked that one out, but he nods patiently and asks, "Why?"

"I think someone's trying to break in," I reply, and it's as near to the truth as I can get.

"Have you rung the police?"

"No."

"I'll do it."

"No!"

He looks at me then. "What's going on?" he asks, and I just stare back at him. I can't think what to say or what to do. I'm a dithering wreck.

"Sam, calm down. Tell me what's going on. I can't help you properly unless I know."

"I can't," I say, and it's almost a wail. I *can't* tell him, I don't want him to know what happened to me. I don't want to run the risk that it spoils things between us.

He can see my distress (let's be honest, it's not difficult) and he says, "Sit down," and he leads me to the sofa. He sits next to me and he wraps my hand in his and it's reassuring. He doesn't ask why I think someone's trying to break in, or who, or why I can't go to the police, or anything. God, he's great.

"Do you want anything?" I ask, suddenly remembering my manners. "Coffee, or a beer, or anything?"

"I'll have a coffee, please," he says, and follows me into the kitchen while I sort out the pot and put it on and we wait for it to boil. I find the mugs and put the milk in and I'm on automatic pilot and it's soothing. He watches me quietly while I pull a packet of biscuits from the cupboard and take it into the living room.

I pour the coffees and my hand is hardly shaking at all. I carry them through and put them on the table and turn to him. I feel I have to say something.

"Thank you for coming."

"It's ok."

"I'm sorry to drag you here."

"I don't mind. Where's Thor?"

"England. Well, he'll be on his way here now."

Paulo nods.

"I'm so frightened." I whisper it without thinking, I can't help it.

"Why?"

Again I stand and stare at him.

"Is it them?" he asks at last, "Is it the men who killed your family?"

And my mouth drops open in shock.

CHAPTER TWENTY

I nearly keel over backwards, I'm not kidding. I continue to stare at Paulo with eyes like saucers. My head's whirling again and I feel like my life is a jigsaw and the pieces have just been rearranged and fitted together differently. My thoughts are shattering and scattering at my feet. I'm speechless.

He says no more, but he puts his hands on my shoulders. I think he can see I might go over at any minute. Eventually I manage to say, "You know?"

He nods.

"How?" I ask. "Donna?"

"No."

"Thor?"

"No."

"Then how? I don't understand."

"I've always known," he says, and I'm going to snap, I know I am, and I try *very* hard not to.

"What do you mean?" I ask, and I can't believe that he knows, he's always known, and he's never said anything, or given any sign, or given me away. He's just waited patiently for me.

"Do you remember the first time you came into Paco's, with Donna?" he says, "I'll never forget it. I'll never forget how you looked."

I have no idea what this means. I know I was a mess back then but I'm sure I'd have remembered to button up my blouse properly.

"Donna did most of the talking," he continues, "and you stood there beside her. You were so timid, but there was something about you." He sighs. "I couldn't help it. You interested me so much."

I'm surprised. This is about the most non-nosey man I know. The thought creeps into my head, *Well, now I know why, don't I?*

"Anyway, I didn't do anything about it - you were none of my business - until a couple of weeks later when I was walking past your villa. I didn't even know it *was* your villa at the time. It was an unusually hot day, I remember, because I was walking along the beach, and I heard a noise. I didn't realise the villa was occupied so I looked over the wall to see what was going on. You were sitting in the sun, and I was about to say hello when you got up and turned around." He stops.

I think back. I made the most of every opportunity to sunbathe when I first moved to Spain and the weather can be surprisingly hot even in winter if you find a sheltered spot. God, my back would have been so much worse then than it is now, and I can imagine the jolt he must have got when he saw it. I stare at him in silence and he begins to look a bit uncomfortable.

"I was so shocked that I didn't say anything, I walked off. But I had to know, and when I got home I went onto the internet. I'm sorry, it was none of my business, I know, but I really liked you and I couldn't stop myself. I went back through the archives until I found you. You looked different but I knew it was you. I couldn't believe it. I couldn't believe what had happened to you, Emma."

I nearly collapse at this use of my old name, and I can see the dark anger in his face. I can't speak. Not only does he know but he must have read all the gory details - the press are never slow to sensationalise. Tears are spilling down my face as I realise that he knows me better than I had ever imagined, and he loves me despite what he knows.

"I'm so sorry," he says, whether at his intrusion into my business or what happened to me I have no idea. Probably both.

"When Thor walked into Paco's," he continues, "I thought he must be Mark. When I saw your face - he had to be Mark, I could cope with that - I could appreciate your reaction, I could even understand." He stops and rubs his nose. "But then I learned he wasn't Mark at all..."

"Oh, Paulo." I'm overcome. I can't keep up. Paulo knows, he's always known and always been there for me, regardless of everything else, supporting me and keeping my secret, even from myself. I look up at him and he drops his head to mine.

Oh my God, he's going to kiss me, I think, and I don't mind. Perhaps it's the after effects of this extreme day, I don't know, but I don't mind at all. His lips meet mine and his arms inch around me and I welcome him. He's holding me close and I'm kissing him back and I feel him respond and it feels good. Oh, God, I'm so confused. Paulo is here, looking after me as he always does, he knows about me and he loves me - and Thor? Thor is a stranger. I'm lost, floundering helplessly as I try to find my way.

It's too much. I feel my composure (actually composure is far too strong a word, but it's the best I can do) begin to slip as I falter, and immediately Paulo stops. I lean my forehead against him and he rests his cheek on my head as once more I try very hard not to snap.

The next minute I hear a cool, "Well, well, what have we here - *very* cosy," and I know that voice. I think I nearly break Paulo's nose as my head snaps up and I spin round. Thor is standing in the doorway and his face is like thunder.

How apt, I think, and I'm so strung up I almost giggle. Then I think, *It's a good job he didn't see us two minutes ago,* and this time I do giggle, I can't help it. God knows what he makes of that. Oh *fuck*, and I thought the day couldn't get any worse.

Paulo backs off. How sensible. Thor looks from me to him, then back to me again. I'm dumbstruck, completely useless, gawping like an idiot as usual.

"Sam's scared," Paulo says in an attempt to explain, and Thor's eyes move to him once more. His face is inscrutable and this makes me more scared still.

"I'd like a word," Thor says, and he takes Paulo into my study and shuts the door.

Oh my God, I can't stand this. I can't stand waiting outside in the living room so I go into my bedroom and sit on the bed with my head in my hands. Christ, I hope Thor isn't going to thump Paulo. I don't think so, he isn't that stupid. I don't know what the hell's going on. I'm totally confused, very frightened and at a loss to know what to do. I've made *such* a mess of things. All this time I've been so determined never to get myself into a situation again where I rely on another man, and now I realise that not only have I failed miserably but I now rely on *two* men, I'm so fucking useless. *Shit!* I don't know what to think.

I sit and wait and eventually I hear the door open and I go back into the living room.

"Paulo's going to take you somewhere safe," Thor tells me, "until this is over."

I stare at him in horror. What does he mean? I open my mouth to speak but the words won't come out.

"I'll go and get some things," Paulo says, "I'll be as quick as I can." He looks from me to Thor. "I'll text when I'm on my way back," he adds.

I watch him, frozen to the spot, as he walks out. My mind is numb. Thor eyes me coolly, and I can't tell what he's thinking. I wonder what was said in there.

"What's happening?" I manage to ask eventually.

"Paulo will take you somewhere safe," he repeats.

"What about you?"

"I'm staying here. When Wayne comes for you, I'll be waiting."

My hand goes up to my mouth. "No! You might get hurt."

"I can look after myself."

"You might get hurt because of me."

"I won't. He won't be expecting me. I'll be all right."

"Don't do this. Don't do this, *please*." I'm begging him, nearly in tears.

"Is that what you want?" he asks harshly. "Do you want to live in fear for the rest of your life? Do you want to always be waiting for him to catch up with you? The police can't do anything unless he actually attacks you - is that what you want?"

I stare at him with wide eyes. "No," I say.

"Because I can't stand it," he continues. "I can't have you living like that, in fear. I couldn't bear it if he hurt you and I hadn't done anything. I need to put an end to it. Even if you don't want me any more, I have to stop him."

Oh, *Christ*. I think of Mark, and of what not doing anything did to him. I'm trying very hard not to cry. I don't know what I want, so help me God. I look up into his eyes and his face is changing and suddenly, after so long, I'm reminded of the leopard. Oh God. I'm trapped.

He advances on me and at the last minute I move forward to meet him. I can't help it, I really can't. Even now I can't resist this stranger. We stare at each other and he puts his hands on my waist and I'm gone.

170

Nothing else matters as we scramble to remove each others clothes, then his hands are touching my skin and he pulls me into the bedroom. Oh my God, I can't stop myself, and I won't stop him, I want him too much.

A little voice inside my head which I'm refusing to listen to says, "Last time," and it frightens me more than anything you can ever imagine.

Afterwards I'm lying in his arms and trying to forget what's happening. I know we have to move but I want these minutes. I cling to him for a moment and he kisses me and I whisper, "Don't let him hurt you." I might not know him any more, and I might not know how I feel, but I desperately want him to be safe.

"I won't," he says, "Don't worry."

Oh, *God*.

We get up and I pull some things together.

"You won't need much," he says, "You'll be indoors all the time. Make sure you have something with you, something to do."

So I grab some books and things as well as my clothes and his mobile goes to say Paulo is on his way. I look at him in alarm and he takes me in his arms and kisses me. I'm so bewildered, I'm so frightened - now for him even more than for me. Everything is out of my control and happening so fast, and I don't know what to think.

"Wait for me, Sam," he says urgently. "Please. Don't do anything rash. Don't make any decisions until this is done. Please."

I look back at him. I guess I know what he means, but if he thinks I'm capable of making a decision he's way off the mark. That's the last thing he should be worrying about. My throat is constricted so I nod.

"Promise me," he says, "Promise me you'll wait."

"I promise," I say weakly, and he nods, satisfied.

We both hear the car at the same time and he takes my bag and my hand and leads me outside to where Paulo's waiting. Thor opens the car door and I get in while he throws my bag onto the back seat. I'm shaking with fear and stress and anguish. He leans across me and hands Paulo a mobile.

"It's a prepay," he says, "Keep it at your work. It mustn't go anywhere near Sam, or be traceable to you. I'll text you to let you know I'm ok."

Paulo nods. Thor looks at me. "Give me your mobile," he says.

I fish it out of my pocket and pass it to him. "I'll keep it here and handle your calls," he tells me. He hands me another phone. "This is for emergencies only. Keep it turned on but don't use it. Don't speak to anyone. Nobody is to know where you are or that you are not at home."

I stare at him with wide eyes.

"Do you understand?"

"Yes," I whisper.

"It has my number and Paulo's number in it. Emergencies only, as a last resort."

I nod. He leans in and kisses me, and I don't want him to stop, and then he pulls away and says, "Go." My eyes start to blur as he walks into the villa and closes the door behind him.

Paulo drives in silence. I have no idea where we're going, and I don't want to know. He seems to drive for ever, although I guess it's less than an hour. Finally we pull up at some huge gates, and there's a security guard. Paulo shows his ID or something and the gates open. We drive through and again wait for a garage door to open before heading down into an underground car park. I have to admit the security seems impressive. "What is this place?" I ask.

"My uncle has an apartment here," Paulo replies.

I know Paulo's uncle and father own the business he works in, and I see that business must be booming. Paulo grabs my bag as well as his own and we take a lift to the top floor. He leads me into a spacious, modern apartment and locks and bolts the door behind me.

He gives me a quick tour. There are three big bedrooms and he puts my bag in an en-suite one. We go into the kitchen and he pulls some milk and so on out of his bag. "I'll go shopping tomorrow," he says. "Make me a list."

I gaze at him in confusion. "You are not leaving this apartment," he explains. "Don't go near the windows or onto the balcony. Nobody is to know you are here." Thor must have given him a good talking to because now Paulo is seeming like a stranger, too. I can't stand this and I give him a wretched look. His face softens.

"I'll stay here tonight," he tells me. "I have to go to work and keep to my routine as much as possible, but I'll come and see you as often as I can."

I can feel the dreaded tears pricking at my eyes. "How long am I going to be here?" I ask in a trembling voice.

"I don't know," he replies.

Of course he doesn't, I can't believe I could ask such a stupid question.

"You should have something to eat," he says.

I'm not hungry but I manage some cereals before collapsing onto the sofa. My mind has thankfully given up trying to think for a while and it's a relief. Paulo comes and sits beside me, but he doesn't try to kiss me or touch me or anything. Thank goodness. Once more I wonder what was said in my study, and I shudder to think, I really do.

Paulo puts the telly on and we sit and stare at it for some time. I know I'm putting off going to bed because I'm sure my brain will wake up when I do and I won't be able to stop thinking and worrying. I'm scared to go over the events of the day or to imagine what might happen and I can't believe that it was only this morning I took Don and Jill to the bank and I didn't have a care in the world. It seems like years ago.

In the end I know I have to go so I move and Paulo turns the telly off. I look at this man who is doing all this for me despite the fact that I am

172

with someone else, and I don't know what to say. Anyway, I think my face does my talking for me because Paulo gets up and takes it in his hands. "Thank you," I manage, and he kisses me, but this time it's a gentle, friendly kiss; one which can't be misconstrued. I lean my forehead against his chest for a second before heading into my bedroom.

Paulo comes back the next evening with the shopping. I make us something to eat. Like a normal couple. Thor sent him a text earlier and there's no news. We eat, and sit, and watch TV and in the end Paulo stays again. He says he won't come the following evening, which is Thursday, because he is due out with the lads. That's ok, he can't be seen to be disappearing off all the time, I understand that. He finishes work early on Fridays, so will come and see me before going to Paco's, again, because not to do so would be unusual. Once more Thor has sent his text and there's no news.

I feel like I'm living in a daze. I spend the days reading and watching TV and doing some exercises because I am stuck inside and generally trying not to go mad with boredom and worry. Even the worry starts to fade after a while, to be honest, because you can only worry about the same thing for so long. Paulo doesn't come near me in *that* way, and I'm grateful. The weekends are the best and the worst. The best because Paulo can spend more time with me and I'm not so alone, and the worst because he isn't at work and so cannot check the mobile Thor gave him. So I don't know what's happening, or if he's ok. The nights are the most difficult, because I can't distract myself and I keep imagining Thor being surprised by Wayne and …

I have to stop thinking like this.

And I have so much time to think about what to do and what I want, and I'm lost. Everything's changed. Paulo knows, Paulo has always known, I still can't believe it, and Thor I have no idea about any more. Even Mark turns up in my thoughts and confuses the mix. I can't get my head around it all, and the knowledge that Thor is in danger and God knows what might happen prevents me from thinking straight. Not that I've ever been any good at that anyway. I go over and over it all in my head, but I get nowhere. Christ, I'm always so pathetic, and never more so than now.

And the days drag on, and I wait.

A few times Paulo brings a bottle of wine to share but otherwise I won't have any alcohol in the apartment because I know I will end up walloping it down to try to numb the anxiety and in the hope that it will help me sleep. Because the night is still the worst time and I dread going to bed because my mind is free to wander and I still don't know what to think and I worry myself sick about Thor and how he is coping in my villa and if he goes out at all and whether Wayne might see him and lie in wait for him and catch him unawares. So I go to bed later and later but it doesn't help, and when sleep reluctantly takes me I end up dreaming terrible dreams. Christ, it's awful.

I'm in bed and I must have been asleep because suddenly I wake with a start. I can feel the bed depressing behind me. *Fuck!* My heart drums wildly. Someone is sliding into my bed! Someone is sliding into bed behind me! *Oh my God! What the fuck?* My body goes rigid with fear and my eyes snap open. I can't breathe. It must be early morning because light is beginning to filter through the shutters. *Jesus Christ! Who is it? Who is it, lying behind me?* I'm petrified. I can't speak. I can't move. Oh Christ, what if it's Wayne? What if he's found me? Is Thor lying dead somewhere? Is Paulo hurt? Christ Almighty, is Wayne raising the hand with the knife right now? Oh God, if it is Wayne it's too late now. I wait for the searing pain and feel a strange sense of resignation, before thinking, *No, please, it can't be.* He wouldn't be so subtle.

Paulo? Could it be Paulo? Is he finally giving in to his feelings?

No, Paulo wouldn't do this, I'm sure. He's waited patiently for so long. It can't be Paulo. I'm trying not to let myself hope for anything else.

The body behind me moves. Oh my God! Oh my God, *please* help me.

It moves, and it curls itself into mine, and now I know. He doesn't touch me in any other way, but I just know. Slowly I turn over to look. It's him. He's finally here. He looks at me from the pillow and his face is composed, but I see the uncertainty deep in his eyes. My God, I realise that for once in my life I am looking at someone who is wondering what to do even more than I am, and in that moment my perspective shifts, and my heart seems to swell beyond all possibility.

I gaze at this man who has given me so much. This man who has rescued me from Simon, who has come to find me twice, who has dealt with Bradley, and who has now risked his life for mine.

And all he's asked in return is for me to go to his sister's wedding.

I can't help snuffling a small giggle as this final thought jumps into my head (where *do* they come from?) and I see his eyebrows rise a fraction and his face start to relax. I reach up and touch him above his eyebrow where he was cut that first time, and now *he* knows. This time it's me who reaches out to him and pulls him to me. He wraps his arms around me and kisses me. I bury my face in his chest and finally, at long last, I'm sure. I'm finally absolutely sure that I never, ever want to stop relying on this man, and I never, ever want to let him go, ever again.

Printed in Poland
by Amazon Fulfillment
Poland Sp. z o.o., Wrocław